WITCH TOWN

WITCH
TOWN

CORY PUTMAN OAKES

Houghton Mifflin Harcourt
Boston   New York

The text of this book is set in Horley Old Style MT Std.
The illustrations are done in pen and ink.

Library of Congress Cataloging-in-Publication Data
Names: Oakes, Cory Putman, author.
Title: Witchtown / by Cory Putman Oakes.
Description: Boston ; New York : Houghton Mifflin Harcourt, 2017. | Summary:
When they arrive in Witchtown, everything changes for a teenager and her
mother, who travel to witch-only communities, lying, cheating, and
stealing everything they can—leaving behind only a powerful spell that
erases them from the memories of everyone they have ever met.
Identifiers: LCCN 2016014684 | ISBN 9780544765573 (hardcover)
Subjects: | CYAC: Witches—Fiction. | Magic—Fiction. | Mothers and
daughters—Fiction. | Swindlers and swindling—Fiction. | Memory—Fiction.
| Community life—Fiction.
Classification: LCC PZ7.1.O15 Wi 2017 | DDC [Fic]—dc23
LC record available at https://lccn.loc.gov/2016014684

Manufactured in the U.S.A.
DOC 10 9 8 7 6 5 4 3 2 1
4500657703

For Mark, my own personal safe-haven

A MODERN WITCH'S PRIMER

Chapter 1
Havens in Historical Context

Near the beginning of this century, with occultism on the rise around the world, a whistleblower from within the pagan community exposed a secret that had long been protected by witches everywhere. The secret was that in addition to Learned witches, ordinary individuals who studied pagan practices and who could, with practice, learn to channel a small amount of power for their rituals, there were also so-called Natural witches, people who possessed a tremendous amount of inborn power and who required little or no formal training to wield it.

In response to the public outcry over this "unregulated threat to public safety," the United States government instituted a National Witch Registry and required all Natural witches, under pain of imprisonment, to submit their name, city of residence, and place of employment to a publicly searchable database.

There was a good faith movement within the Natural witch community to comply with this registry.

Over the next few years, in what would eventually become known as the Second Inquisition, the witches who volunteered their identities were systemically ostracized from their social circles, became unable to retain jobs, and in some cases, were hunted down and abducted by private-citizen "safety brigades." The runaway bestseller *The Inquisitor's Handbook* provided these groups with instructions (mostly badly translated from a sixteenth-century copy of *Malleus Maleficarum*, a.k.a. *The Witch's Hammer*) as to the proper method of torture and execution of witches. Law enforcement was slow to recognize these atrocities as hate crimes and generally lackadaisical in its prosecution of the perpetrators.

The government's solution was to seize small parcels of (mostly undesirable) land around the country in order to establish witch-only communities known as Havens. This, it was argued, would remove the threat to public safety and the temptation for hate crimes, while allowing both Learned and Natural witches to live among their own kind, keep their traditions alive, and practice magic in safety.

The greatest of these Havens was a private township created by the late billionaire insurance magnate Reginald Harris, one of the richest and most influential men in the United States and, until his final years, an unregistered Natural witch. Unlike the small, poor, mostly rural communities that established themselves in most of the government-funded Havens, Harris's town, deep in America's heartland, was intended to be a pagan utopia: a model of green building, spiritual enlightenment, and, above all, magical living.

It was called Witchtown.

CHAPTER ONE

*W*itchtown looked more like a prison than a town.

For one thing, it was surrounded on all sides by a three-story wall. The massive structure was overgrown with ivy and moss, but when we got within a few hundred yards, I could see plenty of places where ugly, manmade concrete was peeking through the greenery. The walls were sloped at a steep angle, probably to prevent people from climbing them. That thought brought on unwelcome images of invaders scaling the slippery, mossy surface, armed and planning to inflict untold horror on the people—the witches—inside . . .

I chased the thought away.

Those times are over, I reminded myself. *For the most part.*

She pulled over right beside the sign.

BURN IN HELL was spray-painted diagonally right across its face, in red. Below that, the phrases SATAN'S SPAWN and EXODUS 22:18 were carved into its surface. The usual anti-witch slurs. Not particularly original. But once I managed to squint my way through all of that, the original lettering on the sign erased any remaining doubt I might have had about our destination:

WITCHTOWN
POPULATION 402
BLESSED BE!

I straightened up a little and looked across the front seat at my mother.

"You're kidding, right?" I asked.

My mother sipped her coffee and didn't respond right away. After days of near-total silence in the car, my words felt uncomfortably loud, even to my own ears. I wasn't sure how long our stalemate had lasted. It's hard to define days based on rest-stop bathrooms and drive-through meals.

She took several more leisurely swallows of coffee. Then she asked, "Why would you think I was kidding?"

"You think now is a good time for this? *Now*? After everything . . ." I cringed. Even just that little bit of talking had distracted me. Caused me to let my guard down. And the sinkhole of pain I had been keeping at bay reopened itself inside my chest. It felt bigger. Like it had grown stronger. It grabbed me now with an intensity that made it difficult to breathe.

"That's all behind us now," my mother said, but I barely heard her.

Too soon. Too soon for reality.

I had to shut it down. I abandoned the conversation, closed my eyes, and sank back down into the passenger seat. I felt for my weathered leather jacket, which I had been using as a blanket, and found it on the car floor. I picked it up and covered myself in it, trying to ignore everything but its familiar scents of sage and something else, something even earthier than sage, as I tried to lull myself back into my silent, senseless cocoon.

Oblivion. Oblivion. Take me away . . .

But a hard tug on the jacket brought me back to the here and now. To my mother, glaring down at me with disapproval.

"It's in the past," she insisted.

I jerked the coat out of her hand and turned my face toward the window.

"*Not* for me."

A harder yank pulled the leather from my grip entirely. I sat up in protest. My mother gave the garment a disgusted look and tossed it down at my feet.

"Let it go," she commanded. Then she added pointedly, "You know you're the only one dwelling on it, don't you?"

I bit my lip. That was true enough. But it didn't make the hurt any less.

The thought brought on a new squeeze of pain, a new struggle to breathe. I retrieved the jacket from the floor again, settled my head against the back of the seat, and closed my eyes.

My mother sighed. "Fine. Have it your way," she huffed, and I heard her door open. A gust of cinnamon-scented air flew up my nostrils as she exited the car.

After a moment, I opened my eyes.

The annoying thing was I knew, I *knew*, I was going to follow her out of the car. I could feel it now: the quiet, persistent, unshakable pull she had on me. Calling me after her. Forcing me to see things her way.

I burrowed my nose into the soft lining of the coat, making one last attempt to hold on to my anger. Part of me wanted to believe that every second I stayed mad at her would give me a tiny bit more power. Which was nonsense. I had never had any kind of power over my mother.

Nobody had.

I left the jacket on the seat when I went after her.

She had popped open the trunk and unzipped the top suitcase. I leaned against the bumper and watched as she rooted through a messy pile of clothes.

"Here, hold this."

She tossed something black and strappy at me. I caught it, instantly wishing I had just let it fall into the dirt instead.

With only a quick glance at the empty road beside us, she stripped off her T-shirt and jeans. She exchanged her flip-flops for the heels, one foot at a time, gripping one of my shoulders for balance. The blue-gray moonstone she wore on a chain around her neck caught the light of the setting sun as she fumbled with the delicate straps on the shoes.

She caught me looking at her necklace, and gestured pointedly at the matching one around my neck.

"Haven't I always protected you?" she asked. "Hasn't it always been you and me?"

I took a breath instead of answering. Separately, those two statements were accurate. But together, they seemed to mean something more. Something that wasn't quite true.

She slipped the dress over her tall, slim body, pulled the clip out of her hair, and shook out the ashy blond strands until they bounced, wavy and alive, against her shoulders. You wouldn't have known she'd been in a car for days.

I was wearing severely rumpled jeans and a tank top. Neither of us suggested that I change. Or do anything with my own long, dirty blond hair, which was piled in a greasy knot on the top of my head. I could only imagine how I looked, next to her.

"We're not ready for this," I said.

She put one hand on each of my shoulders. We were the same height, but now that she was in heels, I had to crane my neck up slightly to make eye contact.

"I shouldn't have to tell you what this place means to us," my mother said quietly. "*Look* at it."

I looked. And when I did, I saw a cluster of buildings, so carefully tucked into the shadow of the Witchtown wall that I hadn't noticed them before. The structures looked temporary —tents, shacks, and old RVs. They gave me the creeps. Even more than the wall did.

"This is it," my mother continued. "Everything we've ever wanted, ever dreamed of, is inside those walls. We are *this close.*"

She let go of one shoulder and grabbed my chin.

"But you have to pull yourself together. Right now. Or we haven't got a prayer. Understand?"

I nodded, more to show her I was listening than anything else. If she chose to take that as a sign that I agreed with her, that was her problem.

She tightened her hand, squeezing my jaw to the point of pain.

"I did it for you," she said evenly, moving her hands so they were on either side of my face. "You know that, right?"

I flinched. I was still one big, open wound. Hearing her talk like that, in that casual way of hers, was too much to bear.

I glared at her. I had seen my mother's glare many times before. It was beautiful. And terrible. It could make things, and people (myself included), wilt under its power.

My glare was nothing like that. But I was surprised to discover it had a small effect on her; she dropped her hands from my face and took a step back.

"Too soon," she muttered to herself, and went back to the driver's-side door.

I walked back to the passenger door, feeling like I had won a tiny victory. I had made it clear that *this* time, *this* pain, was not something she could just breeze past, the way she did with most things.

And yet, even with my small triumph, she had still managed to get the better of me. Here I was, getting back in the car. Without an argument. Just like she wanted.

I twirled my moonstone around my finger.

Witchtown. *Really?*

CHAPTER TWO

*T*he road led us to a large gate in the northernmost part of the wall. The sun had started to set, and the harsh lights on top of the gate shone down on a half-dozen men in black fatigues, carrying machine guns.

Private security. Forget prison. Witchtown was a fortress. Reginald Harris had seen to that when he mapped out the place. I had heard enough stories about the guy to know he had been a nutcase about security.

One of the guards had a vicious-looking German shepherd on a leash. I was too busy watching the dog sniff every inch of our car to hear what my mother said that caused the guards to fall back and the enormous metal gate to open.

We were soon surrounded on all sides by trees, but not before I caught a glimpse of what looked like farm fields. It was hard to tell for sure, as the sun was almost completely gone and the thick trees were blotting out most of the light.

The road changed from dirt to bumpy cobblestones as

we approached what I was tempted to call the town square, except it was in the shape of a circle. The space was surrounded by a ring of whitewashed buildings with dark, exposed beams and thatched roofs. My mother pulled the car up in front of one that looked like all the others. The shingle hanging off the front read MAYOR'S OFFICE in quaint lettering.

A smaller shingle underneath said WITCHTOWN REAL ESTATE.

"We're here," she said, unnecessarily. She turned the ignition off and grabbed my left hand hard so I couldn't yank it away.

With her free hand she reached up to touch the headless, toga-clad statuette that was hanging from our rearview mirror.

"Laverna, bless us," she said to the figurine, then looked at me expectantly.

I muttered the same words and reached up with my free hand to brush my fingers against the Goddess. She was marble, but she was never cool to the touch the way marble was supposed to be. She was always kind of warm. Like skin.

I pulled my hand back from the statuette as soon as my mother dropped hers.

She opened her car door and gestured toward the almost-empty coffee cup in the holder between us. I handed her the cup. With her right hand still grasping my left hand, she poured three drops of the leftover coffee onto the ground.

"Darkness and clouds," my mother said, and squeezed

my hand once before letting it go. She unhooked the small figure from the mirror and tucked Laverna carefully into the side pocket of her purse.

The Witchtown Real Estate office was still open. At the door, we were confronted by a woman with frizzy red hair, a skintight pencil skirt, and a slightly panicked expression.

"I'm sorry, but there must have been some kind of mistake," she said bluntly, positioning herself so that we could step just inside the door but no farther.

My mother frowned. "Oh?"

The frazzled woman held up her hand; her fingers were clenched around a cell phone.

"The guards called to say they let you in, but they must have been mistaken." She glanced out the office window at our dusty green Volkswagen and bit her lip. "We have no openings at the moment. My apologies, but I'll have to ask you to leave now."

The door to an inner office opened behind her and another woman emerged. She was shorter than the frizzy-haired woman, but I could see she had ten times more gravity. She was wearing a tailored skirt suit and heels. Her white-blond hair, which was cut short, contrasted sharply with the deep olive color of her skin, and she had the slightly distracted expression of someone thinking about too many things at once.

She took in the scene before her and raised an eyebrow at Frizz.

"Lois?" she asked.

"Handled!" Frizz assured the woman, who had to be her boss.

The blonde nodded absently.

Lois flashed us a falsely bright smile. "I'm so sorry for the mix-up. If you'd like to fill out an online application, you'll be entered into the lottery with the other applicants and contacted in due course."

She gestured behind us, obviously indicating that we should leave.

Instead, my mother braced herself against the side of the door so her right hand was at eye level, her knuckles facing the room.

"I see," she said, smiling, as though she was not put off in the least by Lois's rudeness. "And do you have something I might use to write down the website address? I have a terrible memory for such things."

She drummed her fingers against the door frame. The gesture was lost on Lois, who turned to rifle through some loose papers on the desk as she presumably searched for a pen. But Lois's boss paused at the threshold of the inner-office door, her eyes fixed on my mother's hand.

Or, more precisely, on her silver ring.

It wasn't a very flashy ring. It wasn't even very attractive. It was just several strands of silver woven together into an intricate double knot the exact shape of two tangled-up infinity symbols. But it was enough to make the blonde in the suit stop in her tracks.

She exchanged a brief look with my mother and tossed a file on the desk, right under Lois's nose.

Lois jumped.

"I've got this," the suit told her curtly. "Take a break."

"But—but I was just—"

"Break, Lois. Now."

Lois bowed her head and skittered backwards, toward a smaller desk on the other side of the office.

The blonde strode forward and put her hand out to my mother.

She introduced herself. "Brooke Bainbridge. Mayor of Witchtown."

"Aubra O'Sullivan," my mother said, taking the offered hand and shaking it. "This is my daughter, Macie."

"Nice to meet you, Macie." The mayor shook my hand too and then gestured to a waiting area with an uncomfortable-looking couch and several armchairs.

I made a beeline for one of the armchairs, but my mother cleared her throat, sat down gracefully on the couch, and patted the cushion next to her.

You and me, her eyes reminded me. *You and me.*

I gritted my teeth and sat down beside her, as the mayor took the armchair closest to my mother's side of the couch.

"Please forgive my assistant," the mayor said, picking up a clipboard. "She was rather hasty. I'm sure we'll be able to accommodate you and your daughter. Let me just take you through a few lifestyle questions . . . Yes, here we are. Which pagan tradition do you practice?"

"We're Eclectic, for the most part," my mother answered. "Mainly Northern European traditions. Some Greek and Roman. Smattering of Egyptian."

The mayor checked several boxes on the form.

"And how long have you identified yourself as a witch, Aubra?"

"All my life," my mother answered patiently. She tapped her ring, which caused the mayor to give her an embarrassed smile.

"Of course. My apologies. I'm just so used to interviewing Learned witches."

"Oh?" my mother raised an eyebrow. "There are no other Naturals here?"

"Well, we do have one," the mayor said, with a grimace. "But she's quite old, I'm afraid, and not quite all there, if you know what I mean. She doesn't practice anymore."

"I see," my mother said, and she was sitting close enough to me that I could actually *feel* her tense up and then relax.

"You'd be the only true Natural in town," the mayor said, and then glanced over at me. "Unless Macie . . ."

She trailed off as her gaze fell to the fingers of my right hand. I tucked my naked digits self-consciously underneath my leg.

"No," my mother cut in. "Macie is not a Natural."

"Shame," the mayor muttered to herself as she checked the box marked "Learned" next to where she had written my name. I did not correct her.

There was no box on the mayor's form for what I was. If she knew the truth, we wouldn't all be sitting around, bothering with paperwork.

But she didn't know, so she continued on in a cheery kind of a way.

"How old are you, Macie dear?"

"Sixteen," I answered.

"And how long have you been a Learned witch?"

"I've been teaching her since birth," my mother jumped in, before I could respond. "Macie is a very gifted herbalist."

That, at least, was true. The herbalist part. Not the teaching part. My mother didn't know a comfrey from a clover. I was entirely self-taught, and proud of it, but now didn't seem like the best time to point that out.

"And have you previously lived in a Haven of any kind?"

"Yes," my mother replied. "Several."

"I see. Where?"

"Here and there," my mother smiled and then sat forward, her eyes full of secrets. "Let me be honest with you, Madame Mayor —"

"Brooke, please," the mayor insisted.

My mother kept smiling. It looked predatory to me, but it must have seemed friendly to the mayor because she leaned in closer as my mother continued.

"My husband was killed in the Second Inquisition. Since his death, my daughter and I have found it necessary to move around quite a bit. I am unregistered, you see. I hope that isn't a problem?"

"Oh, no," the mayor assured her. "We don't discriminate here."

The mayor's voice was calm, but her eyes were darting back and forth excitedly. I could practically see her going down her mental checklist, ticking off the categories my mother could fill for her.

Widow of a martyr. Devoted mother. *Natural.*

My mother was a gold mine for any Haven. A catch.

I, for one, was stuck back at my mother's mention of a *husband*. That was a new one. I was fairly certain that my mother had never been married to my father. Not that we had ever discussed the subject at any length. All I had been told about my father was that he left. And it had been made clear to me that asking any more questions would not be tolerated.

"Macie and I both feel that we have been on the road for long enough," my mother went on. "We are looking for somewhere to settle permanently."

"You won't be disappointed," the mayor said, with a smile. "Just a few more questions. What level of formal education do you have, Aubra?"

"I have a master's degree in accounting," my mother replied. "And I'm a certified public accountant."

Unbelievably, that was true.

The mayor raised an eyebrow.

"*That* will come in handy," she said, mostly to herself.

It always did. Even witches need accountants.

"Any dietary restrictions?" the mayor asked.

"Macie and I are committed raw vegans," my mother told her, and I was barely able to hide my groan. "We believe in putting our spiritual needs above our physical ones."

"That is very dedicated of you," Mayor Bainbridge said admiringly, then capped her pen and turned the clipboard over in her lap. "Well, I am happy to tell you that by lucky co-incidence, we have a need for an accountant. Our previous one left us rather abruptly . . ." Her words trailed off and she made a face, but pulled herself together quickly. "I can offer you his residence. It's a one-bedroom apartment. Will that be suffi-cient for the time being, until something bigger opens up?"

"That will be lovely," my mother said, and I saw a flash of a triumphant grin behind her appropriately grateful smile.

A blur of signatures and forms later, the mayor walked us down the street. She whisked us through a lobby, mentioned something about an initiation ritual tomorrow, and opened the front door of our new apartment with a flourish.

"Welcome home!" she said grandly.

I managed only a weak smile in return. Because I knew that we hadn't come to make Witchtown our home.

We had come to rob it.

CHAPTER THREE

*T*he next morning, I grasped the edge of the bathroom sink and watched my wet hair drip into the deep white basin.

Get a grip, I commanded myself. *Get. A. Grip.*

The couch in the former accountant's apartment both looked and smelled like it was made out of old jeans, but it was surprisingly comfortable. I had passed out on it not long after my mother claimed the apartment's only bedroom (and the queen-size bed that went with it). I didn't wake up until sunlight started fighting to get through the ugly blue curtains.

The calm, the exhaustion—whatever it was that had allowed me a good night's rest—was gone now. I was wired. But not in a good way. My mind refused to settle into the focused, hyperaware state that it normally assumed at the start of every job.

And this isn't just any job, I reminded myself, wringing the water from my hair into the sink. *This is Witchtown. You can't screw this one up.*

For as long as I could remember, my mother and I had robbed Havens. We knew our jobs well. Hers was to hide in plain sight, to distract, to captivate, to get people's attention. She was like the beautiful, exotic street performer who drew the crowds. I was the lowly assistant who moved, unnoticed, through her spellbound audience and eased the fat wallets out of people's pockets.

The thought gave me a twinge. I tried to shake it off, but it was no use.

Things were different now. They had been, ever since Rafe.

I grimaced as the now-familiar pain squeezed my chest. I gripped the sink harder, willing the pain to go away, but I drifted instead down a dusty road, thousands of miles away, toward a Haven that had cornfields instead of walls. I had seen the cornstalks close-up. Seen them grow blurry as I blazed through them, with the wind in my face and solid arms around me, keeping me from flying off—

I raised my eyes from the sink and glared at myself in the mirror.

Stop thinking about him.

I kept staring. I didn't like what was staring back at me. The girl in the mirror looked wrecked. Defeated. Her eyes were mournful and faraway.

All those towns. A never-ending string of them. For as long as I could remember. All that money. It had never been enough.

But Witchtown would be. The money that Reginald Harris had left Witchtown would be enough. She had promised. It had always been our endgame. Our final con. After Witchtown, we could go anywhere. We would settle down. Stop moving. But it all depended on getting a big enough score out of Harris's town, the crown jewel of all the Havens.

If I was going to pull this off—big *if*—I was going to have to do something about the dead-eyed girl in the mirror.

An idea came to me, and the girl in the mirror raised an eyebrow.

You wouldn't dare, came my mother's voice, from deep inside my head. For a moment, the eyes in the mirror flashed vividly green.

Wouldn't I?

I flipped my damp hair over my shoulder and went to search the kitchen. Luckily, the former occupant seemed to have left behind all of his kitchen supplies. I rooted through drawers full of measuring cups, ladles, and whisks until I found what I was pretty sure were poultry shears. Perfect.

Back in the bathroom, I felt a shiver of the old excitement as I pulled my long hair back into a ponytail. The eyes in the mirror grew slightly less foggy as I positioned the shears just above my hand. I cut once, then again, and then one more time until I was holding the severed ponytail over the sink.

The eyes approved. I blinked at myself in the mirror once and then kept going.

I had never cut anyone's hair before, to say nothing of my

own. The result was a little bit shorter and choppier than I had intended. Kind of like a shaggy pixie cut. I couldn't even tuck the front part behind my ears. And I was pretty sure that one side was slightly longer than the other.

I smiled at the eyes in the mirror as I set down the shears and fluffed up the jagged layers in the back.

This girl looked bold and daring. Ready for anything. She had never left anyone behind. I didn't know her yet, but anything was better than the shattered soul that had stepped out of the shower just a few minutes ago.

I gave the girl in the mirror one last tiny smile before I gathered up my damp, discarded locks and chucked them into the trash can under the sink.

Once I was dressed, I glanced at my mother's bedroom door. It was still shut; I didn't expect to hear a peep from her until at least noon. But just in case she woke up before then, it would be better for me to be gone.

Quickly, I dug through one of our suitcases and pulled out a small black shoulder bag and an oversize jewelry box.

Setting the bag aside for now, I opened the box.

My herb journal, the sum total of all the wisdom I had managed to gather about plants, resins, and other things that grow, sat inside. The compartments beneath the journal held dozens of baggies of dried herbs plus a small scythe, my mortar and pestle, several scraps of cloth, and a tangle of cords for making sachets. My collection produced a strong, heavenly, and strange mixture of scents; I bent my head lower so I could breathe it in. Tradition warned against bringing old herbs into a new home, but those customs must have been invented by an herbalist who could afford to replenish her stash every time she moved.

I evaluated my neatly labeled baggies and found that I was nearly out of valerian root and elder. I would need them both later, so I added them to my mental list, replaced the journal, and closed the box. Surely Witchtown had a place where I could restock. Right after I found some food. I hadn't eaten dinner last night, and right about then I would have given my left arm for a stack of pancakes.

The mayor had given me a map last night, and I studied it as I walked out the door. Downtown Witchtown had a circular layout. I had noticed the ring of buildings around the "square" when we arrived, but according to the map there were actually two rings: the inner one (made up of the real estate office, the mayor's office, our apartment building, and a few other businesses) and an outer ring (which housed more shops and various municipal structures). Everything was within easy walking distance.

Which was a good thing. Because I wasn't totally clear on what had happened to our car. The mayor had mentioned something about Witchtown being a green city, and I didn't see any other cars around. Maybe they weren't allowed.

When I looked up from the map, I was surprised to find that the deserted central area I had seen last night had been taken over by a bustling farmer's market.

My mother's raw vegan pronouncement from last night came back to me then, and my stomach growled anew. Partly in hunger and partly in protest. Reluctantly, I put my pancake craving on the shelf. It would be nothing but uncooked vegetables and fruit for the duration of this job. But given that, I guessed there were worse things than stumbling upon a town square packed full of produce.

Everyone seemed to have a basket. I spotted a pile of them on one side of the circle and picked one up for myself. Thus armed, I waded into the fray and tried to look like I belonged.

Strawberries must have been in season, because they were everywhere. I walked up to the nearest vendor and picked out two overflowing cartons of them, plus a smaller container of raspberries.

I went to pay and then paused, considering my options.

A lot of Havens used the barter system, but I had nothing to barter with. Except herbs, but I wasn't going to part with anything in my box until I had a better idea of what my restocking options were in this town. I was relieved to see the person in front of me pay with an ordinary ten-dollar bill. My mother had given me some cash to get the con going. That was the obvious thing to reach for at the moment. But I hesitated.

The three twenty-dollar bills my mother had given me

were part of our take from the last Haven. And I didn't feel like paying with someone else's coin today.

I had earned some money in the last Haven. Earned, not stolen. It pained me to part with any of it, for a number of reasons. Before I could think about it too hard, I dug into my own cash and handed the berry vendor several bills.

"New here, are you?" he asked, smiling at me through his thick mustache.

"Yes," I said. Everyone in Havens always knew everyone else. There was never a place to hide, especially not when you were "the new girl." "My mother and I arrived yesterday afternoon."

"Welcome, then!" he said. His smile broadened as he loaded the berries into my basket. After a moment, he added a plastic bottle of juice.

"A welcome gift," he explained. "That's pure strawberry juice—nothing healthier in this world."

"Thanks," I said.

I made a slow circle of the market as I munched on the berries. They were not pancakes, but they quieted down my angry stomach and gave me a needed surge of energy. By the time I was done I had added some beets, an armload of carrots, a container of cherries, a bundle of spinach, a bag of assorted nuts, a large jar of freshly made peanut butter, and a bag of salt to the basket. I also had a new broom, wedged awkwardly in the crook of my arm. The haul had cost me a fair amount of my cash, but the weight of the basket made me feel more confident about the prospect of a decent meal in the near future.

The only things remaining on my mental list were elder and valerian, but there had not been a single vendor selling herbs. In the short term, this was inconvenient. Especially for the protection sachet I was planning to make later. But in the long term, the lack of a resident herbalist might provide me with a means of making some money. So I was in a surprisingly good mood as I carried my heavy basket and my broom back in the direction of the apartment.

Until I saw something that made my stomach drop down to my knees.

Rafe.

It was just for an instant, and then he disappeared into the crowd. I followed without thinking, terrified I'd lose him. I darted between shoppers, dodging baskets and elbows, until my eyes fixed on the familiar head of dark, slightly shaggy hair hanging down over the collar of his favorite black shirt. I could recognize that back, and the slope of his shoulders, anywhere.

Unable to stop myself, I reached out my free hand to touch his arm. He turned.

"Yes?"

I drew back, deflated.

The guy who turned to face me had a friendly but questioning look on his face. It was a handsome face, with deep-set blue eyes and a defined jaw. But it was not Rafe's face. Now that I got a good look at this guy, I realized his hair had looked black only because it was wet. The dry strands in front looked closer to chestnut brown. And although his skin was tanned, like he spent a lot of time outdoors, it was decidedly white. He also wasn't quite as tall as Rafe. What had I been thinking?

Of course it wasn't him.

"I—" I could barely get that syllable out. It was hard to catch my breath.

The guy extended a hand.

"Kellen Stewart," he said. When I just continued to stare dumbly at him, he added patiently, "And you are . . . ?"

I took a step backwards, pivoted, and walked back through the crowd in a daze, far too lost in thought to consider how rude I was being. I must have been hungrier than I had realized. It wasn't like my brain to just short-circuit like that. I didn't have visions. Or hallucinations. Or whatever that had been.

I don't think I breathed again until I made it back to the apartment. Once there, I sank to the floor and let out a long, slow breath as the broom handle hit the ground with a sharp clatter and the contents of my basket spilled out in front of me.

I didn't venture back out again until it was nearly dark, time for the initiation ritual the mayor had mentioned yesterday. I wasn't sure if all of the four hundred and two souls that Witchtown claimed on its sign were present in the center of town, but it was a very respectable showing. It made sense; it was the full moon, after all, and even the most apathetic members of pagan communities usually get it together to do *something* witchy at that time of the month.

Personally, I was just glad to see that most of the towns-folk were robed. I had never been a big fan of the whole skyclad routine. My mother didn't mind it, but frolicking in the nude with a bunch of strangers had never been my thing.

Earlier, when she had at last emerged from her bedroom, my mother had seen my hair, done a double take, and given me a look she usually reserved for the likes of traveling Bible salesmen. But she seemed to have gotten over that now. She steered me through the crowd, one hand on the shoulder of my crimson ritual robe, straight toward Mayor Bainbridge, who was standing near the altar. It was a large and obviously per-manent chunk of marble, inscribed with what I assumed was the Witchtown motto:

To grow in knowledge

To live in harmony

To harm none

I couldn't honestly see myself getting onboard with any of that. But I guess it was a nice collection of sentiments. Sweet. Bordering on obnoxious.

There were a number of older people around, especially near the mayor, but not a single one of them was wearing a sil-ver ring. Well, the mayor had said the Natural didn't practice anymore. Maybe she was too old even to attend rituals.

My nerves started to hum. An elegant gray-haired lady who was introduced to us as the High Priestess signaled the beginning of the ritual. I tried to take deep breaths and not let my nervousness show, even as the High Priestess took her place behind the altar, sent the Quarter Guards to their respective posts in the outer circle, and motioned for my mother and me to stand to her right.

Breathe, I reminded myself, as I followed my mother to the High Priestess's side. *Just breathe.*

My mother had failed me in countless ways over the years, but never in this. She had almost as much to lose as I did, if the good people of Witchtown were to discover what I was.

It will be okay. This part is always okay.

The twin moonstones around our necks would ensure that.

The High Priestess took up a silver wand and left the altar. Starting in the east, she walked clockwise around the edges of the crowd, drawing a circle around us.

"I consecrate this circle to the Gods," she chanted. "A safe space between the worlds."

When she had completed the circle, the High Priestess returned to the altar. As she called each element, a torch in the corresponding quarter of the circle blazed to life. Two of the Quarter Guards used lighters, I noticed. The other two used channeled power.

As I looked around, I realized that something about this assembled group was nagging at me. There was something odd. Something that I couldn't quite put my finger on.

I puzzled over it until the High Priestess raised both arms

above her head and nine glass orbs that I hadn't noticed previously rose into the air. Each one of them caught the light of the full moon overhead and began to glow with a gentle but vivid silver light. It had been comfortably light outside before, but now it was as if someone had flipped on a switch: it was as bright as daylight.

"The circle is bound!" the High Priestess called, sealing it with her words. "Our work begins!"

A fairly standard circle casting, really. Aside from the orbs. I had seen hundreds of variations on what, when you got down to it, was a fairly simple procedure of sealing off sacred space and summoning the elements to balance the energies of the circle. I'm not sure why I had expected the Witchtown ritual to be any different, but I had.

I was going to have to watch that. Letting this town's reputation get the better of me was going to throw me off my game.

"Welcome, everyone," the High Priestess continued. "The Goddess has blessed us with a beautiful full moon this night."

The High Priestess smiled. The orbs caused her black robe to shimmer and her face to glow with a light that made her look younger than she probably was. And very beautiful. The focal point of power within a circle always takes on a certain unearthly beauty, I had discovered.

"Will Aubra and Macie O'Sullivan please approach the altar?"

I tried not to visibly shake as I obeyed her command. The High Priestess was quite tall and I felt like a small child, gazing up at her the way that our respective positions required.

"Aubra first," she instructed quietly. Then, raising her voice so that all might hear, she intoned, "Aubra O'Sullivan, have you come to us tonight, under the full moon, freely and of your own free will?"

"I have," my mother answered.

"Do you seek the ancient knowledge, the old ways, and the promise of rebirth?"

"I do," my mother answered again.

I busied myself searching through the faces around me as my mother responded to the ritual questions. And then it dawned on me what was weird about the group assembled around us:

No teenagers.

There were little kids and adults, but I was the only one here within five years of my age. Maybe Witchtown teenagers were too cool for rituals?

"I *do*," my mother repeated, and this time there was more of a finality to it than her other replies. She took a silver chalice from the High Priestess's hands and as she raised it to her lips, I felt a warm wind blow through the ritual space, playing with my newly shorn hair. The torches at the four quarters of the circle flared up, as if they had suddenly been called to attention. The flames turned a dark, crimson red, the exact color of the ritual robes my mother and I were wearing. All nine of the

orbs above glowed red as well. There were murmurs of excitement and surprise.

"Natural," I heard more than one person mutter.

My mother opened her eyes. The flames returned to normal, and the red light faded from the orbs.

She returned the cup to the High Priestess's hand, caught
my eye, and winked.

The High Priestess turned to me and all of a sudden, my
palms felt sweaty. I fought the urge to wipe them on my robe.

"Macie O'Sullivan," the High Priestess went on. "Have
you—"

She was interrupted by several loud popping sounds. A
split second later, all of the orbs shattered, raining bits of broken glass down on us.

I ducked instinctively and covered my head. Beside me,
I could see my mother doing the same. There were several
more popping sounds—gunshots? Were those gunshots?
—and more glass fell down all around me. There was a lot of
screaming.

I kept my arms over my head until the glass stopped
coming down and an odd silence settled across the square.
Cautiously, I raised my head.

The High Priestess was still standing on the other side of
the altar, but now she had her back to me. She, and everyone
else in the circle, was staring at the roof above the mayor's office.

There were three men up there, all wearing brown robes

tied at the waist with a rope. The ones on either end were holding rifles, which I assumed meant they had just shot down the orbs. They stood motionless, flanking the middle figure, who held a large, leather-bound book and had his hood pulled up so high it covered most of his face.

All three priests were wearing crosses made of thin branches with featherlike leaves and heavy bunches of red berries. Rowan. I would have recognized it even if the branches hadn't been tied together with red twine. The old rhyme popped into my head, unbidden.

> Rowan tree, red thread;
> Holds the witches all in dread.

Rowan. As toxic to witches as silver is to a werewolf or Kryptonite to Superman. Learned witches, anyway. You need angelica to take down a Natural. But the priests probably hadn't heard about Witchtown's newest arrival yet.

The central figure stepped forward and pulled back his hood, revealing hollow, cavernous eyes and an almost-bald head. He opened his book and began to read, and for a bizarre moment I thought he was going to read us the rowan rhyme. His words, loud and deep, shook the entire square and sent uncomfortable vibrations up through my feet.

> Evil shall come upon you,
> Which you will not know how to charm away;

Disaster shall fall upon you,
For which you will not be able to atone;
And ruin shall come upon you suddenly,
Of which you know nothing—

"Stop!"

My mother's voice rang out, strong and clear, beside me. She raised her arms toward the men on the roof. Her eyes rolled back into her head, as though she was going into a trance.

For a long moment, nothing happened. Then one of the men holding a gun let out a yelp.

His rifle clattered to the roof and bounced twice on the shingles before it dissolved into a puddle of liquid metal. The second priest held on longer, too long, so that when his gun melted into goo, it oozed over his hands, leaving him stuck holding a pile of dripping molten metal. He screamed just as half a dozen other figures, dressed in black and carrying guns of their own, appeared on the rooftop.

"Freeze!"

The Witchtown security forces closed in, but as they did, the center priest reached into his robe and pulled out three metal canisters. Without hesitation he threw them down into the square.

There were three explosions, a lot more screaming, and three swiftly spreading clouds of smoke.

The screaming went on and on, and there was a strange smell, kind of sulfurlike, to my sensitive nose. The curly tendrils of smoke blanketed the sacred circle in seconds, blocking out the light from the moon and turning the space into an eerie void. I couldn't see much beyond the end of my own nose, but I could feel the jostling of people around me, all scrambling in different directions.

"No!" the High Priestess's voice rang out in the midst of the chaos. "No! Do not break the circle!"

But it was too late for that. People were running blindly through the smoke, desperate to get out of the square. The circle had no power to stop them.

I was beginning to wonder if I shouldn't run as well, and if so, to where, when I felt a very solid hand grab me and pull me into the smoke.

"I've got her!" a voice yelled. *"I've got her!"*

CHAPTER FOUR

*L*et me go!" I yelled.

I tried to pull away, but succeeded only in getting my feet tangled in my robe and falling down.

The person who held my arm stopped for a second, yanked me back onto my feet, and then continued to drag me along.

"Come on!" he said. "We're almost out of the smoke!"

He was right. The smoke was starting to thin out. We had left the chaos of the ritual area behind us and were making our way quickly through the downtown area.

North. I was pretty sure we were headed north.

I was a little bit confused about my abductor. He was in front of me, so all I could discern was that he was tall, with broad, muscular shoulders and very short brown hair. I was relieved to note that his robe was blue (not brown) and that he was not carrying a gun. He was not one of the men from the roof.

Since the size of his shoulders alone made it clear there

was really no point in fighting him, I picked up my pace so he wouldn't have to pull so hard.

Weirdest kidnapping ever . . .

We passed through a moss-covered archway into a wooded area. There were pine trees all around and I felt claustrophobic until we broke into sudden open space.

My captor let go of my arm.

We were in a grove, probably fifty yards of circular space surrounded by tall trees. The main light, aside from the moon above, came from a large torch that had been stuck in the center of the circle, next to an overturned log. There were people milling around on the other side of the circle, maybe three dozen or so. About half of them carried flashlights.

One of the ones without a flashlight strode across the circle to meet us. When she passed beneath the torch, I saw she was an intense-looking brunette in a dark green robe.

"Took you long enough," she chirped to my kidnapper.

His massive shoulders shrugged.

"They got pretty far into the ritual before they were interrupted," he explained.

"What was it this time?" the brunette inquired, sounding annoyed. Her hair was impeccably styled into casual-looking waves that almost made me regret my hasty hack job on my own hair.

"Guns and a Bible reading," my kidnapper answered, sounding bored. "Snipers took out those orbs Maire likes so much."

That made the brunette smile. She was very pretty. In a ferocious kind of way. Neither the smile nor the smattering of freckles across the pale skin of her nose did anything to soften her appearance.

"Good," she said. "I hate those stupid things."

"And there were smoke bombs," the giant added. "They smelled terrible. Didn't they, Macie?"

"Terrible," I agreed, trying to make my voice as casual as his. "Um, what am I doing here?"

The brunette slugged my kidnapper on the arm.

"You didn't tell her? What did you do, drag her off like some barbarian thug?"

The thug leaned down and kissed her sweetly on the mouth.

"I was being dramatic. I know how you love it when I'm dramatic."

The brunette rolled her eyes, not quite hiding her smile. Then she turned to me and put out a businesslike hand.

"I'm Autumn Forster," she said, then gestured toward the thug. "This is Royce. Please excuse him."

"Sure," I said, as I shook her hand. What else was I supposed to say?

Autumn grinned, her eyes sparkling with intrigue. She gestured to the grove at her back. "Welcome to your *real* initiation, Macie."

"I'm not following," I admitted, squinting in the dim light to get a look at the people gathered behind her. Some were in robes, but most were not. Not that anybody was skyclad, thank goodness—they were mostly in jeans. There was one girl in head-to-toe black with spiky, angry-looking hair, but everyone else looked fairly harmless. They were all within a year or two of my age.

Apparently the young people of Witchtown preferred to initiate their own.

"She gets it," Autumn surmised, watching me closely.

I looked back in the direction we had come from. I couldn't be quite as blasé about what had just happened as they could.

"What exactly was that back there?" I asked. "Did anybody get hurt?"

Autumn laughed at that, and Royce let out a snort.

"Oh, no," he said, snorting again. "That was just the Zealots."

"The Zealots?" I repeated.

"Yeah. They're like extreme Christians. They're camped outside the wall, and they pull stunts like that every now and then." Autumn went to explain further, but then her attention shifted to something behind me. "Kellen, are we ready?"

I froze at the name.

"All set" came a familiar-sounding voice. He stepped into my eye line a moment later, carrying four unlit torches and a white candle. I wondered again how I could have possibly mistaken him for Rafe. It wasn't just the details, like his lighter hair. Kellen gave off an entirely different vibe. And from the available evidence, his smile came a lot easier.

"Macie, this is Kellen," Autumn said, relieving him of the white candle. "Kellen, this is Macie."

"We've met, sort of," Kellen said, and grinned at me. He pulled a small vial out of his pocket, which I thought was kind of weird until he tossed it to Autumn and said, "Water. The rest is already on the altar."

"Great. Let's get started."

At Autumn's direction, everyone spread out around the edges of the grove and linked hands to form a circle. Out of the corner of my eye, I thought I saw the girl in black fade quietly into the woods, rather than join hands with anyone. Autumn stood importantly on the other side of the log, facing me. Royce hurried to stand on her left and after Kellen handed out the torches, he came to stand on her right.

It was all a lot more relaxed than the formal ritual in the square. Autumn used a random tree branch for a wand and the elements were called with a saltshaker, a stick of incense, a candle, and the water vial from Kellen's pocket.

If anything, the lack of formality just made me more nervous. When Autumn raised her arms to invoke the Goddess of the Forest to guide the ritual, I clutched my moonstone and invoked a Goddess of my own.

Laverna, I implored. *Extend your darkness and obscurity over my misdeeds.*

Autumn lowered her hands and cupped them widely around the candle flame. The smile drained from her face and a look of concentration took its place. When she raised her eyes to meet mine, they were full of utter seriousness and something else . . . something that meant she was channeling power. From the candle, from the circle, from all of us. I couldn't feel it, of course, but that didn't mean my vows weren't going to be bound by more than just my words.

The thought made me shiver a little. I tried not to show it.

Darkness and clouds. Darkness and clouds . . .

"Macie O'Sullivan," Autumn began, her voice rich with ritual authority. "Do you claim the name of 'witch'?"

"Yes," I said, and tried not to look like I was bracing myself for a thunderbolt, or whatever else might strike me down for trying to claim a title I didn't deserve.

Let me seem just and pious.

Autumn continued.

"Do you vow to serve the ancient ways?"

"Yes," I said. Not as big a lie as the first one.

"And are you committed to advancing the positive image of witch culture, politically, spiritually, and in whatever other way may become necessary?"

"Huh?" I asked. I felt like I'd missed a step somewhere.

Autumn rolled her eyes and switched back to her normal speaking voice.

"Basically," she said impatiently, "I want you to promise that your actions will not perpetuate the popular notion that witches are nothing but delusional, crunchy fuck-wits. Or, alternatively, that we are dangerously powerful, psychotic heathens bent on world domination."

"Uh—" As I struggled to keep a straight face, I got a glimpse of Kellen, just a bit behind Autumn, doing exactly the same thing.

He caught me looking at him and winked.

I frowned back, irritated by the familiarity, and turned my attention to Autumn.

"Uh, sure, I guess I can promise that . . ."

"Good. Welcome to Witchtown." Autumn clapped her hands. "The circle is undone, but let it never be broken."

She grinned at me, and all the trappings of ritual disappeared from her face.

"Now we can drink."

It was over. I had done it.

I sat down shakily on a log. I hadn't allowed myself to feel the full extent of my nerves during the ritual. If I had, I wouldn't have had the strength to stand there, vulnerable, letting all of that magic get channeled around me. The young people of Witchtown were a powerful lot. That much even I could tell.

But none of them had realized there was a Void in their midst.

"Drink?"

I jumped at the voice, and looked up to see Kellen offering me a plastic cup.

I took it and he sat down, uninvited, on my log. About an

arm's length to my left. He had removed his black robe and was wearing jeans and a gray cotton jacket. It made me feel a little bit overdressed in my crimson robe. The robe was making me feel a bit hot, as it was a pretty warm evening, even for June. But I couldn't quite bring myself to take it off. There was a strange kind of safety in its velvety soft pleats.

I took the cup and peered suspiciously at the mystery liquid inside. It was too dark to get a good look at it.

"Wine," Kellen assured me. "Witchtown's finest. Did you know we have a winery here?"

"No, I didn't," I said, as a small movement caught my eye. The girl in black emerged from the trees on the other side of the grove. She stood still for a moment, just inside the circle of torchlight, then turned and sat down against a tree at least twenty paces from the nearest group.

I nodded toward her.

"What's with her?"

Kellen leaned forward to follow my eye line. "Talya? Don't know, really. She's only been here for about a month or so. She keeps to herself. Doesn't like to participate in rituals."

"Is she a Solitary?" I asked.

"She says so," he said, and leaned toward me, affecting a melodramatic tone. "There's a rumor that she's a Void."

"Oh?" I said. And that made up my mind about the wine. I took a drink, hoping that it would wash down the slightly choky feeling in my throat. "Is she?"

"Nah," Kellen scoffed, his voice returning to normal. The dim torchlight made his profile look very sharp, almost angular. "I mean, I've never seen her channel, but that doesn't mean she can't. I'm pretty sure Autumn started the whole 'Void' rumor after Talya wouldn't let us initiate her."

I raised my eyebrows. It hadn't occurred to me that getting initiated was a choice, but it *had* occurred to Talya. She had defied Autumn and gotten away with it. That gave me a surge of respect for her.

I must have given my thoughts away with my expression, because Kellen laughed suddenly.

"I know, right? Autumn doesn't hear the word *no* very often."

"Not from you, anyway," I quipped. "What are you? Like, her lackey?"

Kellen choked in midsip. "Excuse me?"

I scanned the circle until I found the forceful brunette. She was making out with Royce on the other side of the grove. Actually, there were quite a few people making out. That had a tendency to happen after rituals. Something about raising all that power. So I'd been told.

I inclined my head toward Autumn.

"You were pretty much doing her bidding today," I pointed out, thinking of the torches, the candles, and the rest of the setup, which had obviously been his doing.

"So?" he said evenly. His face was hard to read.

"So why would you do that?"

"Do I need a reason?" he asked. He was watching me curiously, in kind of an amused way. "I'm a nice guy, Macie. I help out. What's wrong with that?"

"Nothing," I said, staring at my wine. "Nothing at all."

People who are legitimately *nice don't have to spell it out like that.*

I wasn't sure why I was being so hard on him. The only thing I could really accuse Kellen of was not being the person I had thought he was at the farmer's market. Which was hardly his fault. Maybe the wine was clouding my judgment.

But I doubted it. My instincts were telling me there was something here that needed figuring out.

Kellen took another sip of his wine and sat forward on the log. He was a few inches closer to me now than he had been, and I caught a whiff of a woodsy, piney scent. Juniper, I thought. But I wasn't sure if it was coming from Kellen or from the trees around us.

"I have a knack for ritual," he admitted. "I'm good at it. Autumn is our self-appointed High Priestess, which makes Royce the High Priest by default. But they're not very good with details."

"And you are?"

He grinned.

"Maybe."

I'll bet you are.

I grinned back at him. He was quite good-looking. In a decidedly non-Rafe kind of way. The thought made something in my chest start to ache.

I ignored it. This was strictly professional. All business. Nothing that should wake up the sinkhole.

He took another sip of his wine.

"Enough about me. What about you? What's your problem, Macie?"

"My *problem*?" I asked, not sure I had heard him right.

"Yeah. Witchtown is a refuge. A haven, literally. Lowercase *h*. And people generally don't end up in havens if everything is going great for them on the outside. So what's your problem?"

I stalled, taking several sips of wine as I thought about my answer. The dry, slightly sour taste was starting to grow on me.

"Nothing, really," I said at last. Then, as an afterthought, I added, "I mean, my mother is kind of a pain in the ass."

"She's a Natural, right?"

"Yeah." I licked my lips. "We move around a lot. I've been hoping we could stay in one place for a while."

I drank some more wine, mostly to stop myself from saying more. There had been a little bit more truth in there than I had meant to throw in. I squinted into my cup, which was nearly empty now, and tried to recall how the conversation had shifted to me.

Because he shifted it, I realized. Maybe I was right to be wary of him.

"What about you?" I countered. "What's *your* problem?"

He shrugged innocently. "I'm pretty boring."

"Oh, really?" I raised an eyebrow.

"Yup," he said, smiling now. "Nothing to tell."

"I doubt that," I said. I could feel my smile fade. I was frustrated at the smirking stone wall that was suddenly sitting next to me.

And a little bit impressed. Most people had a tendency to blab on and on about themselves when given the slightest excuse. I usually counted on that. But this guy . . . somehow he had gotten me to do the blabbing.

Having one of my best tricks used against me put me on edge. I made a face and drank the last sip of wine in my cup before I looked over at him again.

"So, I guess we're the only two people in Witchtown without any problems, huh?"

He cocked his head, seemingly considering this as he moved even closer to me on the log. There were only a few inches separating us now. Just the width of my left hand, which was lying on the rough bark between us.

"I can think of worse things to have in common," he said.

He was close enough that I could feel his breath on my cheek when he spoke. The juniper scent was stronger now — it was definitely coming from him. It must have been the wine, but for a second, when he leaned toward me, I actually considered what it would be like to kiss him. To pretend, for just one night, to get caught up in the power of my own initiation ritual, drink a bit too much wine, and make out with a cute, mysterious stranger in the woods. That's what a normal girl my age would do. Wasn't I supposed to be fitting in?

Then I thought of Rafe, and I jerked back so suddenly that I would have fallen off the log if Kellen hadn't reached out a hand to steady me.

"I—I can't. I have . . . I mean, there's . . . there's somebody."

At that moment I felt like Rafe was *right there*, watching me. I felt it so strongly that I tore myself away from Kellen's beautiful eyes—wow, they were really, really blue—and looked furtively around the grove, searching for Rafe.

Kellen followed my gaze, looking confused.

"What, here? That was fast. Didn't you only get here yesterday?"

"He's not . . ." I trailed off, inwardly berating myself. *He's not here, you idiot. Get a grip.* "He's not here. He's from . . . before."

"Oh," Kellen said knowingly. "So you're doing the long distance thing?"

"Something like that . . ."

"Got it," he said, letting go of my arm. "Sorry, I didn't know."

"It's okay." I still could *not* shake the feeling that I was being watched. I got to my feet slowly, holding on to the log until the last possible second in case the wine chose that moment to catch up with me.

Kellen stood up as well. He had that look of curious amusement on his face again. After a moment, he put his hand out to me.

"It was nice to meet you, Macie O'Sullivan. I'll be seeing you around."

"You too."

"You know your way back? I can walk you—"

"I'll manage."

He frowned at this, then reached into his jacket pocket and pulled out a small flashlight.

"Take this. Due south will bring you downtown. The woods aren't big. If you keep walking long enough, you'll find your way out."

"Thanks," I said.

At the edge of the clearing, I passed the girl in black. Was *she* the one who had been watching me? Her eyes seemed locked on something behind me, on the other side of the circle, but when I got within a few feet of her, she turned her head to look at me.

She gave me a very slight nod.

I nodded in return, even though she had already looked away from me. Back to whatever she had been staring at before.

As I walked south, as instructed, I caught my eyes

automatically scanning the ground, looking for usable plants. I thought of the last time I had been in the woods at the full moon. There had been a guy there that night as well. But unlike Kellen, he hadn't tried to kiss me.

Quite the opposite. The first night I had met Rafe, he had damn near almost killed me.

I smiled at the memory. My feet took me through the forest gate, back toward the dim lights of downtown. But my mind was in an entirely different Haven, on an entirely different night . . .

I let myself into the rickety wooden building my mother and I had moved into earlier that day . . . and almost immediately let myself back out again, slamming the door behind me.

My mother was not alone. She and her friend, whoever he was, were getting to know each other. All over the futon that I had staked out as my bed.

Gross.

I rubbed my bare arms to keep warm and walked away from the tiny group of houses, all similarly run-down and in bad need of new paint jobs. I walked toward the rougher part of the Haven, where the trees were.

At least that explained what we were doing here. I had been wondering all day what had brought us to this Gods-forsaken, broken-down rural Haven in the middle of nowhere, built on land that nobody wanted anyway—the kind of Haven that pro-Witch activists liked to point to as evidence of witches' second-class treatment. We weren't going to find much money here. We'd probably end up losing money here.

So of course there had to be a guy in the picture. Why hadn't I seen that sooner?

I didn't have the stomach to think about that for long, or the energy to face nursing her through yet another failed relationship. So I just kept walking.

The trees closed in around me and it got darker, but the light from the full moon overhead filtered through the scraggly pine needles just enough to light my way.

There didn't seem to be much to find at first. Not in this sorry excuse for a forest. I was on the verge of giving up, on sitting down and just letting time pass, when I found the mandrakes.

There were dozens of them, all clustered around the roots of a particularly large pine tree. Mandrakes are unassuming above the surface, just clusters of purplish flowers surrounded by lush green leaves. It's their roots that are noteworthy. They have a creepy tendency to look like people; gnarled, twisted, scowling people. They are deeply poisonous but they are also very popular things to put on altars. I could always sell them pretty much as fast as I could find them.

I had a half dozen dug up and set out in a line on the ground before I found something else.

One mandrake had claimed a plastic bag by growing a thin

tendril of root around it. When I worked the bag free, I stared in disbelief at several clusters of tightly rolled hundred-dollar bills.

I peered into the hole that the mandrake plant had left behind. The glare of moonlight on wrinkled plastic stared back at me. More bags. At least three that I could see, and the hole was deep.

When I reached my hand down to get the rest, I was immediately thrown back. As though someone had shoved me, even though there was no one else there. Before I even hit the ground, a very intense pain blossomed in my middle.

I curled up in the dirt in agony, the money forgotten. I couldn't move. I was making a horrible sound, something between a screech and a groan. A few endless minutes later, when something prodded me painfully in the ribs, I couldn't stop myself from being rolled over onto my side. A dark shape loomed over me, and to my pained eyes it looked as gnarled and misshapen as the mandrake roots.

I recoiled as it crouched down beside me.

"What are you doing with that?"

The plastic baggie was yanked from my hand, and the pain stopped immediately. It left me so abruptly that I gasped. When I was able to sit up, the shape was still there. I blinked away black clouds and tried to focus on the eyes that were glaring down at me.

There was a face around the eyes, a guy's face, made of dark brown skin and framed by shaggy black hair the same color as his eyes. It was a combination I might have found attractive if I hadn't been pretty sure I was about to throw up. And if the eyes had not been staring at me so murderously.

"Who are you?" he asked, still glaring. "How did you know to look here?"

"I'm Macie," I told him. I saw no point in lying. My voice sounded hoarse from screaming. "Macie O'Sullivan. I just moved here—"

"Get out of here, Macie O'Sullivan," he commanded darkly. "And don't come back. Do you hear?"

I nodded, and stumbled a bit as I struggled to get my feet beneath me.

"Go," he said impatiently.

"I'm going," I said unsteadily. Then, when I finally got to my feet, I added, "Jerk."

I woke with a start, back in Witchtown, back on the previous accountant's couch. I was clutching Rafe's jacket to my face and crying.

This is ridiculous, I told myself, and sat up.

Much as it pained me to admit it, my mother had been right about one thing. I had to let it go. Or at least, I was going to have to fool myself into thinking that I had. There would be plenty of time to cry about Rafe. Later. But now I had to focus. There was only one Witchtown, and I couldn't afford to make any mistakes here.

I gave the jacket one last squeeze. One last, long inhale so I could commit its scent to memory. Then I stuffed it underneath the couch cushion.

When I lay back down, I took comfort in the slight lump I felt beneath me. It was a crutch, I knew that. I didn't have the strength to get rid of the jacket entirely. But at least it was a step in the right direction. It was enough.

Enough for now.

CHAPTER FIVE

*M*ayor Bainbridge summoned my mother and me to her office first thing in the morning. To address the tiny, niggling issue that I hadn't technically been initiated the previous night.

The mayor rectified that by casting a small circle around us on the floor of her office and taking me through the vows herself. It happened too spur of the moment for me to get nervous, and it was over too quickly for me to get more than mildly stressed out about it.

"Cursed Zealots," she said, after she had closed the circle. "What do they think they're going to accomplish anyway? They can't believe they're going to convert anybody. Not *here*."

"Did the guards catch the priests?" I asked.

"No," the mayor answered, sounding regretful. "They got away in the smoke."

"The real question," my mother said, "is how they got

into town in the first place. Why didn't the wall keep them out?"

The mayor bit her lip. This was clearly not a subject she wanted to discuss with Witchtown's newest high-profile resident.

"We think they might be getting some help. From *inside* the town," she admitted.

"You mean, like a spy?" I asked. I was intrigued, in spite of myself, at the thought of a Zealot spy hiding out among the Witchtown residents. There was definitely more to this town than I had thought.

"I wouldn't be that dramatic about it," the mayor mumbled. "Those particular clowns have been camped out since we started building Witchtown, and they've never done anything truly violent. Yet."

She exchanged a fretful glance with the ground for a few seconds before she looked up at my mother and changed the subject.

"I'm having Lois assemble the town books for you to have a look at. While she's working on that, perhaps you'd like to see your new office?"

"Very much," my mother said.

"Great! I'll take you myself. I have to make one quick call . . ."

While we waited for the mayor outside in the square, my mother grabbed my arm.

"You never told me what happened to you last night," she pointed out.

"I just hung out in the woods with a couple of kids," I said vaguely.

A look of tired disapproval came over her face.

"Why are you wasting your time there?" she sniffed. "Kids don't know anything."

"*I'm* a kid," I snapped.

My mother gave me a long look.

"I'm worried about you, Macie. I think you need to pull a job."

"*Now?*" I asked, incredulous. "It's too early! We can't steal something the second we get to town!"

That was practically Thievery 101. And my mother knew it.

"We need some seed money—" she started.

"No we don't," I barked. "We still have the money we got from the last town."

"Fine. Then maybe I just need you to prove to me what side you're on. I'm having doubts."

She caught my eye. And before I could look away, I could tell that she saw the same doubts reflected there. Dammit.

"Something small," she cautioned. "Nothing flashy. Just something to get your confidence back. Today. Tonight, at the latest."

"You're not even going to help me?" I pleaded.

She shook her head.

"I think it's about time we see what you can do on your own. Impress me."

"You know that I—" I paused, and ground my back molars together. "You know I can't do what you can do. How am I supposed to—"

"You'll figure it out. Use *your* strengths. Stop depending so much on mine."

"What if—hey!"

My mother grabbed my hand without any sort of warning. I tried to pull away, but her grip was bone crushing. She was staring, wide-eyed, at something behind me.

I turned my head to see.

It was an old lady, coming out of the Witchtown Post Office. One of those impossibly old women, with skin as thin as paper and prominent bones that look too delicate to hold them upright. I could tell she was petite even though her frame was concealed beneath multiple layers of ratty sweaters and shawls. Her long gray hair looked like it had been carefully styled about a decade ago but left to fend for itself ever since; two messy French braids hung down like dreadlocks to her waist.

I was at a loss to explain this woman's effect on my mother, until she shifted a grocery bag from her left hip to her right, and the silver ring on her hand flashed in the sunlight.

"The other Natural," I said, mostly to myself, staring at the ring.

"Well," my mother murmured. "I never thought I'd see *her* again."

I blinked over at my mother in disbelief. "You *know* her?"

We did not know people. Witches (with the exception of my mother) like to put down roots, so they tend to stay in one place. And since we never went to the same Haven twice, we never saw the same people more than once.

Not that it would have mattered if we did. We always made sure no one would remember us. Which is to say, *she* made sure.

We did *not* know people.

The vicelike grip on my hand suddenly loosened, and my mother's expression shifted from shock back to her usual knowing smirk.

"I *knew* her," she corrected me stiffly. "A long time ago. Too many Havens back to count."

I looked over at the woman again and tried to imagine her younger, less wrinkled. I couldn't, but even so, I was fairly certain I had no memory of her. I must have been very young when we had encountered her before.

A thought occurred to me. I bit the inside of my lip and braced myself, proceeding carefully.

"If it's been that long," I began, "are you sure the spell is still—"

"Of course I'm sure," she snarled. She was always touchy about that spell. The one that erased our very existences, over and over again. The one that made us ghosts in the memories of everyone we had ever met. She performed it at the conclusion of every job; it was the last thing we did before we left a Haven.

I had no reason to doubt her, or the spell. But I had never actually seen it in action before—we had always left too quickly. My eyes flickered back over to the old woman, who was rooting through her purse with her free hand and muttering to herself.

"Watch," my mother said irritably, and slid around me until she was in front of the woman. "May I give you a hand?"

"My glasses," the woman mumbled, still staring down into the purse.

"Perhaps I can find them," my mother suggested, smiling so sweetly it made my insides clench. "May I?"

The old Natural looked up, squinted for a moment, then shrugged and placed her tattered, moth-eaten purse into my mother's waiting hands.

My mother fished out a beat-up silver case.

"Pardon me for saying so," she said, as she removed a pair of glasses with the thickest lenses I had ever seen and held them out for the old Natural to take. "But have we met before? You seem very familiar to me."

The woman slid the enormous frames onto her nose and I held my breath as she gave my mother a thorough going-over, from head to toe.

"Don't think so," she pronounced finally, and put out a hand. "I'm Pendle. Pendle Bishop."

My mother introduced herself, and me, and Pendle Bishop gave no sign that she had ever seen us before. Once, I thought I caught her looking at my moonstone. But at second glance, I saw that her eyes were so cloudy and unfocused it was a wonder she could see anything at all. Even with the thick glasses.

Eventually, she puttered away. My mother flashed me an "I told you so" expression just as the mayor reemerged from her office.

"A job," my mother reminded me, lowering her voice. "By tomorrow."

Then she smiled and tossed something at me. I caught it. I didn't even need to look to know that it was Pendle Bishop's wallet.

"Easy as that," my mother trilled, then winked as she turned to meet the mayor. "Darkness and clouds!"

"Darkness and clouds," I muttered at her back.

I turned sharply in the opposite direction, my nerves still humming slightly at the memory of Pendle Bishop's milky, unfocused eyes. I concentrated on keeping my feet moving, telling myself forcefully that her eyes were only like that because she was very, very old.

Rafe's eyes did not — could not — look like that.

I didn't have my map with me, but yesterday I had noted the location of the Magic Supply Depot. It was one of the buildings on the main square, just a few doors down from the mayor's office. I still needed elder and valerian, and I had been too freaked out by my faux Rafe sighting yesterday to venture out in search of them after the farmer's market.

Stalling, a pesky voice in the back of my head accused. *You're stalling.*

I shook it off. I was *not* stalling. The early stages of a con are all about getting the lay of the land. You have to understand how a Haven works in order to figure out where the money is. The *real* money. Every Haven has a town fund or some other bank account where they keep the funds the government gives. In the poorer Havens, sometimes that was all there was to steal. But we were counting on Witchtown having something better than that.

If I was going to find it, I was going to have to figure out how things worked here. What the power structure was. Because all of my instincts were telling me that the mayor was not it. Mayor Bainbridge may have been the head of Witchtown, but I was after the heart. That would be where the money was. That would be our "in," the spot where we had to strike.

Per my mother's command, I also had to find something quick that I could steal by tonight. Downtown seemed like the logical place to start looking.

I had only gone a few steps before I started to get a weird, prickly feeling on the back of my neck. Like somebody was following me. I didn't let on. I just kept strolling casually, even as I spotted the shingle with the words MAGIC SUPPLY DEPOT on it and my hopes of finding my herbs quietly died.

The Depot's door was boarded up and the windows were papered over. Odd, because the building itself seemed quite new. The white on its walls was slightly brighter than the buildings on either side of it, and when I sniffed the air I caught the faint whiff of fresh paint and just-sawed lumber.

Was I imagining things, or was the shingle over the door a little bit singed at the corners?

Sigh. I was going to have to think of another way to get my herbs.

I continued walking, as though the Depot had not been my destination at all. There was still someone behind me, I could tell. And suddenly, I was tired of playing this game.

I turned the corner onto Swords and Cups Avenue, then stopped walking abruptly and turned around so I would be face to face with my shadow when they came around after me. Whoever they were. I didn't know many people in town yet, so my list of suspects was pretty short. Kellen? Perhaps. Autumn? No, she wasn't the kind to do her own legwork. She would most likely send Royce. It was probably Royce.

But the pigtailed girl who came around the corner a moment later could not have been less Royce-like. She was wearing an electric blue tank top, white sequin leg warmers over fuzzy, purple pants, and a pink cowboy hat. She was also carrying a broom.

She skidded to a halt at the sight of me.

"Gotcha!" she said, with an embarrassed giggle. "Now it's your turn, okay? Chase me!"

She turned on her heel and looked eagerly over her shoulder to make sure I was going to follow her.

I could think of no good excuse not to do as she asked. After a moment's hesitation, I followed her around the corner, back to the front of the Depot, where I ran right smack into the girl in black.

"Oooofff!" The girl—what had Kellen said her name was? Talya?—recovered first, took a step back, and glared down at the small girl in the hat.

"Aimee!" she said accusingly, and grabbed the girl by one arm.

"I told her to chase me," Aimee admitted, and the brim of the cowboy hat obscured her face as she looked down at her feet.

Talya turned to me. She was wearing all black again: jeans, boots, and several layered T-shirts, the same as last night. But today she was also wearing a black bandanna over her short black hair. The broom in her hand was a size larger than the little girl's.

"I'm Macie. Macie O'Sullivan." I said, extending a hand. I wasn't quite sure why I did it. I couldn't think of a way that knowing the girl in black would be of any help to me. But still, there I was, offering her my hand.

She hesitated before letting go of Aimee.

"I'm Natalya. Talya. Cohen," she said at last, taking my hand lightly in what my mother would've called a weak handshake. "And this is my cousin Aimee."

She gestured down to the little girl, but she didn't take her eyes off me. She stared at me, her brown eyes expectant. Like she was waiting for something.

The staring went on for so long that I started to feel like I should do something. Like dance, or burst into song. But instead, I just stared back. Her gaze was unflinching. Her eyes were that light shade of brown that makes eyes look lit up from the inside. They looked especially bright alongside her black clothing and hair.

"What?" I asked.

"Nothing. You're new here, right?" she asked. "Are you lost?"

I gestured toward the boarded-up building behind us.

"I was looking for the Supply Depot, but it seems to be closed."

"It's been closed since I got to town," Talya informed me. "Most people here order stuff online. What do you need?"

"Some herbs," I said vaguely.

"Which ones?" she pressed me.

I scowled again. I didn't like being pressed.

"Elderflower," I told her. "And some valerian root."

She nodded slowly, as though filing this away, then looked over her shoulder toward a group of people who were gathered around the altar in the square. "Aimee and I are supposed to be over there," she said. "You can come with us if you like."

It was impossible to tell from her tone whether she was extending the invitation out of politeness or if she actually wanted me there. She didn't seem like someone who was overly concerned with social niceties. So I decided to call her bluff.

"Sure. Let's go."

Talya turned without a word and began to walk away, dragging her cousin along behind her.

What a weird girl.

But was she a Void?

I shook off the thought and, with one last glance at the defunct Depot, I hurried to catch up to her.

The people in the square were industriously sweeping up the shattered orb glass and assorted other odds and ends that remained from last night's ritual. I recognized Autumn and Royce.

There was no sign of Kellen, I noted with relief.

Autumn bent to sweep a pile of broken glass into a dustbin. When we approached, she straightened up and glared at Talya.

"You're late."

"That's my fault," I jumped in. "I got lost and needed directions."

Talya looked at me curiously. It wasn't quite true, of course, but at least it got Autumn off her back. The junior High Priestess looked away from her and shot an uncertain glance at Aimee, who was smiling up at her.

"Let's just get on with the ritual," Autumn resolved.

The rest of the sweepers gathered around us and took

turns dumping their dustbins into a trash bag that Royce was passing around.

"What ritual?" Talya asked Autumn, her voice sounding tight. "I thought we were just here to clean up the glass and stuff."

"We finished that part," Autumn informed her, "no thanks to you. Now we have to balance the energy."

She looked at Talya like she was daring her to argue. Talya drew in a breath, then pursed her lips and took a step backwards, falling into line with the rest of the broom squad.

Autumn picked up an earthenware jar from the altar, then turned to assess the dozen or so people assembled before her. Her eyes fell on me and my lack of broom, and she thrust the jar into my arms.

"Macie will scatter the salt around the square," she announced. "The rest of us will sweep. Clockwise, of course. And let's make it quick, people. We all have more interesting things to do today, I'm sure. *Stupid* orbs."

Oddly, Talya's obvious lack of comfort with the ritual was making me totally forget my own. I reached into the jar, grabbed a handful of salt, and tossed it onto the ground. The others, including Talya and little Aimee, spread out behind me to sweep the salt, along with all of the negative energy the Zealots had brought with them, out of the ritual area.

As I worked my way clockwise around the circle, as directed, I pretended that I was scattering sprinkles on top of a cake. *Mhmmmm, cake.* I had been a raw vegan for less than forty-eight hours, and already it was getting old. I had eaten only a large spoonful of peanut butter and a handful of straw-berries for breakfast, and my stomach was starting to growl.

Out of the corner of my eye, I saw Autumn light a white candle on the altar. She stood in front of it, raised her arms to the sky, and mumbled a few words. She was still scowling.

My usual ritual nerves were just starting to spring to life when Royce came up alongside me and whispered into my ear.

"Don't mind Autumn. She's grumpy today."

"She really hates those orbs," I remarked, also in a whisper.

Royce laughed quietly at this.

"Yeah, Autumn prefers rituals to be simple. More nat-ural."

"Oh," I said, remembering my no-frills initiation in the woods. "What about you?"

Royce leaned on his broom as he pondered this.

"I don't know," he said again, shrugging his mountainous shoulders. "I guess—"

He stopped, his attention suddenly caught by something on the other side of the square.

It was Talya, and she was staring straight at Royce. But not in that awkward way she had stared at me earlier. This time she was standing motionless, one hand on the handle of her broom, driving the bristles into the ground. Her eyes were fixed in Royce's direction, but it looked like they were ze-roed in on something behind him. As though she was looking through him.

"Talya? What's wrong?" Royce asked.

She didn't move, except to abruptly cover her mouth with her free hand.

Behind the altar, Autumn opened her eyes at the sound of Royce's voice, followed his gaze, and narrowed her eyes severely in Talya's direction.

I don't know where the thought came from, but suddenly it was very clear to me that I needed to distract everyone from Talya. So I did the only thing I could think to do; I dropped the jar of salt.

It hit the ground with a loud thud and shattered, spilling broken pottery and salt all over the cobblestones at my feet.

All the eyes in the square, including Autumn's, shifted from Talya to me.

"Great!" Autumn said, her voice oozing sarcasm as she snuffed out the candle in front of her. "Now we get to start all over. Thanks, Macie."

On the other side of the square, Talya lowered her hand from her mouth and tried to put it nonchalantly on her hip. But I noticed that her other hand, the one holding the broom, was shaking.

I had never really known another Void. I had seen one once, when we had passed through the city of San Francisco. She had been living on the streets in a pile of rags and garbage, and I had known her by the red, blistery *V* that had been branded on her left cheek.

No one knows why some people just can't channel. In theory, becoming a Learned witch is not that complicated: as opposed to Natural witches (who work with their own, internal power), Learned witches use power channeled from external sources, like the moon or the wind. The only way to become a Natural is to be born one. But with enough study and practice, anyone can learn to channel and become a Learned. In theory, anyway. Voids are the exception to the rule. They are rare, but even so, Havens go to great lengths to keep them out.

Every Haven keeps an iron cattle brand. They mark you before they banish you so no other Haven can ever be tricked into taking you. And so the outside world will know you for what you are. Or what you tried to be, anyway. There's no evidence that Voids are contagious, but this is one area where witches are unwilling to take chances. Not even Witchtown allowed Voids, and they were as progressive as Havens got.

I had nightmares for years after I saw that woman. About how easy it would be to get found out. And how the red-hot metal would feel as it seared into my face. I still thought about it sometimes.

I wondered if Talya ever did. I wondered if she ever felt empty, the way I did. Like a hollow, worthless vessel, which no power could be coaxed to enter.

Except that one time . . .

No, that time did not count. It had been a rain spell and it had been in Seattle. Seattle. Where it was pretty weird for it *not* to be raining.

Besides, even if I had channeled that day, it took more than one accidental rainstorm to make someone a witch. "Witch" was not a title I could ever hope to claim.

When the square was clean, both spiritually and physically, Autumn released everyone. I watched Talya grab Aimee by the hand and begin to march her quickly out of the square, right past me.

She paused and turned around to face me. "Thank you," she said stiffly, and I got the distinct feeling these were not words she said often.

"Sure," I said, although I wasn't really certain what I had done.

She went to take a step and then paused again.

"What herbs did you say you needed?"

"Elder and valerian," I repeated.

"Do you mind wild herbs?"

"I prefer them," I said truthfully.

I thought I saw a ghost of a smile appear on her lips. Then she pulled on Aimee's hand and led her away without further comment.

I stared after her. There was a lot to ponder there, but I couldn't afford to think about it right now.

I had a robbery to plan.

CHAPTER SIX

*T*here were at least eight color-coded bins in the alley behind the mayor's office. Part of Witchtown's ridiculously complicated recycling program. The mayor had tried explaining it to us last night, but I had tuned out most of it. I doubted we'd be here long enough to tarnish Witchtown's zero carbon footprint anyway.

To the left of the bins, there were two doors. The streetlights overhead provided just enough of a glow for me to see that one was labeled ARCHIVES. The other was unmarked, but looked like it led into the office itself.

I stood in front of the blank door, with a small black bag in my gloved hand. Fighting against my better judgment.

Just get it over with.

I took out a flashlight and wedged it into my armpit to get a better look at the lock.

Pick or bump?

Picks are quiet and elegant, and leave no trace. Bumping is faster, but there's always a chance of damaging the lock. And it would be better if the mayor thought this was an inside job.

But as I looked around, at the scant cover provided by the alley, I decided that speed was more important. It was close to two in the morning, and the streets of Witchtown had been silent on the walk here, but I didn't know this town well enough to risk loitering around the alley for long.

Which is the whole problem with pulling a job too early.

I opened the bag and pulled out a ring of keys and a small rubber mallet. Screwdrivers or tension wrenches were more traditional, but I had always found mallets easier to grip. Plus, they make a lot less noise.

I noted the lock type, found the correct bump key, and slid it home. Three sharp, muffled taps with the mallet to make the pins jump and *bam,* I was in. And the lock was still in one piece.

Thanking Laverna for small favors, I opened the door. I paused briefly on the threshold, but there was no alarm. I hadn't really expected one. Witches, I had discovered, were secretive and paranoid and good at hiding things like spell books. But they were shockingly low-tech when it came to protecting things of *actual* value.

Some witches used protective spells, but I didn't think that would be an issue here either. Just in case, I had Laverna tucked into my bag. Her presence was usually enough to render those kinds of spells ineffective.

I walked to the center of the office.

Normally, when I was with my mother, this was when my part of the job would be over. She was much better than I was at finding money. It seemed to call out to her, like it wanted to be found. It had never been that way for me.

Use your strengths, she had told me.

Right, I thought back. Standing in the middle of the crammed office, which smelled strongly of stale coffee, I couldn't picture a situation where a working knowledge of herbs would be less helpful. Trust my mother to rub my nose in my own uselessness. That was probably her real reason for sending me out on my own.

Think, Macie, I ordered myself. *Everything you need is right in front of you.*

There had to be money here somewhere. Petty cash, a community fund, something. At this point I would have settled for the office clerk's lunch money. Anything monetary I could take home, to convince my mother my head was in the game.

My attention was drawn to the lone plant in the room, which was sitting in a pot on top of a squat wooden file cabinet. It was a much-neglected silverweed plant, sometimes called "five-finger grass" because its leaves look like a hand. It was an herb said to assist in "anything five fingers can do," particularly lucky in money matters.

My eyes traveled down the cabinet. The bottom drawer had a lock on it, which made me smile.

I always found it amusing when people put big beefy padlocks onto cheap, put-it-together-yourself furniture.

I set the silverweed on the mayor's desk, safely up and out of the way. Then I turned the file cabinet around and picked out the eight nails that were holding the faux-wood backing in place. After that, I just had to unscrew four cam locks before I could take the back off the locked drawer.

There were a bunch of files inside, mostly labeled with things like "Insurance" and "Important—Save." I was tempted to read through the one labeled "Private—Brooke," but then I found a manila envelope marked "Beautification Donations—for Deposit."

Inside was a stack of cash. Jackpot.

I stuffed the bills into my bag without bothering to count them. Then I replaced the empty folder and set about reassembling the file cabinet. When everything, including the silverweed, was back in its proper place, I slipped out the back door.

Just in time to see Talya come out of the door marked ARCHIVES.

In her black bandanna and entirely black outfit, she looked like even more of a thief than I did. But her face, with its slightly tuned-out expression of thoughtful boredom, said to me that she was not in the act of doing something wrong.

I highly doubted I had a similar look.

I stood, frozen, and watched her take in every detail. My black gloved hand on the doorknob of the office. The small black bag over my shoulder. The lateness of the hour.

I needed to think of something to say. Something to spin it: to make her think that *I* had caught *her* and not the other way around. But before I could think of anything Talya turned away, locked the door of the Archives, and slipped the key into her back pocket.

She nodded in my direction.

"'Night," she said, then turned, walked down the alley, and disappeared behind a brown bin marked COMPOST.

There had been $814 in the locked drawer. First thing the next morning, I left it all on the kitchen table, where my mother would find it.

Now that I had completed her stupid, unnecessary thief test, it was time to start planning the real heist. And that meant continuing to get my bearings in this strange new Haven. So I grabbed the mayor's map and headed out, with a steady stream of thoughts for company and a highly unsatisfying meal of leftover salad in my stomach.

I probably should have been more worried that I had gotten caught. Not that Talya had actually seen me do anything wrong. Even if the mayor noticed the money was missing and started asking around for suspects, Talya couldn't call me out for being there without placing herself at the scene of the crime as well.

If it came down to it, who's to say that the mayor wouldn't take the word of the innocent new arrival who just happened to be out for a late-night stroll over the word of a rumored Void?

I didn't love the thought of using that particular piece of gossip against Talya. But if it came down to her or me, I knew what side I would take. Still, I doubted I would have to go there.

I had a weird feeling that Talya wasn't going to tell anybody.

Putting the odd Goth out of my head for the moment, I paused to check the map. I had meant to walk north, toward something marked "the Tor," but I had been so lost in thought that I had somehow wandered west. I was standing on the shore of Witchtown Lake.

There were voices nearby. I darted behind a tree just as a small girl with white-blond hair ran by.

She was clutching a stick and looking over her shoulder. Before long, a mop-haired boy ran up behind her and made a grab for the stick.

"Kellen!" the girl called shrilly. *"Kellen!"*

I gulped, hopefully not audibly, as Kellen emerged from the nearby woods and walked right past my hiding place. Through the scraggly leaves of the stunted tree I was using for cover, I could see that in spite of the warm weather, he was wearing the same jacket he had worn at my initiation. He was also wearing a pair of jeans that, I had to admit, fit him nicely.

Stop it, I scolded myself. *You were going to be more careful with him, remember?*

"He's trying to steal my wand!" the girl cried as the boy lunged toward her again, missed the wand, and grabbed a chunk of her hair instead.

Kellen walked up to the squabbling kiddos, seized the disputed stick, and tossed it into the lake. Both kids gasped in protest.

"You don't want a wand you fought over," he explained. "The energy will never be right. You have to find one that feels right to you. *Only* to you. Got it?"

"Okay," the little girl mumbled, and ran back into the woods.

The boy said nothing. He stared wistfully at the spot where the wand had disappeared into the lake, until Kellen tickled him and hauled him toward the trees by his armpits.

"Come on, I saw a lot of good ones in here."

The little boy giggled and gazed up at Kellen, hero worship shining brightly in his eyes.

I smiled in spite of myself.

"Hi, Macie!" An alarmingly loud voice piped up behind me, startling me so completely that I shot to my feet. I spun around and found myself staring down at Talya's cousin Aimee.

"What are you doing here?" she asked, so loudly again that I cringed.

I looked warily over my shoulder. Kellen had stopped at the edge of the trees. He turned around and spotted me easily.

If he was surprised to find me here, he didn't show it.

"Looking to join the class?" he asked.

"Huh?" I asked.

"Kellen is our teacher!" Aimee announced. "He's the best!"

"I help out with the little ones a couple times a week during the summer," Kellen said.

Of course you do.

Assisting with rituals, hanging with the kids. What, was he running for Town Golden Boy? "A nice guy," he had called himself. Sure. Nobody was that nice for no reason.

He walked toward me until he was directly on the other side of my tree. "Right now we're trying to find wands."

"I found mine!" Aimee told him, holding up an arm-length branch.

"Great!" Kellen cheered, without looking away from me.

I narrowed my eyes at him; he smiled innocently in return.

"Care to join us?" he asked. It sounded like a dare.

"Sure," I said.

Once the kids had all found wands, Kellen led us to a grassy area beside the lake and explained that today's lesson was on channeling wind. For a heart-stopping moment, I worried that he was going to ask me to demonstrate. But instead he lit a candle, lined the kids up, and each one took a turn trying to summon up enough of a breeze to put out the flame.

Relieved that I was not required to participate, I stretched out on the grass a good distance away, with my head on Kellen's backpack. When I could tell that his attention was focused entirely on the kids, I put one hand behind my head and slipped the other inside the pack.

There wasn't much in there. A plastic bottle (probably water), a book, and—yahtzee!—a wallet. I extracted the small leather rectangle and rolled over partway so I could examine its contents in private.

The front pocket held a driver's license for one Kellen Stewart, age seventeen. Which was odd, considering that he lived in a place that didn't allow cars. There were also two twenty-dollar bills, a CPR certification card, and a frequent buyer card for someplace called the Crescent Roll that had five hole punches through it.

That was it. No pictures, no receipts, no notes.

I wasn't a master pickpocket, but I had lifted my share of wallets and I had never seen one so free of clutter. Pendle Bishop's, for example, had been stuffed so full of junk that I had had to dump the whole thing out before I found a lone five-dollar bill in the midst of the garbage.

Just another thing confirming my hunch that there was more to Kellen than met the eye.

I slipped the wallet, with the two twenties still inside,

back into the bag and rolled over, shielding my eyes against the warm sun and watching as he patiently took each kid through the exercise. He applauded them when they succeeded and reassured them when they came up short. One time he summoned a gust of wind himself, so strong it almost knocked the kids off their feet. They giggled hysterically at this and demanded more. A thought came to me out of nowhere: *Rafe would love this.*

It was an odd thought to have about the guy whose cold glare had kept me up for most of the night. Anger had been a part of who Rafe was, and angry Rafe had been the first version of him that I had become acquainted with. But there had been a lot more to Rafe than his anger. There were far better versions of him.

The sun, combined with my restless night and my long walk that morning, was making me drowsy. I felt my eyes start to close and I didn't fight it. It was nice here. Warm. And something about the ceaseless kid chatter and Kellen's calm explanations in the background made me feel safe.

I settled my head into a more comfortable position against the backpack and drifted off. Rafe would have felt at home here too. The *real* Rafe. The one I had met the day after I had found the mandrakes in the woods . . .

The knock on the door sent me stumbling toward it. I opened it without thinking and when I saw who it was, my stomach clenched in on itself, like it was reliving the night before. I mentally calculated how long it would take to slam the door in his face and run out the back.

Until his voice made me pause.

"It's Macie, right?"

It was a nice voice. Much better than the growly, menacing voice he had used before. It was hard to square the dark, murderous presence of last night with the thoroughly unthreatening guy on my doorstep. He was dressed casually in jeans and a very worn leather jacket. He had a somewhat embarrassed expression on his face. And he was holding a dirty plastic bag.

"That's me," I said, keeping one hand on the door. Ready to slam it if necessary.

"I wanted to apologize for last night. And to make sure that you're okay. You are, aren't you? Okay?"

"Yeah," I said.

Now that he wasn't glaring at me, I could see that my earlier assessment of him maybe being attractive had not done him justice. His black hair was shiny, just longer than his chin, and it was curly in some places. It would have been pretty on a girl; on a guy, it was something else entirely. His skin was smooth and brown and his eyes were as dark as I remembered, but softer in the light of day. He was adorable, frankly. And I think that annoyed me even more than his nearly having killed me the night before.

"You found my stash," he continued, and a glint of humor crept into his eyes. "I had it warded. But I had no idea it would be so strong. I'm sorry."

"It was probably the mandrakes," I told him.

"Mandrakes?" He frowned. "Is that what these things are?"

He held up the plastic bag; it was full of the roots I had dug up last night.

"Yeah," I said. "Mandrake roots amplify magic. And there was a crap ton of them around that tree."

"I didn't know that. If you need more of these, I know where there's a whole field of them."

"A whole field?" I repeated, unable to stop myself from adding up in my head how much an entire field of mandrake roots would be worth.

"I'll show you, if you like."

"Okay . . ."

"I'm Rafael, by the way. Rafe."

He held out his free hand and I hesitated. There were so many reasons not to touch him.

But then he leaned in a bit closer to me, and suddenly all of the reasons became a shade hazier.

"I'm not warded," he assured me. "I promise."

I took his hand. It was a decision. I knew that it was the start of something. And now, even after all that had happened, I couldn't bring myself to regret it.

"Hey! Sleeping Beauty!"

My eyes flew open. Kellen was standing over me. The sun was behind him, making his brown hair seem to glow.

"Nice nap?" he asked, holding out a hand to help me up.

So many reasons not to touch him . . .

"Not bad," I said, letting him pull me to my feet.

"Want to nap here again tomorrow? Same time?"

So many reasons . . .

"Sure," I said, sounding much more lighthearted than I felt. *Tomorrow. Tomorrow I will figure out what your secret is,* I promised him silently. But out loud, I just said, "Why not?"

The Crescent Roll turned out to be a bakery. It was in the southeast portion of downtown, nestled between the Sweep Shop broom store and the Familiar Care pet supply shop, just behind the Blessed Be Bikram yoga studio.

I didn't plan to go inside. I was only curious to see for myself the store that was associated with the single semipersonal item in Kellen's wallet. But as I stood outside the frosted windows, a woman exited the store, bringing with her an armload of baguettes and a heavenly smell that almost knocked me over. My stomach growled and before I could think it through, I found myself catching the door and letting myself in.

It was a cute place, with distressed gray walls and white, crisscrossing beams. Large glass display cases sat on either side of a marble counter. I tried not to look too hard, but out of the corner of my eye I saw cupcakes with thick white frosting; cookies; danishes with fruit topping; croissants; and cakes. So many cakes.

I had wandered into raw vegan hell.

I wanted to leave but I was too paralyzed by the smell. I'm not sure how long I stood there torturing myself, but eventually I noticed that the High Priestess from last night's ritual was behind the counter, thoroughly kissing a shorter woman who was wearing an apron and a hairnet.

"Pasta tonight?" the High Priestess asked.

"Pesto," the baker replied. "Love you, old lady."

"Love you more, older lady." The High Priestess laughed, then noticed me standing there. "Oh, hello. It's Macie, isn't it?"

"Yes," I said, feeling like an intruder. Even though the High Priestess was no longer masked by the glamour of the ritual, I was still a bit dazzled by her. She was older than I had guessed on initiation night, gray haired and delicately wrinkled but still very beautiful.

"A pity about the interruption to your initiation. I trust the mayor sorted you out?" she asked. A slight edge had crept into her voice, as though she was checking up on the mayor's diligence.

"Yes, Mayor Bainbridge initiated me yesterday," I reported.

"Good." The High Priestess relaxed immediately and smiled. She kissed the baker again, this time on the top of her hairnet, then swept out the front door just as the telltale whistle of a teakettle sounded from behind the counter.

"Will you join me in a cup, dear?" the baker asked me, gesturing to a stool at the end of the counter. "I'm Gayle, by the way. Gayle Giroux-Trescott. Maire was rude not to introduce me."

I hesitated only slightly. Technically, the boiling water in the kettle should be off-limits to a raw vegan. But since it seemed the least of the many baked and sugary evils surrounding me at the moment, I decided I didn't care.

"Nice to meet you," I said, and took the proffered stool.

Gayle poured two teacups of hot water and put a box of teabags on the counter between us.

"It's always a bit startling to see a High Priestess outside of ritual," she said soothingly, as she selected a bag of peppermint tea from the box. "Last year, when it was my turn, I found it quite isolating. Maire handles it better."

I picked out a cinnamon apple tea and plopped the bag into my steaming cup, catching a sudden whiff of information competing with the baked goods.

"You were High Priestess last year?" I inquired.

Gayle nodded, and blew across the top of her cup.

."Yes, we rotate here. All of the Elders, as the mayor insists on calling us, serve a year's term each. There are about fifteen of us on the committee, so I'll probably be senile by the time it's my turn again, Goddess willing."

I giggled.

Look at me, Mother, I thought snarkily. *Talking to an adult.*

"How do you get on the committee?" I asked, sipping my tea prematurely and burning my tongue.

Gayle thought for a moment. She leaned on the counter, crossing her muscular arms in front of her cup. I supposed bakers needed good muscles. All that kneading.

"Well, most of us are over fifty. And a lot of us own businesses. Come to think of it, the Elder Committee *is* basically the same cast of characters as the Merchants' Guild. We could probably save a great deal of time by combining our monthly meetings. That's small-town politics for you. But this can't be very interesting to you."

Inside my head, there was a bell ringing and someone shouting "BINGO," but outwardly I smiled politely and took another, more careful, sip of my tea.

"I just got here, so it's all pretty interesting to me," I said mildly. Then, since Gayle seemed to be giving so freely of information, I added, "Who owns the Supply Depot? I passed it yesterday and it looked abandoned."

"Oh, it looks better now than it did a month ago. It burned down, you know."

"It did?" That shingle *had* looked singed.

"Twice," Gayle said, then reconsidered. "Actually, three times, if you count the first. Had to be rebuilt from the ground up every time. It just can't keep a tenant."

She eyed me cagily over the top of her cup.

"Why do you ask? Are you interested in leasing it?"

"Me?" I laughed into my tea. "I'm sixteen."

Gayle shrugged.

"I was sixteen when I took over my mother's bakery.

Are you looking for a job? Something to do? I know you're on Solstice break at the moment, and if you got the place up and running by fall, you could find someone to help you out with it during school hours. The Witchtown school system is pretty flexible. Very adaptable to independent study."

I thought for a moment. Running a business was an interesting proposition. Especially given what she had just told me.

"It's only an idea," Gayle said. "I believe the initial buy-in is a thousand dollars, plus there will be monthly rent. But given the history of the place, I bet you could get a deal from the mayor. Maybe even a loan to get you started."

I drank down the last of my tea, thinking hard. I didn't have a thousand dollars. But I did have the eight hundred and change from the mayor's office. Perhaps a reinvestment was in order.

I'm not sure if Gayle could hear my stomach rumbling, or if she sensed my sudden distraction, but she leaned forward with a look of concern on her face.

"Can I get you anything else? The cinnamon rolls are fresh. And the scones are from an old family recipe—"

"Oh, no, thank you," I interrupted. In answer to her raised eyebrow, I added, "I'm a raw vegan."

Her eyes widened.

"How dreadful," she said, and then smiled, softening the words somewhat.

"Yes, it is," I agreed, as my eyes wandered to a tray of

danishes that had thick cream cheese frosting smeared gener-
ously all over them. *Drool.* "I should probably go."

"Of course," Gayle said. "I hope you'll come back some-
time soon. And bring your mother. I'd love to meet her, too."

"Sure," I said. Even though I knew, deep down, that I
would never intentionally inflict my mother on Gayle the
Baker. "Thank you for the tea."

"Anytime, dear."

When I arrived home, there were two plastic baggies Scotch-
taped to my front door, along with a crumpled-up note that
read:

AS DISCUSSED

— TALYA

The first bag contained a handful of pretty white elderflowers that were so fresh the petals hadn't even begun to wilt.
I opened the second bag, and it took only a quick sniff for me
to recognize the distinctive, vaguely foul stench of valerian
root.

Was this her way of saying thank you for drawing focus
away from her in the square? Or a way of telling me that she
wasn't going to mention our midnight meeting at the mayor's
office?

Pushing the quandary aside — I refused to think about
Voids and the old maxim that like calls to like — I reached for
the doorknob and let myself in.

My mother was at the kitchen table.

"We need a thousand dollars," I burst out, smiling triumphantly.

But my smile quickly faded when I got a good look at the scene in front of me.

My mother was lying face-down on the table, her head in the crook of one of her arms. There was a bottle of wine beside her, one empty glass, and a big pile of what I was pretty sure were accounting ledgers.

The Witchtown books. Frizz must have delivered them.

The most worrisome thing was the suitcase at my mother's feet. It was half full of clothes and shoes. And I distinctly remembered having emptied it yesterday.

My mother raised her head slightly, and her glazed eyes met mine.

"Pack your things, Macie. We're leaving. Right now."

CHAPTER SEVEN

*W*hat?" I demanded, sure I couldn't have heard her correctly. I set the two baggies of herbs on the counter, out of the way.

"We're leaving," she repeated, picking up the bottle. Only a drip of wine remained; it sloshed into her glass.

"We can't leave!" I exclaimed. "I figured it out! Our *in!* We need to lease the Supply Depot. That will get us into the Merchants' Guild, which will get us in with the Elders. They're the ones who are really running this place," I explained, re-membering Maire's face as she had inquired about my initia-tion. "I know we have enough. We have the eight hundred I took from the mayor's office. That and a little of what we stole from the last town, and we're there. We'll get it back. It's just a temporary investment until we get to the real money—"

"There isn't any," my mother said, waving her hand over the accounting ledgers. "Witchtown has been losing money for two years straight. It's broke. There's nothing here."

My mouth dropped open.

"That's impossible."

"Oh, it's possible." My mother hauled herself out of her seat and walked, a bit unsteadily, over to the small altar in the living room, then snatched up Laverna. "Witchtown is a mirage," she said, slurring. "A Laverna-cursed mirage. A complete waste of our time."

She tossed the headless statue into the suitcase.

I blinked. Witchtown had been our ultimate con for as long as I could remember. The thing we had dreamed about. It couldn't be broke. It just couldn't.

My mother staggered back to her seat but missed the chair. She caught herself by grabbing the edge of the table, sending two of the ledgers and a plastic cup full of cutlery crashing to the floor.

She scowled down at the floor. Two utensils had fallen free of the cup.

"Visitors," she pronounced. "*Shit*. We'll have to pack later. Help me clean up."

I peered back down at the floor. One fork and one spoon; a man and a woman were coming. But who?

My mother retreated to the bathroom, presumably to make herself presentable. I endeavored to do the same to our front room. I rolled the half-full suitcase into the bedroom and closed the door, pausing only to rescue Laverna and place her back on the altar.

The empty altar. I still hadn't made the protection sachet.

But now I had the herbs to do it.

I pitched the empty wine bottle into the kitchen trashcan, set the almost-empty wine glass aside, and restacked the ledgers neatly on the table. Then I grabbed the valerian root and elderflowers that Talya had brought me from off the counter, plus some dried basil and marjoram from my herb box. I didn't have time for the mortar and pestle, so I crushed the herbs together in my fingers, sprinkled them into a piece of red cloth, and used a piece of red string to tie the bag shut.

I set the sachet on the altar in front of Laverna, then returned to the kitchen and picked up the wine glass. I didn't bother looking toward the bathroom: this was one spell I didn't need my mother for. Herbs don't particularly care if they are being wielded by a Natural, a Learned, or a Void. They have their own magic. And Laverna had never seemed to mind my calling upon her.

Silently, for Laverna liked silence, I implored her:

Laverna, protect this house.
As you protect all those who lie and thieve
Beauteous Laverna,
O give me to deceive . . .

The doorbell rang.

Hastily, I transferred the wine glass to my left hand and poured three drops onto the sachet.

My mother emerged from the bathroom, looking calm, refreshed, and entirely sober.

I ditched the wine glass in the sink a fraction of a second before she opened the front door.

"Madame Mayor, what a surprise. Do come in."

My mother blocked the doorway with her body and gestured behind her back for me to go into the bedroom.

Apparently, I was not invited to the spontaneous meeting.

I glared at her back and stomped silently into the bedroom, shut off the light, and left the door open a crack.

"This is my husband, Percy Bainbridge," I heard the mayor say.

Ahh. The fork.

"Lovely to meet you, Percy," my mother purred. "Won't you both come in?"

I heard the front door close. I peeked through the crack and all three of them wandered into my view as my mother showed them to the kitchen table.

"Where is Macie this evening?" the mayor inquired, taking a seat. She was wearing another tight power suit, a blue one this time. Her husband was wearing an old-looking checkered shirt and ill-fitting khakis. His outfit, plus his severely receding hairline and weak jaw, made them seem a very odd couple to me.

"Asleep already, poor thing," my mother said, setting three glasses of water on the table.

Percy drank thirstily from his glass, but the mayor took only one sip.

"I see you received the books," she said quietly. "Did you have a chance to look through them?"

"Yes . . ." my mother said carefully, letting the word hang as she slipped into a chair across from the mayor, her back to the door and me.

"What is your assessment?" the mayor asked, stone faced.

My mother sipped her water.

"Frankly, Brooke, from what I've seen, it looks like Witchtown has been grossly mismanaged for some time now."

Even from across the room I could see the mayor stiffen, then struggle to regain her composure as she tucked a piece of her ultra-blond hair behind her ear.

"That's why I'm here, Aubra. It's also why I brought Percy. He's the head of the Witchtown Bank. We'd like to explain."

I didn't hear my mother's response, but she must have looked agreeable to hearing more, because the mayor continued.

"I was Reggie — *Reginald* — Harris's private secretary for eleven years, right up until his death. I was very involved in the planning of Witchtown. I have worked tirelessly to make it a reality," explained the mayor.

Percy snorted loudly at this.

"I can assure you of that," he said dryly. "This is the most I've seen of my wife in months, if you can believe it."

The mayor gave him a warning look, and went on.

"For the first three years, things ran smoothly. It's only been in the last two that things have taken a turn."

"A turn?" my mother asked calmly.

The mayor leaned forward.

"I alluded to this before, in my office. But now I can tell you that there is no doubt that someone is sabotaging Witchtown."

"Sabotaging?" my mother asked. "Are you certain?"

"Very," the mayor said curtly. "Two years ago we had a crop blight, which severely crippled our fall harvest. Then there was a small flood in our water treatment plant, an accident in the sewage plant, and then a few of our windmills stopped working. Small things. But they keep happening."

"And last night, some money was stolen from your office," Percy reminded her.

I stiffened, but the mayor waved her hand in the air.

"That had to be Lois. I fired her. She was the only one other than me who had the key to the drawer where the money was kept. Plus, that girl we hired to organize the Archives said she saw Lois lurking around at odd hours."

I felt my eyebrows go up. I had counted on Talya keeping her mouth shut, but not actually covering for me. Her job at the Archives explained what *she* was doing there that night (although not why she was there so late). What did she think *I* had been doing there?

"The Zealots?" my mother mused, bringing my attention back to the conversation.

"Has to be. Although we don't have any proof, of course. Slippery bastards," the mayor growled under her breath, then went on. "All of those problems were easily fixed, but very expensive. Then this past spring, we lost a huge percentage of our wine grapes to a fungus. Witchtown Wine is our biggest moneymaker. We were counting on that revenue to make up for all the additional expenses."

"Surely there's a town fund, something for emergencies?" my mother inquired, sounding innocent.

"There was," Percy answered. "Until our former accountant embezzled it all when he left us last month."

"The truth is, Witchtown is broke," the mayor said plainly. "We, Percy and I, have managed to keep most of this quiet. If word gets out, people will start to leave. But the biggest problem we have at the moment is security. In two months' time, we'll be unable to pay the company that guards our walls. We've already scaled back a great deal, which is why there have been so many instances of shenanigans, like the ones that interrupted your initiation ritual. With the Zealots camped just outside, and everything that has been going on even *with* security, having none at all is . . . unthinkable."

"Not to mention, impossible to hide from the townsfolk," my mother added thoughtfully.

The mayor nodded.

"Reginald Harris had a vision, Aubra. A vision of a place where witches could be safe and free and, most important, where we could depend on one another—not on the government—for everything we need. That's what Witchtown is. It's the only Haven of its kind; the only one that doesn't survive on government funds. If we go down, or worse, if we have to go groveling to the politicians for a handout, think what that would mean. Think what a blow that would be to our kind. The anti-witch factions would be cheering in the streets. We can't allow that to happen."

"I'm very sorry to hear all of this, Brooke," my mother said. Her voice oozed sympathy, but I could tell that she had mentally checked out of the situation. She was probably already planning our next move.

The mayor's face darkened.

"I *refuse* to see that great man's legacy crumble into ruin," she said, and I jumped slightly at the vehement tone that had suddenly crept into her voice. "Witchtown was Reginald's fondest dream, and he left me in charge. This town will not die on my watch. I will not allow it."

Percy reached out and put a hand on his wife's arm, but the mayor shook him off and leaned in closer to Aubra.

"I have a plan, but I'm going to need your help."

"I thought you might," Aubra said, but I could hear the indifference in her voice.

"I found a group of investors who are interested in

financing the town. They are due to arrive in about a week. The townspeople believe they are coming in order to help fund a planned expansion."

"And you need me to do what, exactly?"

The mayor took a deep breath.

"I need you to make a false set of books. To convince the investors that Witchtown is profitable, stable, and a good financial risk."

"Oh," my mother said, and the lack of enthusiasm in her voice was obvious.

"That and one other thing," the mayor added, elbowing her husband. "You tell her, Percy."

"Well." Percy cleared his throat. "You see, Reginald Harris poured a substantial percentage of his wealth into Witchtown. But the bulk of his personal fortune is still intact. Harris had no will and he left behind only distant relatives, so his estate has been tied up in litigation since the day he died. There's a lot of secrecy surrounding his assets. But *we* believe that there is a large chunk of Harris's fortune located in a vault, right here in the Witchtown Bank."

"I see. And you believe this because . . . ?" my mother asked skeptically.

"Because he told me," the mayor cut in. "Reggie told me. And I know, I know *down in the depths of my soul,* that he would gladly hand over a piece of his personal fortune to save Witchtown. All of it, if that was what it took. He was very passionate about this place, Aubra."

I couldn't see my mother's expression, but I could imagine her raising her eyebrow.

"I've tried to get inside the vault myself," the mayor confessed. "But the spells protecting it are complicated, and I'm just a Learned. Reginald Harris was a Natural. A powerful Natural. I was wondering if you would take a crack at it."

"Me?" my mother asked, sounding incredulous. "You're asking me to break into Reginald Harris's vault?"

I bit back a grin at the irony.

"Yes," the mayor said, her expression serious. "And if you succeed, I give you my solemn pledge that whether the investors come through or not, we will take only the money we need to get this town back on its feet." After a moment, when my mother said nothing, the mayor added, "Plus a generous percentage to compensate you for your time and effort, of course."

"Ahh, I see," my mother said slowly, and it sounded to me like she was checking back in. Cautiously, at least.

"I know I'm asking a lot—" the mayor started.

"Yes, you are," my mother said flatly.

"I know it would mean taking an enormous risk—"

"Yes, it would."

"And you have your daughter to think about—"

"Yes, I do."

"But if you could just consider my proposal—"

"I have," my mother interrupted her coolly. "I'll do it."

The mayor looked startled at the sudden acquiescence,

but she composed herself quickly and smiled with obvious relief.

"Thank you for trusting me with this information, Brooke," my mother continued. "In return, I'd like to make an investment of my own. I'd like to lease the Supply Depot. I heard somewhere that the buy-in is a thousand dollars?"

"Yes, that's correct," the mayor said.

"I know it's not much," my mother went on. "Not enough to make any kind of a difference, surely, but it's all I can manage. I mean it to demonstrate my loyalty to the town."

"Well," the mayor said, sounding overwhelmed. "I don't know what to say, Aubra. I assume you know the history of the Depot?"

"Of course," my mother said, even though I knew she didn't. I would have bet everything I had that she hadn't even known of its existence until I mentioned it to her earlier.

"Well, then, I'm sure you understand why I would hesitate to rent the place to just anyone, given the poltergeist and all. But I'm sure that, being a Natural, you'll be able to get a handle on it right quick."

Poltergeist? I thought. *Oh, crap.*

"I'm sure I won't have any trouble," my mother said pleasantly, but I could practically hear her teeth grinding. Oh, she was going to kill me.

"I can have a new set of books done in a day or two," my mother went on. "As for the vault, I really won't know until I've had a look at it."

"I'd be happy to show it to you," Percy assured her. "At your convenience."

"Thank you, Percy. That's very kind."

I winced as Percy's ratlike face lit up and he nearly melted into his chair. Another male turned to goo after the slightest bit of attention from my mother.

"Thank you, Aubra," the mayor said, walking over to my mother's chair and clasping her in an extremely awkward-looking hug. "I can't tell you what it means to have your help. I had a feeling about you when you first walked into my office. I think . . ." she trailed off, choking up. "I think you're going to save us."

I rolled my eyes behind the door.

Lady, you have no idea.

"I'll do everything I can," my mother said, holding the mayor at arm's length after the hug and turning slightly so that I could see her give the simpering woman her patented Aubra O'Sullivan, friendly-neighborhood-Natural-to-the-rescue smile.

On the other side of the table, I saw the dopey look that Percy was giving my mother, and I started to feel sick to my stomach. Men like that had proved to be nothing but a massive distraction to my mother in the past.

Please, Laverna. Don't let her get distracted by this one.

After the mayor and Percy left, my mother opened the bedroom door and leaned against the doorframe.

"Well? What do you think?"

My mouth fell open in shock. My mother had never asked me my opinion before. Not on anything. Not even dinner, let alone anything relating to a con.

I swallowed. An epic question deserved an epic answer, but all I could do was shrug.

"A vault . . ." my mother tapped her lip thoughtfully. "Can you open one of those?"

I shook my head.

"They're totally different from normal locks," I pointed out. "And besides, the mayor said it's protected by spells. That's your department."

"Do you think there's really any money in there?" my mother pressed me.

"I think that the mayor thinks there is," I said carefully.

My mother nodded.

"My thoughts exactly. We can still bail, you know. Right now. Tonight."

I stiffened. Bailing meant that everything my mother had promised me about this being our last con would be nullified. We'd have to find another prize. Somewhere else where we could presumably make enough money to leave thieving behind. But there weren't any other Havens like Witchtown.

Could I really continue to live like that indefinitely? In little windows of time. A few months here, half a year there. An endless string of almost connections, almost friends, almost loves . . . never hanging around anywhere long enough to let anyone get past the surface.

I swallowed, chasing all thoughts of Rafe from my head. I could *not* afford to lose myself in him right now. I needed to *think*.

My mother knelt down in front of me.

"It's up to you, Macie. We'll do whatever you want to do."

I raised an eyebrow. Pulling off that job at the mayor's office must have convinced her of more than I thought.

"No, Witchtown is our endgame," I told her. "Our last con. We get the money, then we leave here and we find somewhere to settle down. Somewhere we can really *live*. That's what we agreed."

"But if there's no money—" my mother started.

"There *is* money," I informed her. "The *town* might be broke, but have you looked around? The businesses are thriving. The merchants must be making money. The Merchants' Guild is what we should be looking at—just like I was trying to tell you earlier."

My mother nodded.

"And that's the con you want to run?" she asked. "The Depot? Getting in with the merchants?"

I nodded. She looked at me sharply for a split second before nodding back.

"Then run it," she said.

"Me?" I squeaked.

"Yes. I have to help Brooke with those investors. And then I have to do my best to get inside that vault—who knows, maybe Brooke is right and there's a fortune hidden there. But I won't have time to run a business. It has to be you."

She smiled wickedly.

"It's brilliant, actually. You're so young, they'll never see you coming. Those shop owners will take you under their wing *like that*." She snapped your fingers. "You'll be in before you know it."

I bit back a grimace at all she was insinuating there— that I was some helpless little thing, that the business owners of Witchtown were idiots. The important thing was that I was getting what I wanted. It didn't matter what my mother thought of it.

To my amazement, my mother reached out a hand and stroked my hair.

"I know I have some ground to make up with you," she said wistfully, pulling gently on the freshly severed ends. "I want you to be happy. You know that, right?"

"Yes, Mother," I said, afraid to move.

Who are you and what have you done with Aubra?

"I like this plan," she said. "It may even end up paying off. Maybe we'll get more money out of Witchtown than we thought."

I felt a small smile tug at my lips, and her face hardened.

"I want nothing to do with that poltergeist," she said,

not quite suppressing her shudder. "I don't even want to hear about it. You know how I feel about ghosts."

"I'll take care of it," I promised her.

"Good."

She held out her hands and pulled us both to our feet.

"Come on. Let's have a glass of wine and talk details."

CHAPTER EIGHT

*T*he next morning, I was itching to go check out the Depot.

My Depot. My very own con. The thought that I was going to be able to run it however I liked, without my mother's interference, was equal parts exciting and terrifying.

The mayor had brought over the lease papers that morning; my mother had signed them, written the mayor a check, and handed me the keys. They were burning a hole in my pocket.

But there was something else I had to do first.

The door to the Archives was open. It led to a steep flight of dingy stairs, which in turn led to a small, dungeonlike room with no windows. I suspected that some people would go nuts spending long periods of time in such sensory isolation, but I doubted Talya was one of them. No wonder the mayor had hired her for this job.

There were bookshelves along all four walls. A long table ran down the center; Talya was seated cross-legged in the middle of it, hunched over a notebook, with open books all around her. No surprise, she was in all black again: this time, black overalls over a black long-sleeved thermal. Even her black Chucks had black doodles on the white parts.

I cleared my throat.

She looked up and froze. Her eyes darted quickly to the door and she grimaced, seemingly realizing that her only escape from the room was behind me. Caught, she put down her notebook and watched me warily, from behind thickly eyelinered eyes

"What are you doing here?"

"I wanted to bring you this."

Careful to stay at arm's length so as not to spook her, I tossed a plastic baggie into her lap.

"In exchange for the herbs you brought by yesterday," I explained, when she gave me a puzzled look. "It's a mandrake root. It'll enhance your spells."

She looked down at the bag without touching it.

"I know what it is," she said. "It's worth a lot more than the herbs I gave you."

"Not to me. They were exactly what I needed. Thank you."

"You're welcome," she said carefully. "Thank you for what you did in the square."

"No problem."

Neither of us mentioned our strange midnight encounter.

Talya finally picked up the bag, fixed her eyes on me, and stared.

"Why do you do that?" I asked her, surprising myself with the question.

"Do what?" she countered, her eyes still locked on my face.

"*Stare.*"

She paused a bit before answering.

"I'm waiting for something."

I spread my hands.

"This is all I do. I don't turn into anything. I don't dance. I'm sorry if that disappoints you."

She smiled. She also blinked, and dropped her piercing gaze down to the mandrake root.

"Well, thank you for the herbs," I said, and turned to go.

"What are you?" she said to my back.

"What?" I whirled back around. My heart suddenly skipped a beat, and my hand flew to my moonstone.

She looked at me again. Not staring this time, just looking.

"They think I'm a Void," she said. "Autumn and the others. Don't they?"

"That's the rumor," I said truthfully.

She smiled grimly.

"I stay away from them. But it's not because I'm a Void; it's because I see things."

"What kinds of things?" I asked, trying to sound casual.

"Things people don't want me to see," she answered, just as casually. "Secrets. I see them. Some of them. And then I have to say them. That's why I avoid people."

"Oh," I said, my head spinning slightly. Talya was a

psychic? "Like in the square? Were you seeing things about Royce?"

"Yes."

I had always avoided psychics like the plague, for obvious reasons. Now that I knew what she was, my entire body was tense. I recognized the sensation: fight or flight.

"I see things," she repeated, "but not about you. This makes three separate times I've been around you and I haven't seen anything. That's never happened to me before."

"Oh," I said, and forced myself to let go of my necklace. "Maybe I'm just not very interesting."

"Everyone has secrets," Talya retorted. "*Everyone*. Why can't I see yours?"

Because I'm empty inside. Hollow. A Void.

"I don't know," I said. "Why do you want to know things that people don't want to share?"

Her face darkened.

"I don't want to know them at all."

I let out a small sigh of relief. A tortured psychic, then. Somehow, that seemed less dangerous than a motivated, enthusiastic psychic.

"What did you see about Royce?" I asked, honestly curious.

She shook her head.

"I can't tell you that. It wouldn't be right."

A psychic with ethics. It was definitely time to change the subject.

"Fair enough," I said. "Thanks again for the herbs. They seemed fresh; you must have found them around here, right?"

"There're lots of good gathering places in Witchtown. I could show you," she offered, looking vaguely shocked at the words coming out of her mouth.

"I'd like that," I said, equally shocked at the words coming out of mine.

Get out of here, Macie, a voice inside my head ordered me sharply. And I decided to obey.

What are you doing? the voice demanded, as I turned and let myself back out onto the bright streets of Witchtown. *She's a threat! You should be staying far, far away from her. No making friends.*

Part of me agreed wholeheartedly with the voice. But another part of me was finding it difficult to think of Talya as dangerous. A third part was wondering what she might have seen in me, if I had stayed down in that room just a little bit longer.

I gritted my teeth and walked faster.

It didn't matter what the weird Goth girl thought of me. She was just a mark. Witchtown would be no different from any other Haven we had ever visited: when we were ready to leave here, my mother would cast her spell, and Talya would forget she had ever known me. Just like everyone else I had ever met. That was the way it had to be.

It made no sense that in some weird, twisted way I was already sad about it.

CHAPTER NINE

*T*he board that had been nailed over the door of the Depot was no longer there; the mayor must have gotten someone to remove it. My key slid into the lock easily enough, but it didn't want to turn. I strained, jiggled the key, and turned the knob as sharply as I could, but it refused to budge. I was on the verge of running to get my lock picks when one final jerk of the key did the trick.

The shop was very similar in size to the Crescent Roll; it was long and narrow, with high ceilings. It even had the same U-shaped counter, but the Depot's was wooden instead of marble. There were a few empty display cases near the counter, and the center of the space was dominated by a pile of boxes. The mayor had mentioned that morning that some of the previous tenant's inventory had been kept offsite, so it had been spared from the fire. She had thrown it in with the price of the lease.

I was curious about the boxes and what might be in them,

but when I recalled the mayor's words from the night before, I hesitated on the doorstep. I had never dealt with a poltergeist before. One of the Havens we had robbed a couple of years back had had an old library that everybody thought was haunted, but I had never seen the ghost. I wasn't sure how to proceed, or even whether a poltergeist would be around in the daylight. But I thought I might as well take a stab at showing it who was boss, right from the start.

"Hello?" I called up into the rafters.

I was answered with silence. But not an empty, lonely silence; the quiet of the Depot made it feel strangely *inhabited*. Full, almost stifling, even though there was practically nothing in the shop. I had the same prickly feeling I had had the other morning when Aimee had been following me. But this time, the presence seemed to come from all directions. Like the building itself was watching me.

The longer I waited for a response, the more creeped out I got. So I tried again. This time I tried to add a little bit of entitled indignation to the word, the way my mother would have done:

"Hel-*lo?*"

Nothing. Weirdly, my voice did not echo, even though it should have, what with the high ceilings and all. And was I imagining things, or was the temperature in here quite a bit cooler than outside?

I shook off a shudder and forced myself to take three confident steps farther into the room.

"I don't know who are you, or if you're here now," I said loudly, even though I was almost positive I wasn't alone, "but this is my shop."

This time I was answered by a blast of icy wind, which could not possibly have come from the warm June day outside. I shivered in my thin T-shirt and wrapped my arms around myself as another, even stronger gust of air engulfed me.

My teeth began to chatter, and I thought about what I must look like to the poltergeist—small and shivery, and probably two seconds away from running out the door. The image brought on a sudden surge of anger. Getting the Depot up and running was key to our plans for Witchtown. For *my* plans. And this ghost thought it was going to drive me away with a little bit of cold?

No way. I'd buy a space heater. Or six. This poltergeist didn't know what it was dealing with.

Dropping my arms as though the cold was not affecting me at all, I marched around behind the counter, stopped at the very bottom of the horseshoe curve, and faced the shop's door. This seemed like the most proprietary place to position myself: it was where Gayle had been standing when I walked into the Crescent Roll. I put my hands firmly on the slightly beat-up wood and raised my chin so that my voice would carry through the whole space.

"This is *my shop*," I repeated, loudly, over the wind. "And I will not tolerate any interference."

The wind stopped abruptly and a quiet, growly whisper spoke up from directly behind me.

"Oh, really?"

I jumped, whirled, and found myself trapped between the curve of the counter and a pair of bloodshot eyes. The eyes had no irises, just pupils: wide black disks floating in two pools of red. I couldn't see my reflection in them; I couldn't see much of anything. The eyes had to be attached to something, like a face and a body, but they were taking up my entire field of vision.

We stood frozen, the eyes and I, while my heartbeat ticked off the seconds.

The dark disks were calculating, looking me up and down, hard. Were they examining me? What would happen when they reached a conclusion?

Say something, my brain commanded.

Though the wind had stopped, my body was still shaking with fear and residual cold. I managed to part my lips. I had no idea what I intended to say, but before I could get a word out, the eyes blinked once, and I thought I heard exactly one syllable of a haughty, irritated laugh.

"I don't think so," the poltergeist said, in that same quiet, barely audible voice. Then the counter that surrounded me burst into flames.

I ducked. I was stuck inside a horseshoe of fire. The poltergeist backed up a couple of steps until it stood in the open end. I could see now that it—he—was a man. Or he had been a man, back when he was alive. In death he was a tall, shadowy figure in a long black coat. He seemed to shimmer a little around the edges, although that may have been from the heat of the flames. I couldn't see the expression on his face, but I saw him cross his arms and plant his feet.

Cutting off my escape.

The air was rapidly becoming too hot to breathe. I bent my head lower, closer to the floor, where there was still some oxygen. I was afraid to consider my options because I knew I didn't have many. The poltergeist had clearly settled in to watch the show; there would be no appealing to him, even if I could think of something to say.

I thought of praying to Laverna, but I was fairly certain that the Goddess of Thieves couldn't help me now. I didn't need darkness. And I didn't need clouds.

I needed wind.

I closed my eyes and I reached, just as I had reached countless times before. I knew it was pointless, but it was the only thing I could do besides quietly burn to death. I wasn't surprised when nothing came. Nothing except what was always there whenever I tried to channel: the wall. The thick, impenetrable wall that stood between me and the power that came so easily to others. The power my mother had been born with; the power that even the six-year-olds in the meadow had been able to summon at will.

But not me. That wall had always declared me unfit,

unworthy to get near magic. And it wasn't going to make any exceptions now. Not even to save my life.

The smell of charred cloth brought my attention back to the floor of the Depot: the frayed bottoms of my jeans were starting to smoke. The moonstone's chain had grown hot around my neck, and my lungs felt like they were breathing in the fire. I was just starting to contemplate the notion that I might actually die here when I heard a shout. And suddenly I was cold again instead of hot.

The fire was gone. There was smoke everywhere and my eyes burned with it. Through streams of tears I could see that the poltergeist was gone, too. In its place was a flour-streaked apron and a pair of hands reaching down to help me up.

CHAPTER TEN

*D*on't be embarrassed, dear. It's very difficult to channel when you're scared."

I didn't respond; it was taking all my energy to keep my hands from shaking. Which was important because I was holding a cup of hot tea.

My thoughts were coming too fast for me to do anything but sit and wait for them to slow down. So I had parked myself at a corner table inside the Crescent Roll and watched as Gayle rustled up tea and a heaping plate of scones, mouthed something to Maire (who was behind the counter), then came and sat down across from me.

"It's something we can work on," Gayle continued, nudging the scones closer to me. They were fresh and cakey looking, and they smelled like lemons. Lemons and some sort of herb—thyme? Was that thyme? The heavenly scent was too much. I had had salad for dinner last night, then again for breakfast that morning. My stomach, which had ceased to be amused by an endless parade of vegetables, was in full-on rebellion mode and was trying to recruit my head over to its cause. My need to devour one of the scones, to sink my teeth into that thin, crackled sugar glaze on top, was almost primal.

I stuck my nose into my teacup and flooded my senses with apple cinnamon instead.

"In the fall, when school starts, we can set you up with a mentor," Gayle mused, and took a casual sip of her tea. As though everything were perfectly normal and she was not, in fact, sitting across the table from a girl whose clothes and hair were singed, whose left shoe had been partially melted at the heel, and who smelled like a campfire. "Maybe Odin. Someone who can help you get past the fear."

Well, that's something, I thought, as I flashed Gayle what had to be a pretty feeble smile. *At least she still thinks you're a witch.*

A lousy one, sure. An incompetent, badly trained witch with fear issues. But that was better than the alternative.

I set down my cup.

"What—" I tried, then doubled over and hacked up the remaining smoke in my lungs. I was glad I had put down my tea. "What—" I tried again, clearing my throat loudly. "What *was* that thing?"

"That," Gayle said, leaning back in her chair," was the first owner of the Depot. He and his husband both died in the first Depot fire, not long after they bought the place."

"And he enjoyed it so much he stuck around just to do the same thing to others?"

Gayle shrugged.

"It's a little game he and the mayor like to play. Brooke rebuilds the place; he burns it down. Three times so far. He doesn't seem to want the Depot to have a new owner."

I stared at her.

"Geez, Gayle! You must *really* not like me. Why else would you try and talk me into buying that place?"

"Oh, no, dear. It's not that," Gayle said, smiling over her teacup. "I've been pondering the problem of the Depot for quite a while now. I was thinking about it the other day, in fact. I had just asked the Goddess to send me a solution when in you walked. You looked so young, I thought that perhaps the Goddess and I had gotten our signals crossed. But then, before I could find a way to bring up the Depot, you asked me about it. Right out of the blue. That's when I knew."

"Oh," I said, not sure exactly how to respond to that.

Gayle leaned forward and put her hand on mine. Her eyes were heavy with concern.

"I would have warned you about the poltergeist," she said. "I'm sorry. I had no idea you'd swoop in and buy the place so quickly."

"I wouldn't have if I had known it was haunted."

"Then perhaps it's a good thing I never got around to telling you," Gayle quipped, sitting back and sipping her tea again. "What are you going to do about it now?"

I picked up my tea and scowled down at the scones while I thought about how to answer that question. In spite of what Gayle had said, I knew there was only one Goddess who could possibly have sent me here. And Laverna's purposes were not the benevolent, kind ones that Gayle's Goddess would have.

Still, I knew better than to argue with a witch who thought she saw the hand of a Goddess in something. It might even be useful down the line, when it came time to get the Merchants' Guild to trust me. But it also meant I had to figure out a way to deal with the ghost, and fast. Before Gayle figured out that I wasn't the answer to anyone's prayers.

I shuddered involuntarily at the thought of ever stepping foot inside the Depot again. But there was nothing to be done about it. I couldn't admit defeat to Gayle. Or my mother.

"I'll figure something out," I assured Gayle, and stood up. "Thank you for putting out the fire."

Gayle raised an eyebrow.

"I'm sure you would have been just fine without me," she said, and I didn't know her well enough yet to tell if she meant that or not.

I headed for the door.

"One piece of advice?" she called after me.

"The first step to having power over something is to know its name. Your poltergeist has a name: it's Bradley."

The poltergeist, the fire, and my recovery tea with Gayle made me late to my appointment to meet Kellen in the meadow. I thought about blowing him off. For the entire walk toward the lake, I considered it. But I wouldn't let myself turn back, no matter how much I wanted to run to the apartment, snuggle with Rafe's jacket, and take a very long nap. I was a professional. The poltergeist may have destroyed my morning, but I wasn't going to let him derail the rest of my day.

There were things I needed to get done. Like find out how Kellen figured into my plans for Witchtown.

When I arrived at the lake, Kellen and the kids were sitting in a circle, patiently waiting for me. Before I could apologize for my tardiness, he announced that in honor of my presence, he would be using this afternoon to teach the younguns about the local herbology.

Had I ever told Kellen I was an herbalist? I couldn't remember . . .

Kellen directed the kids, and me, to disperse and search the area for interesting plants. He then announced that we would regroup in half an hour, when I would examine everyone's findings and give a rundown of their magical properties.

Was he testing me? Bring it on, Golden Boy.

The kids wandered off in small clumps, and Kellen divided his time between the groups. Still a tad shaky from my eventful morning, I decided to go in the opposite direction from everyone else. I walked alongside the lake, keeping my eye on the tree break where the stubby pines gave way to the shoreline. Poison oak liked to grow in places like that. Might as well teach the kids something useful.

I walked until I came to the top of the dam, without finding anything. The dam created a large reservoir that fed into a water filtration plant. According to what I remembered of the mayor's map, there was also a hydroelectric plant somewhere at the dam's base.

I had to hand it to Witchtown; it used every resource at its disposal to power, feed, and maintain itself. The people of Witchtown had worked hard to ensure that they would need nothing from the outside world. I could see why the mayor was so freaked out about that hard-won independence being threatened.

A small stream veered off from the lake and I followed it into a glen. Shaggy weeping willows hung down into the water from both banks, giving the space a closed-in feel. There was a small island in the center of the stream, dotted with — I had to look twice to make sure — wild angelica.

No way.

I had never seen angelica in person before. Finding it gave me a shivery thrill, and at that moment I could think of only one other person who might appreciate my excitement.

Talya seemed to know her herbs. But she was never going to believe me without proof.

The water looked only about a foot deep, so I stripped off my shoes and socks and rolled my pants up to my knees. With a silent apology to the citizens of Witchtown for contaminating their water supply with my dirty feet, I stepped in and made my way toward the island.

"What are you doing?"

Flapping my arms to regain my balance, I turned around and saw Aimee on the bank behind me.

I pointed to the angelica.

"I found something cool! And secret. Wait there, I'll show you."

I waded carefully into the stream, debating what I would —or should—tell Aimee about my find. Angelica was deceptively innocent in its beauty, with wispy white flowers shooting out from the center of the plant like tiny bursts of light. And it was harmless enough to ordinary people, and even to Learned witches. But it was Kryptonite to Natural witches, just like rowan to Learneds. For this reason, angelica was rare, controversial, and—ever since the end of the Second Inquisiton—spectacularly illegal. The U.S. government had gone to great lengths to eradicate it. Witchtown could get into serious trouble if word got out that it was growing wild here.

"I found something too!" Aimee exclaimed, waving a fistful of daisylike flowers at me. "What are these, Macie? What are these?"

I smiled to myself, and took another careful step toward the island.

"Those taste really yummy," I lied. "Nibble on one, you'll see."

Her eyes lit up, and I couldn't help but cringe when, instead of nibbling on just one flower, she shoved the whole handful into her mouth at once. She chewed a couple of times, then made a terrible face and spat everything out into her hand.

"Yuck!"

"Gotcha!" I said to her, as I reached the island. "Those are chamomile flowers. They *do* taste yummy when they're brewed in tea, but they're really bitter right after you pick them."

"Yuck!" she exclaimed again, and scraped her tongue with her fingers to get rid of the taste. Still making a face, she knelt at the edge of the stream and scooped some of the water into her mouth.

"Aimee," I scolded, as I reached my hand toward one of the wispy angelica stems. "I don't know if that's the cleanest—"

"Ow!" she cried, as soon as she had spat the water out, and then started gagging. Grasping her hand, she tried to wipe the water off on her sleeve, but succeeded only in getting her other hand wet. Which appeared to cause her even more pain. "Ow! Ow! OW!"

Alarmed, I left the angelica behind, without even touching it. I started to splash back over toward the bank as quickly as I could and watched, helpless, as Aimee howled in pain.

The sound brought Kellen at a run, before I could get out of the water.

"It burns!" Aimee yelled.

Kellen pulled a bottle of water from his backpack and poured it over Aimee's hands. The pain drained from her face.

"I drank some, too," she admitted, and Kellen handed her the bottle.

"Rinse out your mouth," he suggested. While she was doing as she was told, Kellen turned and bent down toward the water. He dipped an experimental hand in, cringed, then brought his hand cautiously to his mouth, allowing the tiniest bit of the water to touch his lips.

He spat it out immediately, wincing in pain.

"Rowan," he said, and coughed. Aimee handed him the water bottle, and he used it to rinse his mouth and hands, just as she had.

I tensed. What on earth was rowan doing in the Witchtown water supply?

Kellen spat one more time, then stood up. When he looked at me, there was a strange expression on his face. It took me a second to figure out why, but when I did, my blood ran cold.

There was rowan in the creek.

And I was standing barefoot and ankle deep in it.

CHAPTER ELEVEN

*C*ould this day get any worse?

"Ow!" I yelled loudly, and splashed the rest of my way out of the creek, doing my best to imitate the reactions that Aimee and Kellen had had.

I wasn't fooling Kellen. At least, I was pretty sure I wasn't. His face was expressionless as he took two careful steps out of my way so that I could flail onto the bank.

But Aimee's eyes were huge with concern.

"Macie!" she yelled, grabbing the water bottle from Kellen's hand and pouring what was left of it over my feet. "Are you okay? Are you okay?"

"I'm fine," I assured her, forcing myself to sigh with relief as she had, but feeling ridiculous as I did.

This is stupid. He knows.

Kellen didn't say anything, just took the empty bottle from Aimee and screwed the plastic cap back on top.

"Let's get the others and make sure no one else goes near the water," he said, and turned back toward the meadow.

Swearing silently and to myself, I bent to retrieve my shoes and socks. For a second, I looked longingly over my shoulder at the angelica. What was that innocent-looking white flower going to cost me?

I sighed for real then, and reached over to give Aimee a hand up the steep bank.

While Kellen was busy turning his pupils over to the next teacher, I tried to make a run for it.

Just get out of here, I told myself, as I walked quickly back toward the path that led downtown. *Avoid him for a while. The more time that goes by, the less he'll remember what he saw. He won't trust it. It goes counter to everything he thinks he knows about you.*

That seemed like a fine plan, but it was blown to pieces when, an impossibly short time later, I heard someone running up behind me on the path.

"Macie, wait!"

I picked up my pace, speed walking now, pretending that I hadn't heard him.

"Macie! Stop!"

Kellen grabbed my elbow from behind, and stopped me in my tracks.

I jerked my arm free and glared at him.

"What's your problem?" I exclaimed, feigning astonishment.

He ignored my act.

"Are we going to talk about this?"

"About what?" I asked innocently.

"You know *what*." His eyes narrowed and he looked at me the way I imagined he would look at one of the six-year-olds after catching them in an obvious lie. "The rowan. It didn't hurt you."

"So?" I asked, hoping to buy time. *Think, Macie. Think.*

"I only touched the water for a second, and my hand is still stinging like hell. And my entire mouth is numb. You had your feet submerged in it for a couple of minutes, at least. And you didn't react until I pointed it out to you."

He wasn't going to just let it go. Kellen was not as trusting as Gayle; he wasn't going to give me the benefit of the doubt. I was going to have to confront this, head-on.

"So what?" I asked, throwing the words down like a challenge.

He crossed his arms over his chest.

"I can think of two possibilities," he said. His voice was calm. Downright analytical.

"Just two?" I mocked.

"Yes," he said, still dead calm. "The first is that you're a Natural. Rowan leeches only *channeled* power, or the remnants of channeled power. So it only hurts Learneds. Naturals don't have to channel, since they just use their own power, so rowan is harmless to them."

I said nothing. Maybe if I gave him nothing, no reaction whatsoever, he would talk himself in circles. Arrive at no conclusion.

"Your mother's a Natural," he added thoughtfully, relaxing his arms at his sides."But that doesn't mean you are. And you don't wear the ring. I can't think of a reason you'd hide that. So I'm betting it's possibility number two."

"Which is?" I asked. It was impossible not to ask.

"You don't know how to channel. There was no channeled power in you for the rowan to leech, so it had no effect on you."

I did my best to keep my face expressionless. But inside, I was panicking. I knew deep down that Kellen didn't need false assurances from me. What was I going to do when he figured it out?

What was *he* going to do?

I decided there was no point in waiting to find out.

"I'm a Void, okay?" I told him. The words sounded strange out loud. "I can't channel."

Kellen looked surprised.

"A Void?" he said, as though that was the last thing he had expected me to say. "Who told you that?"

"Nobody *told* me that," I spat at him. "I just *am* that. I have been. My whole life."

He shook his head.

"No, you're not."

I was so stunned at his words that I nearly fell over. *What?*

"What?" I said out loud.

"You. Are. Not. A. Void." He said it plainly, overpronouncing the words. "No one is born a Void. That's not how it works. You have to *do* something to Void yourself. Overreach. Channel too much power. Something like that."

Annoyance washed over me, and I took a deep breath to calm myself.

"You seem to be quite the expert," I snapped.

"Not an expert," he said quietly. "But I did know a Void once. I've seen one, up close and personal. And believe me, they are empty. Soulless and vacant. You're not."

I clenched one fist, and dug my nails painfully into the palm of my hand. My anger was starting to edge out my fear at being found out.

"Do you really think I'd admit to something like that if it wasn't true?" I demanded. "I know they say you can't be born a Void. But I was. I don't know how it happened. And maybe I'm nothing like the Void you knew. But I *am* a Void. I don't know what else to tell you."

He ran a hand through his hair, obviously thinking hard.

"I'd like to prove you wrong," he said a few seconds later.

I just stared at him.

"What are you going to do? Trick me into accidentally

channeling? Force me? Believe me, my mother has tried every-thing you could think of. Nothing has ever worked."

"Not trick you, not force you. Teach you."

"My mother has tried that, too. And she's a Natural. You're just a Learned."

"Exactly," he said, and his usual cocky expression started to return. "She's a Natural. Magic is like breathing to her. Which means she never had to learn. Your mom trying to teach you magic is like you trying to teach someone how to breathe. How can you even begin to teach someone something that is just instinct to you? You need a teacher who had to learn it too."

I scowled at him. But an annoying little voice in my head started asking if he could be right.

No, he's not right. Stop listening to him.

I closed my eyes. My brain was starting to hurt.

"Kellen, there's no point," I said.

"Are you sure about that? I'm an *excellent* teacher. I have references." He gestured behind us to the little witches running around the meadow by the lake, and grinned at me.

I did not grin in return. And the chaos in my head swirled into full-blown panic when he reached for my hand and took hold of it.

Suddenly, I realized how completely I had lost control of this situation. This guy now knew my biggest secret. Or one of my biggest secrets, at any rate. And I had gotten absolutely nothing from him in return. He had me badly off balance.

I had only confided in one other person about being a Void. And *that* had been under different circumstances. Very different.

My thoughts started to wander. I started to smell the sweet, thick scent of sawdust . . .

I shook my head clear of the memory and took a step backwards, pulling away from his hand.

"I told you," I said flatly. "I'm with someone."

He raised an eyebrow and folded his arms across his chest again.

"I have no idea why that should interfere with what I'm proposing," he said, sounding mildly affronted. *The bastard.* "What kind of magic do you think I'm going to teach you, anyway?"

"It doesn't matter what kind," I told him. "It *won't work.*"

He put his hands up in surrender.

"Then I might be wasting my time. I'll consider myself warned. But I'd like to try anyway. What've you got to lose?"

I considered this. He wasn't letting it go. But it didn't seem like he was going to go running to the mayor to tell on me, either. For whatever reason, he wanted to try to teach me. He wanted something from me. *That* opened up possibilities.

"Okay," I said reluctantly. "You can *try* and teach me, but on one condition. Wait, no. *Two* conditions."

"Name them."

"First, this is our secret. You will tell *no one* what you know about me."

"I figured that. Done. What's the second condition?"

I hesitated.

"What do you know about poltergeists?"

It was dark when I approached the Depot door for the second time that day. My hands were shaking and my lungs ached with the memory of the smoke, but I tried to shove all that aside. I was not going to let one measly near-death experience scare me off.

The lock on the door didn't give me as much trouble this time, which struck me as more ominous than convenient. I walked inside with my arms crossed protectively over my face. Which, judging by his smirk, Kellen seemed to find amusing.

"Just wait," I warned him, then peeked through my arms and searched for the poltergeist — for Bradley. I didn't see him, but I was getting that weird feeling of being watched again, so I knew there was no guarantee he wasn't seeing me.

That's right, I said silently, to the ceiling rafters. *I'm back.*

I jumped as Kellen closed the door behind us, the sound shaking my bravado just a tad.

He smiled an apology, shrugged off his backpack, and suddenly, the way that his T-shirt fit over his arms became very distracting. Kellen's shoulders were no rivals for the insanely muscled Royce, but they were broader than I had thought. Strong, in a lean sort of way. Which, frankly, I had always preferred . . .

What are you doing? There's a poltergeist in here who tried to kill you earlier today and you're noticing people's arms? Focus, Macie!

Kellen paused in front of the freshly charred counter and raised an eyebrow in my direction. Then his eyes traveled down, taking in the scorched cuffs of my jeans and my slightly melted shoe. I hadn't told him any of the details of my earlier encounter with the poltergeist; only that I had had one.

I needed something to do, so I walked toward the large pile of boxes in the center of the room. As long as Bradley was taking his time, I figured I might as well get some of this stuff sorted out. This place would feel a lot more like a shop with stuff on the shelves.

"Did you know any of the previous owners?" I asked Kellen. The first box I opened contained dozens of candles wrapped in tissue paper. I set it aside and struggled to lift another, slightly larger box marked "Incense Burners— Assorted."

"No," said Kellen, taking the heavy box out of my hands and placing it on a shelf behind us. "I didn't move here until the Depot had already burned down once. The next two owners weren't around for very long before—" he stopped, catching himself.

"Before the place burned down over their heads?" I finished for him.

"Let's just make sure that doesn't happen again. Oh, I forgot, I have something that might help with that."

Kellen walked back to the door and pulled something

bulky out of his backpack. He hid it behind himself until he was in front of me, then he bowed dramatically and handed me a bright red fire extinguisher with a large white bow taped to it.

I gave him a severe look as I took the surprisingly heavy metal cylinder from him.

"Gayle told me a little about what happened earlier, when I stopped by the bakery on my way home today," he admitted.

"I didn't know you two were friends."

"She's my mentor. Everyone in Witchtown gets assigned an Elder mentor. School here is regular classes in the morning, mentor time in the afternoon. You'll see in the fall."

I winced. Gayle had mentioned school earlier today too. As though it was a foregone conclusion I would still be here to attend classes. But I knew I wouldn't see fall in Witchtown. My mother and I rarely stayed in one place more than a few months. By the time school started again, we—along with every memory of us—would be long gone.

"Gayle told you I needed help?" I asked. I didn't know why I felt offended by this, given that it was completely true.

"She . . . might have suggested I find a way to work on the wind spell with you," he said sheepishly, nodding at the fire extinguisher. "But given what happened earlier, in the creek, I thought this might be more practical."

I turned the extinguisher over in my hands and ran my fingers over the white bow. I couldn't remember the last time anyone had given me a gift.

"Maybe it'll come in handy," he added, with a furtive glance around the Depot. "I hope not, though. But my mother always said it was bad manners to arrive empty-handed at a housewarming. Er, Depot-warming, in this case. So I had to bring you something."

"Thanks," I said. I cleared my throat quickly, embarrassed at the slight wobble in my voice, and set the fire extinguisher on the nearest countertop. Then, to make conversation, I added, "Does your mother know anything about poltergeists?"

"Possibly," Kellen said, looking suddenly uncomfortable. "I mean, she's dead, so . . ."

He trailed off and I felt my mouth drop open.

"Oh, Kellen—" I started, knowing that I had no idea how I intended to finish that sentence. I should have caught the past tense when he first brought her up.

"It's okay," he said hurriedly. "It happened a long time ago."

He cleared his throat too and looked away from me, toward the pile of inventory. After a moment he looked up and his normal smug smile had returned.

"So what are you going to do with all this stuff?" he asked.

I still felt like I should say something to acknowledge what he had just told me. The first piece of personal information he had ever offered. But I also felt like I should follow his lead, and he was clearly done talking about it.

"I guess we can start by unpacking it," I said. "I'll have to order more, obviously, but there's probably enough here for me to open the shop, once I get it all organized."

My eyes were drawn to a plastic box marked "Herbs." This was the part of owning a supply depot—or pretending to, at any rate—that I was the most excited about. I grabbed the box eagerly and as I did, Kellen smiled at me.

"What?" I asked, impatiently.

"Nothing. Just . . . you're excited. About this place. It's cute."

I wrinkled my nose at him. *Cute?*

I worked my thumbnail underneath the packing tape. Kellen was different this evening. Here he was, bringing me gifts, paying me compliments, and finally letting a crack appear in that swaggery armor of his.

It's because he knows you're a Void, I realized suddenly. *He thinks he has you all figured out now.*

An interesting and most unexpected side effect of his finding out. I would have to think about that. There was still something about him I didn't trust. Something that still needed figuring out.

The box was full of small plastic baggies, all sealed for freshness and labeled. I dug in, thinking of how I would display the herbs. Bins, probably. And the more exotic ones could go in glass jars, maybe above the bins . . .

I picked up a bag marked "Dried Feverfew" and opened it, sniffing carefully and bracing myself for the herb's strong, bitter scent. But it didn't come.

I looked more closely at the bag. It contained a handful of green leaves that had been dried and crushed. A lot of herbs were stored this way; they all looked alike and could be distinguished only by their scents. But this one did not smell right.

"What's wrong?" Kellen asked, looking up from a box titled "Assorted Ritual Garb."

I took another sniff inside the bag to confirm what my well-practiced nose was telling me.

"Basil," I muttered. "This bag is marked 'Feverfew,' but it's full of dried basil."

"Are you sure?" Kellen asked.

"Of course I'm sure. I know my herbs."

My curiosity, and the depressing thought that the entire box of herbs might be useless, was eclipsing my fear of the poltergeist, for the moment. I pulled out another baggie. This one was labeled "Rosehips," but the crumbly, dry plant inside was entirely the wrong color. I examined baggie after baggie and I felt my heart sink. In some cases, the herbs were merely misidentified; a dried bulb marked "Wild Garlic" was clearly daffodil, a strip of bark obviously from a eucalyptus tree was labeled "Alder Bark," and so on. But in most cases, it looked (and smelled) like most of the herbs had been swapped for cheaper lookalikes. Dried basil appeared to be the filler herb of choice.

"It looks like the previous owner was running a scam," I said to Kellen.

"Or someone was scamming them," Kellen suggested,

picking up a couple of the baggies. "I wouldn't know the difference between most of these. Maybe they didn't either?"

"You wouldn't know until you tried a spell and it went wrong. Or worse," I added, as he examined a baggie that held a delicate dried plant with feathery green leaves and white flowers. "Be careful with that one. It's toxic."

Kellen peered at the label.

"Queen Anne's Lace?" he read, frowning at the unassuming name.

"Nope. It *looks* a lot like Queen Anne's Lace, so it's an easy mistake to make. But you see those purplish, red spots on the stem? That's poison hemlock. No reputable herbalist would *ever* mix those two up. I mean, someone could *die* if they ate or drank something with hemlock in it! Hello? Socrates?"

Kellen gingerly handed me the baggie. I set it on the counter, wondering how I was going to dispose of it in a way I could be sure would prevent anyone from touching it. That might be pretty hard, given Witchtown's aggressive recycling and compost programs.

I looked mournfully over the rest of my stock.

"Hey, don't sweat it," Kellen said cheerfully. "Maybe we could—hey, is it cold in here?"

He was right; a chill had descended over the shop. I rubbed my bare arms.

"Here we go," I muttered, and fought back a powerful urge to run for the door. I immediately regretted having brought Kellen here. Recruiting him to help had seemed like a fine idea earlier, when we were safely arguing at the sunny lakeside. But now that we were here, all I could think about were the bloodshot, calculating eyes. Not to mention the fire. What could Kellen possibly do to help, even if he did have Gayle for a mentor?

We both jumped when one of the boxes in the middle of the pile exploded and the poltergeist jumped out.

He hung over the boxes for a moment, giving me a much better view of him than I had had earlier. He was young. Early twenties, maybe. Beneath the black trench coat, he was wearing modern clothes that bordered on trendy: distressed jeans and a hoodie that were both so effortlessly casual they had to be expensive. His brown, slightly curly hair was expertly mussed and did not move with the icy wind he stirred up.

With a shock, I realized that my poltergeist was actually sorta . . . *hot.* In an overly groomed kind of a way.

But it was hard to concentrate on that when he was staring at us so menacingly. And by "us," I mean me. His freaky, red-eyed glare reminded me a little of Rafe's, and the thought put me off balance.

His expression was so furious that I expected him to yell. But when he spoke, it was in the same quiet almost whisper he had used before.

"You came back," he purred, menacingly. "Why did you come back?"

I cringed as another blast of wind blew my hair back. But

I stood firm. Having Kellen immediately next to me made me feel braver than I had the last time I had faced Bradley.

"I own this place," I informed the poltergeist coolly. "This is my shop."

His glare deepened. Honestly, if he hadn't been dead, I would have said he belonged on a runway somewhere.

"I don't think so," he said, abandoning the creepy whisper and speaking in a tone of voice that was surprisingly normal. It made him seem more annoyed than homicidal, especially when he rolled his eyes. "I told you that already. Did I not make myself clear?"

"I heard you," I informed him, and his slightly less frightening manner gave me the courage to try using his name. "I heard you, *Bradley.* Why don't you think I own this place?"

He looked around, sweeping his dead eyes over the ruined counter and the empty shelves. When he got to the boxes beneath his feet, he wrinkled his nose. "This place is not yours. It's Stan's. And you are not worthy of it."

"Who's Stan?" Kellen asked, taking a step forward.

Bradley turned in his direction.

"His husband!" I burst out, then flinched as they both looked over at me. "That's right, isn't it?" I asked the ghost. "Gayle said you owned this place with your husband. Was his name Stan? You both died in the first Depot fire, right? How did it happen?"

Bradley's glare faded to a pout, and I could have sworn his lower lip wobbled.

"Get out," he said, and he was back to the scary whisper again. His eyes blazed and he rose higher above the boxes as the temperature in the room abruptly dropped another ten degrees. His voice broke as he said it again: "Get. Out!"

Before either of us could move to obey him, the front door to the shop opened.

Autumn walked in, with Royce right behind her. Witchtown's Queen Bee gave a friendly wave when she saw Kellen and me standing there.

"Hi, Macie! I heard your mom bought this place! Hey, how come it's so—"

She stopped dead and stared, open-mouthed, at the poltergeist. Behind her, Royce was doing exactly the same thing.

"What the—" Royce began.

"GET OUT!"

The poltergeist's voice was a screech now as he swooped down from the roof and flew straight at Autumn. She screamed and covered her head with her hands as she and Royce ran back outside. The poltergeist slammed into the wall above the door, grunted in frustration, then turned and dove straight into the pile of merchandise, tossing boxes and packing material aside. A box marked "Candle Holders" hit the wall with a sharp crash, and I jumped out of the way as an oil lamp shattered at my feet.

Kellen grabbed my hand.

"Time to go."

I let him pull me toward the door. When we were outside,

I cringed at the sound of more glass breaking from inside the shop.

My shop.

"Don't worry," Kellen said, and gave me a smile filled with such genuine warmth that I felt my knees shake a little. Or maybe it was that I had just survived a second encounter with the poltergeist without being burned alive. "Now that we know what we're dealing with, we'll come up with a better plan for next time."

Round two definitely belonged to the poltergeist. But I was nowhere near giving up. Round three was going to be mine.

Gayle had said that the first step to having power over something was to know its name.

And now I knew another one.

Stan.

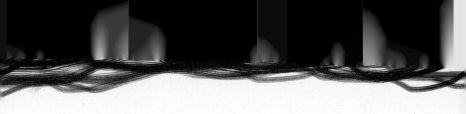

CHAPTER TWELVE

*T*hat evening I stood alone in the apartment, clutching a mug of lemon balm tea. There were a lot of things to ponder about this incomprehensible day. But one thing kept standing out.

Kellen. So he was going to try to teach me, was he?

I did not trust him. My internal alarms had been going off since I met him, and I wasn't one to ignore that strong a gut feeling. Even if there seemed to be less evidence to support it every time I was around him. Part of me still couldn't help but wonder if he was right about me. He had seemed so certain. He had the kind of confidence that was contagious. What if. What if I wasn't a Void after all? What if I *could* learn to channel . . .

I shook my head. I had a lifetime of evidence to stack up against his totally uneducated opinion. Seattle be damned. I. Could. Not. Channel.

But I would go along with it. Be the dutiful pupil. I would

keep him close, mostly because I couldn't afford to have him anywhere else. Not now that he knew.

Only one other person had ever found out I was a Void, and I had known that Rafe wouldn't betray me. I couldn't say the same thing about Kellen, whatever promises he might have made to me. I was reasonably sure we were playing each other. Me, to make sure he wouldn't get in the way of my con. Him? I still had no idea what his deal was. But my connection with Rafe . . . that had been real. At least, it had turned real. Once I figured him out. My first impression of him had been dead wrong.

"You think I'm a drug dealer?" Rafe had asked, incredulous.

"Well . . ." I hesitated, trying to think how to explain myself. "I mean, you're all kinds of mysterious about what you do all day. And you have lots of cash hidden in plastic bags in the woods. What was I supposed to think?"

"Unbelievable," Rafe muttered. "Come on. I have something to show you."

He led me to the larger of the two dilapidated shacks on his property. Inside, the air smelled almost sweet, and it was so thick it felt heavy inside my lungs. There was wood everywhere, all in various stages of becoming something more. Furniture, mostly. There was a stack of half-finished chairs in the corner and a beautiful table in the very center, with a power sander and several piles of sandpaper sitting on it. A workbench took up the far wall, which was also home to a scary-looking saw and lots of tools.

"This is what I do all day," Rafe said behind me, leaning against the center table.

"Oh," I said sheepishly. "Why didn't you tell me before?"

"I didn't think you were interested. You only seemed to care about how many mandrake plants I could lead you to."

Really? That was what he thought? How depressing. And how true.

I looked around the room, trying to take in everything at once. I walked over to one of the chairs.

"So the money in the woods . . . that was from selling furniture?"

"Furniture, carvings, whatever I feel like making. There's a pretty good market for quality handcrafted wood products. I have a guy who sells my stuff outside the Haven. Someday, maybe I'll be able to open a shop myself. In a Haven where the people have more money to buy things."

I sniffed the air. It smelled like sawdust, but also very strongly of sage, a smell I used to associate only with ritual but which was becoming more and more connected to Rafe.

"Do you cast in here?" I asked.

"I don't do formal spellwork, no. But there's a lot of craft that goes into woodworking, if you do it right. Wood is very absorbent of thoughts, feelings." He picked up a piece of sandpaper and absent-mindedly started sanding the table. "Every time you touch a piece of wood, you put your intentions into it. So I burn a lot of sage in here. It gets my mind right, you know?"

I didn't know. I ran my hand over the back of the chair, feeling the surface that Rafe had touched, again and again, as he had shaped it and made it smooth. I felt nothing more than the flawless wood beneath my hands. Was there more? Did other people feel more when they touched something that Rafe had touched?

The idea disturbed me. I changed the subject.

"Why do you stay here?" I asked. "You have enough money to get out, to start your shop. More than enough. I've seen it. What's keeping you?"

"That money's not for me," Rafe explained. "It's for my dad."

"What?" I exclaimed. I stopped petting the chair and stared at him incredulously. "You cannot be planning on giving that to your dad. You know what he'll do with it!"

"I'm not going to give it to him," Rafe agreed, tossing aside the sandpaper and jumping up to sit on the edge of the table, facing me. "I'm going to use it to pay off the mortgage on the farm. I'm paying it now, every month, but once I go he won't be able to keep the payments up. His assistance will cover what he needs for food and stuff, but I can't let him lose the farm. I can't leave him homeless. What?"

I was staring at him, reliving every moment we had ever had together through this new prism of understanding. How had I been so wrong? I blamed the way we had met. It had given me a weird first impression of him, and first impressions were difficult to shake. Even for me.

I will never steal from Rafe.

The thought hit me with such force that I had to grab the back of the chair to steady myself. The truth of it was undeniable. If he had led me to his stash right that very moment and given me an hour alone with it, I would have left every dollar exactly where it was.

I had never in my life been as sure of something as I was about that.

Everybody I had ever met had always been fair game. To the extent that I had ever bothered to find out their stories, their problems, their hopes, I had never let their needs eclipse mine. No one had ever been off-limits.

Until now.

I was gripping the chair with both hands. Slowly, I looked back across the room at him.

He was still sitting on the table, watching as I warred with my own thoughts.

"You must be some kind of terrible," he remarked, holding my eyes. "To have spent all of this time with me, thinking what you thought, and never worrying about it."

"Yes," I said simply.

"Tell me."

"I'm a Void," I said. And I watched his eyes carefully, looking for a reaction.

There was no surprise. No shock. No . . . revulsion. Instead, his eyes gradually grew darker, until they reminded me a little of the eyes that had stared down at me in the woods. But this was a different kind of darkness. This was wanting. This was curiosity satisfied, which in turn opened up another need.

My stomach clenched and felt like it was flipping over itself, and I felt my fingertips press harder on the back of the chair.

He eased off the table.

"Is that supposed to scare me?"

"I don't know," I said, looking at my feet.

"Would it scare you if I were a Void?"

"No," I muttered. No more than his face was scaring me right now. This was unexplored territory. And I wasn't sure yet whether I wanted to run from it or straight toward it.

Straight toward him.

"All right then," he said, and took a step toward me.

I scooted backwards and put the chair between us.

"What are you doing?" I demanded.

"What do you think?"

I kept the chair between us.

"You don't think I'm going to infect you?" I asked, my voice sounding almost pleading. "Burn you out, just by being near you?"

"Nope," he said. He was standing right on the other side of the chair now. I could have backed up farther toward the corner, but I was afraid of what would happen if I let go of the chair.

"There's more," I said desperately. "A lot more."

I am so much worse than you think.

"I don't care."

"You should. You really should —"

"I don't."

He sidestepped the chair so that he was standing directly in front of me. He put one calloused hand on top of both of mine, pinning them to the chair railing. He snaked his other hand up into my hair, and tilted my face so that I was looking at him.

"I don't care," he said again, pronouncing the words very carefully before covering his lips with mine.

I felt the kiss not just where his lips and his tongue touched me, but down the entire length of my body. I felt his hands on me and I wondered if they could change me, the way they had changed the wood. Shape me, smooth me, transform me into something different. Something better . . .

The apartment had grown dark. I put down my cold tea and felt my way toward the couch.

It's not backtracking. I just need to hold it for a moment.

I reached a hand under the couch cushion, feeling for where I had hidden Rafe's jacket. There was nothing. Had I noticed the usual lump in the couch when I went to sleep last night? Or had I been so busy trying to forget about it that I had actually succeeded?

I threw the cushion aside, and the moonlight coming through the window illuminated the empty space underneath.

———

I waited all night for my mother to come home, but she never did. She must have been putting in some serious time trying to get inside the vault with Percy. At least, I hoped that's what they were doing. There were a myriad of other possibilities, none of which I wanted to think about.

While I waited, I searched.

It didn't take long. The apartment was not big, and nomads that we were, my mother and I had very few personal belongings. My mother's room smelled strongly of cinnamon, like she always did, and a few minutes of poking around was all it took for me to conclude that Rafe's jacket was definitely not there.

What *was* there, underneath a sweatshirt in the bottom drawer of the bureau, was a large bag full of beef jerky. At any other time, finding out that she had been cheating on the diet she had forced on me would have infuriated me to the point of tears. But I was already so angry that there was no way her latest petty betrayal was going to make any kind of dent.

What had she done with it?

Everything she had said about having "ground to make up" had been crap. It was always crap. And I fell for it every time.

There was nothing to do but wait, so I paced circles around the living room. By the time the sun peeked through the hideous blue curtains, my anger had built up so much that my hands had clenched themselves into shaky fists.

That's it, I thought suddenly. *I'm done.*

I stormed out of the apartment.

I had no idea where my mother might be. Or what I was going to say to her once I found her. All I could hear inside my head were the same two words over and over again.

I'm done. I'm done. I'm done.

I stomped in the direction of the bank — the most reasonable place to begin looking for her — and got about two steps in that direction before I slammed right into someone.

The person was dressed in a black skirt, black leggings, and black boots. So I just assumed it was Talya until I regained my balance enough to look up and see Autumn scowling down at me.

"Macie!" she exclaimed. "Watch where you're going!"

"Sorry," I muttered, frowning. Why was Autumn dressed all in black?

Now that I was able to focus on something besides my anger, I noticed that there were black banners flying all around the square.

"What's going on?" I asked Autumn, who was brushing nonexistent dust from her shoulder.

"Pendle Bishop," she said. "Didn't you hear?"

"What about her?" I asked, with a mounting sense of dread.

Autumn finished fussing with her clothes and looked over at me sadly.

"She died last night."

CHAPTER THIRTEEN

*T*he rowan in the water supply turned out to be more of an annoyance than a genuine danger to the town. The mayor handled the whole thing with her usual efficiency, even though I could tell she was cringing from yet another unexpected expense and she took to muttering about the "cursed Zealots" more than usual. It took three days, two cleansing spells (both of which I managed to avoid participating in), and the installation of a fancy new filter before the water was declared rowan free and safe to use again—just in time for Pendle Bishop's funeral.

I had never seen the square more crowded. I suspected that almost every resident of Witchtown was there, including the ones who hadn't bothered to turn up for my initiation. It looked like all of the town teenagers, with the exception of Talya (who was nowhere to be seen), were standing in a clump around Autumn and Royce.

I stood at the edge of the group, fingering my moonstone as Maire finished casting the circle around us. The nerves that normally hit me like a freight train in ritual situations were being kept at bay, for once. I suspected that had a lot to do with the large wooden structure beside the altar.

And with the body on top of it.

I couldn't see the actual body, of course. Just a cloth-wrapped bundle that looked too small to contain the earthly remains of an entire person. Even a person as small as Pendle Bishop had been.

Maire approached the pyre. She opened a small jar, and there was just enough of a breeze to bring a whiff of cypress oil to my nose. Maire dipped her fingers in it and touched the top of the cloth-wrapped head.

"We bless your head. May you carry the wisdom you have gathered here to the next life and beyond."

"She's not going to be buried?" I whispered to Kellen. Most witches preferred a natural burial. No casket, just a cloth wrapping. No muss, no fuss. As close to the earth as possible.

"It's casket or cremation here," Kellen explained. "Most people choose cremation. The urn can be buried directly in the earth."

"We bless your eyes, all that you have seen and have yet to see," Maire continued.

I flinched. I still had Pendle's wallet tucked somewhere in our apartment. Could she see *that*, now that she was presumably free of the dementia that had clouded her vision in life?

I fidgeted uncomfortably, and Kellen must have noticed because he looked over at me strangely.

"I've never been to a funeral before," I admitted.

"I have," he said dryly, and I knew he was thinking about his mom.

Whatever suspicions I still harbored about him, this was not play-acting. There was real pain on his face.

I slipped my hand into his. He did not look at me, but he gave my fingers a warm squeeze, just as Maire raised a hand slightly to the other side of the altar, to where my mother was standing.

My mother closed her eyes and a ball of flames engulfed the pyre.

The new town Natural burning the old. There was something comfortingly circular about it.

And something profoundly unsettling, too.

Kellen disappeared quickly, almost the second Maire closed the circle and dismissed us. I wasn't sure quite what to do or where to go myself, so I followed the group that headed to Odin's Tavern.

Witchtown's one and only drinking establishment was all polished wood. The back wall was dominated by a carving of a topless woman with flowing hair, which looked like it had been pried off the bow of a ship.

The man behind the bar was wearing a Viking helmet, and he was so enormous that I dismissed him at first as just another oversize decoration. But when my entrance caused the little bells attached to the door to jingle, the helmet turned in my direction and the horns swung slowly from side to side.

"No minors," he growled.

"It's okay, Uncle O, she's with me."

Talya was waving at me from a table next to the window.

I glanced back toward the bar. The horns dipped forward slightly, in what I assumed was permission, so I walked over to join her.

"Odin, I presume?" I asked, referring to the formidable bartender.

"My uncle," Talya confirmed. "Aimee's dad."

"You live with them, right?" I had heard that Talya's parents were not in Witchtown.

"Yeah," Talya said, playing with the straw in her drink. "Once my parents figured out the witch thing wasn't a phase, they shipped me off so that I could be with 'my own kind,' to use their words."

"Nice," I said sarcastically.

A bowl of nuts crashed down onto our table, and I jumped. When I looked up to find Odin standing over me, I jumped a second time.

"What else can I get you?" he rumbled, then gestured to Talya's drink. "You want the ginger ale too?"

I was about to say yes, since it seemed the polite thing to do, but the smallest of warning headshakes from Talya made me reconsider.

"Um, I think I'll start with water. Thanks," I squeaked. Then, because my stomach had woken up at the sight of the nuts, I pointed to the bowl. "Um, are those raw?"

"I sure as hell didn't cook them. I'll be right back with your water."

Good enough. I took a handful.

"Wise choice," Talya said, making a face at her ginger ale and pushing it away. "He makes it himself. He tries. But it tastes like socks."

I stifled a laugh as more black-clad funeralgoers streamed into the tavern.

"Did you watch the funeral from here?" I asked Talya.

"Yes. Rituals are a problem for me," she admitted. When I said nothing, she sighed. "If I concentrate really hard, I can usually prevent myself from saying the things I see out loud. Except in ritual. Being around channeled power just makes me blurt things out."

"Oh," I said. "I can see how that would be a problem."

Odin brought me my water, and I told Talya about finding the angelica. She seemed to believe me, even without evidence. I offered to show her where it was and in return, she promised to lead me to some of her favorite herb-hunting spots around town.

After that, a strange silence fell over us.

"So why do you hang around the rituals?" I asked her, after a while. "Why take the chance?"

"I like to watch," Talya mumbled. And to my surprise, she colored slightly.

I raised an eyebrow.

"Like to watch *who?*" I baited her.

Oh Gods, don't let it be Kellen.

But honestly, Kellen didn't seem like her type. And he hadn't been a part of the group sweeping the square. He hadn't been the one she was staring at . . .

"Royce?" I ventured hesitantly. "Is it Royce?"

Talya's blush deepened.

"It *is* Royce!" I exclaimed, triumphantly.

"He has nice shoulders," she admitted.

I started to giggle, and she glared at me for a second before laughing herself.

"He's also attached at the hip to Autumn," I pointed out gently.

Talya stopped laughing and eyed me gravely.

"Don't be so sure about that," she muttered.

I raised an eyebrow. I was about to ask her again what she had seen about Royce when my mother breezed through the door of the tavern.

"Hello, girls." My mother swooped down on us and kissed me on the cheek before I could duck. "Fancy meeting you here."

"Mother, this is Talya," I mumbled. "Talya, my mother. Aubra."

"Delighted to meet you, Talya," my mother gushed, sticking her hand out.

Talya reached out a lacey, black-gloved hand, her eyes wide.

"Talya?" I asked.

She did not respond. She was staring at my mother, the same way she had stared at Royce. Frozen, slack-jawed, and looking a little bit beyond her. Her lips twitched like she was about to speak, but she clapped a hand over her mouth before she could make a sound.

She stood up and had to grab the table to keep from stumbling backwards.

"I'm fine," she said, when I jumped up to help her. "I'm . . . um . . . late for work."

She ran for the door. My mother stared after her.

"What's her problem?" she asked me.

I shrugged my shoulders and returned to my seat, like I hadn't noticed anything strange. But I could feel my heartbeat quickening. What had she seen about my mother?

"Um," I started, then bit my lip. I would rather have had this conversation in private.

"Yes, dear?" my mother asked, turning slightly to scan the bar.

"You . . . You didn't have anything to do with Pendle Bishop's death, did you?"

My mother whipped her head around to face me.

"Of course I didn't!" she snapped. "The mayor said that

Pendle Bishop died of a heart attack. Even I can't make that just *happen*."

"Okay . . ." I said guardedly.

My mother made a face and sank gracefully into the chair that Talya had just vacated. She folded her hands and looked at me primly across the table.

"Why would I harm that old woman?"

Why would you steal Rafe's jacket?

"I don't know," I said honestly, answering both questions. I *wanted* to believe that she wasn't capable of murder. There was a time where I would have believed it without a second thought. But now . . .

I had seen too much to rule it out. I wasn't entirely sure where my mother would draw the line anymore.

Or if she would draw the line at all.

"How's the vault coming?" I asked, mostly to change the subject.

"Slowly. I've been too busy drawing up the fake financials for the investors to make much headway on anything else. But the books are all done now, so Percy and I are going to put in some serious time at the bank later today," she said, waving at something over my shoulder. I craned my neck and saw the mayor's rodent-faced husband waiting eagerly at the bar.

Great. Just great.

My mother stood up.

"Have a lovely day, darling," she said, beaming wildly at me as she flitted across the room toward Percy.

With a sigh, I took a handful of nuts for the road and started for the door.

"Hey," came a gruff voice from behind me.

I spun around to see Odin coming around the bar, walking purposefully toward me, his face unreadable beneath the fierce Viking helmet. It took real effort for me to take a deep breath and stand my ground, planting my feet into the wooden floor beneath me. But I was glad that I didn't give in to the urge to flee when he stopped in front of me and put out a meaty hand.

I took it, and he nearly shook my arm off.

"It's nice to see Talya with a friend," he said, still growling slightly despite a hint of a pleasant tone. "It's Macie, right?"

"Right."

"You come back anytime, Macie. Okay?"

"Okay," I agreed.

CHAPTER FOURTEEN

*T*he next morning, I had my first magic lesson with Kellen.

Kellen lived just north of downtown, in a neighborhood made up of cute little homes with thatched roofs, picket fences, and large gardens. The streets in this area were all roughly cobbled and had names like Evening Primrose Lane and Meadowsweet Way.

Of course Witchtown's Prince Charming would live in a place right out of a fairy tale.

Kellen let me in the front door and led me into the kitchen by way of a snug living room. He introduced me to a man with his same firm jaw, blue eyes, and floppy brown hair.

"My dad," Kellen said.

"Just leaving," his dad assured us, and he shook my hand and gave Kellen an amused smile. "You kids have fun."

After his dad left, Kellen motioned for me to sit. I pulled out a chair from the cozy kitchen table, sniffing the air as I did. The scent of juniper was there, of course, because Kellen was. But the dominant scent in the room was a sweet, doughy, slightly charred aroma, which meant Kellen had eaten partially burnt pancakes for breakfast.

My craving from that first morning in Witchtown came back with a vengeance. I sat down quickly in the chair, trying not to breathe through my nose.

Kellen set two pewter candleholders on the table of front of me and wedged a white taper candle into each of them.

"Since you seem pretty dead set on this 'I can't channel' business," he said, with only a touch of mockery in his voice, "I'm not even going to bother taking you through the summoning, accepting, and channeling of power, the way I would with someone normal."

"Gee, thanks," I said, and I had just enough wounded pride to add, "I did it once, you know."

"Really?"

He sat down across from me.

"Sort of," I hedged. Seattle was kind of hard to explain. I didn't remember much about it. And strangely, thinking of it always made me wonder about my father. Or maybe I was thinking about him because I had just met Kellen's dad? "I mean, I was little. But I'm pretty sure I channeled."

"That should make it easier for you to do it again," Kellen said, moving the candles so that they were between us on the table. "Still, given your issues, I'm going to try to come at it from a different angle."

With a flick of his fingers, a tiny ball of flame appeared, lighting the candle on the right.

"Showoff," I scoffed.

"Look at the flame," he said, in the same teacher voice I had heard him use on the six-year-olds. "Take a good, hard look at it. Notice all the details. Then I want you to close your eyes and picture the flame in your mind."

I stared at him in disbelief.

"Candle meditation? This is kid stuff!"

"Humor me," he said. When I continued to glower at him, he added, "You promised you would do what I say, no questions asked."

I blew out a lungful of air, causing the flame to dance but not go out.

"Fine."

Dutifully, I stared at the candle flame. It was your basic, orangey yellow flame that faded to blue the closer it got to the wick. It wasn't long before my eyes started to hurt. I closed them, and brought up an image of an identical candle in my mind's eye.

"Got it?" Kellen asked. His voice was quiet, gentle so as not to distract me.

"Yes," I said. I still felt like an overgrown six-year-old. But the part of my brain that was not absorbed with fueling the candle image was aware that while my eyes were closed, Kellen was free to stare at me at his leisure. *Was* he staring?

I would probably never know. Unless I peeked, which would ruin the exercise.

Did I want him to stare? I wasn't sure of that either.

"Okay," he said. "Now that you have a clear image, I want you to manipulate it. First, make the entire flame yellow. Go."

I concentrated, and the orange and blue parts of the flame in my mind melted away, leaving only the yellow behind.

"Now orange. Go."

The yellow flame darkened into a bristling burnt orange.

"Now expand the flame; make it fatter. Go."

"Shrink it; make it tall and skinny. Go."

"Make it green."

"Pink with yellow polka dots."

I obeyed all of his commands, smirking a little at the last one.

"Okay," he said, and his voice took on a slightly more serious tone. "Now picture another candle in the background. Unlit. Just like the real one on the table in front of you. Got it?"

"Got it."

"Now make the flame jump from the lit candle to the unlit one. Go."

I tried, really I did. But the tiny flame in my head, which had so obligingly changed colors and shapes, stubbornly refused to jump. It didn't matter how much I commanded it, threatened it, sweet-talked it, or even begged. It wouldn't go near the second candle.

The problem was I knew what was supposed to happen.

Or, at least, I knew what Kellen wanted to have happen. His plan was for me to make my mental candle flame jump, then I would open my eyes, and both of the candles on the table would be lit. *Boom*, channeling, without thinking about it. But the wall, that damned wall, was sitting stubbornly between the two candles. Mocking me.

The frustration must have been showing on my face, because I suddenly felt Kellen's hand on mine.

"Open your eyes," he said.

I did. Only the candle on the right was lit.

I looked over the candles at Kellen. He looked disappointed. And he was looking at me the way one might look at a puzzle.

"You see?" I said. "It won't work. I can't channel."

"That was only our first try," he reminded me. His hand was still on mine.

He has such nice eyes.

I hadn't noticed his eyes since initiation night, immediately after he had tried to kiss me. The candle's flame was reflected in them now, making them look even bluer than they had then.

Stop it.

"Did the real flame ever change?" I asked him. I was annoyed to detect a hint of hope in my voice. "With the visualizations? Did it change colors or size?"

Kellen smiled apologetically, and I sat back in my chair, defeated.

"What does it feel like to channel?" I asked him.

Before Kellen could answer, I heard the echo of my own voice in my head. I had asked that question before.

I sat up straighter and extracted my hand from his.

"I should go."

He stood up.

"I'll walk you back downtown."

As we made our way down the cobblestone streets of Kellen's neighborhood, I put a hand to my stomach and stifled a belch, wincing slightly at the sudden taste of garlic in my mouth. Last night, completely and totally unable to face another salad, I had unearthed my copy of *The Art of Raw Vegan Cooking*, which I had bought the first time my mother had forced us to "go raw" (several Havens back). My attempt at the featured cover recipe of carrot pasta with raw marinara sauce had come out remarkably edible, I thought, if a little heavy on the raw garlic. But my mother hadn't been quite as impressed.

"You know," she had said, throwing down her fork, "we don't have to eat this crap when it's just us."

"Yes, we do," I had replied firmly. Then, choosing to ignore her having just called the meal I had made for her "crap," I added, "It's too easy to slip up if we act differently in public than we do in private. You taught me that yourself."

I had met her gaze then, and tried to tell her with my eyes that I knew exactly what she was hiding in her bottom drawer.

She hadn't said anything. She just marched into the bedroom, leaving me to finish my meal in silence.

At least she was probably burping up garlic today too. The thought cheered me as we reached the outermost circle of buildings of downtown and passed by an old Victorian house.

I paused. The house would have fit in perfectly in the Victorian Village, which was just south of downtown. But here, among all of the identical, whitewashed commercial buildings, it looked very out of place.

"That was Pendle Bishop's house," Kellen explained.

"Really?" I wasn't surprised. The peeling paint, the shabby shutters, and the slightly leaning porch looked exactly how I would have pictured the batty old Natural's house.

"This whole area used to be housing, back when Witchtown was smaller," Kellen told me. "When downtown expanded, they built another neighborhood in the south, with bigger and nicer houses. Everybody agreed to move except Pendle."

"She refused?" I asked, looking harder at the house. There was something odd about it. A fiercely sad vibe was emanating from the place, as though it missed its owner. But there was something else . . .

"Yeah, she refused," Kellen said, smiling a little. "So they built downtown around her. That was right around the time I got here."

I continued to scrutinize the house. It was the yard, I

think, that bothered me. It didn't look right. The vividly green grass and the freshly mulched flowerbeds looked too labor-intensive to belong to a slightly crazy old lady. Even if the lawn was just a tad too overgrown to be described as well mani-cured.

Beside me, Kellen was looking closely at the lawn as well.

"Grass could use some mowing. I was going to try to come by today or tomorrow, but . . ." He spread his hands.

"You mow her lawn?" I asked. "I mean, mowed?"

"Sure," he said, looking surprised at my surprise. "It's not like she could do it herself, you know."

I followed him silently into town. He ducked quickly into the Green Man Organic Grocer, promising that he would only be a moment. Rather than follow him in, I browsed the out-door racks of Widdershins Wardrobe, the secondhand cloth-ing place next door. It looked like a fifty-fifty mix between ritual wear and everyday wear. I flipped mindlessly through a jumble of coats, wondering if I would ever find the outer limits of Kellen's do-goodedness.

Then my fingers touched something familiar.

I shoved an armful of hangers aside to get a better look, and there it was: Rafe's jacket. Just hanging there. With a red tag tied to the zipper.

My heart started beating in my throat.

I snatched the hanger off the rack and marched inside. I walked right up to the girl sitting behind the counter and threw the jacket down in front of her, right on top of the tarot cards she had laid out beside the cash register.

"Hey!" she protested.

"Where did you get this?" I demanded.

She gave the jacket a lethargic stare, then shrugged. She looked about my age. She had probably been at my second initiation ritual.

"Don't know," she said. "Half the stuff we get is donated. There's a bin. We also buy stuff that's in good condition."

"But you don't know who brought this in?" I pressed her.

"Not my job," she said, peeling the jacket off her cards and handing it back to me.

I knew who had brought it in. But confirmation would have been nice.

"Are you buying it or what?"

"There you are!" Kellen said, coming up behind me and holding a reusable bag full of oranges. "Are you buying something?"

I glanced down at the jacket in my hands and fumbled for the red tag. It said twenty-five dollars.

My heart sank. I had gone food shopping again yesterday and as a consequence, I had only eleven dollars of my own money left in my wallet.

"I can give it to you for twenty," the clerk offered. I had no idea why she was being nice. Probably just to get rid of me. But twenty dollars was still too much.

I wanted to kick myself. It was too late to come back later and steal it — not when I had made such a scene.

My mind was telling me to lay the jacket on the counter and go, but my hands would not cooperate. They held on like I was drowning and the jacket was the only life preserver in sight.

"Do you need money?" Kellen whispered.

I opened my mouth to say no, but there was already a twenty-dollar bill in his hand. He set it down on the counter and gave the clerk one of his trademark grins.

I wanted to protest. Letting Kellen pay for this jacket was wrong on a number of levels. But I couldn't summon the words. I just hugged the jacket to my chest and followed him out of the store.

When we were back on the sidewalk, he stopped. I looked up and struggled to cobble together two words.

"Thank you."

He folded his arms and assumed an expression that I was becoming familiar with: the Macie-contemplation expression. A mixture of scrutiny, curiosity, and smaller but equal parts wariness and amusement. I was expecting him to demand an explanation, and I was busy trying to figure out a plausible story, when he said, "I never figured you for a fan of leather."

There was no good response to that. I didn't want to lie to him. Not when he had just done something nice.

I think he saw at least some of that on my face, because all of a sudden he called up a very fake-looking smile and gestured for me to lead the way down the sidewalk.

When we arrived at the door of my apartment building, I smiled a quick goodbye and went to duck inside, to sort my feelings out in private.

He stopped me with a hand on my arm.

"You asked me what it feels like to channel . . . do you still want to know?"

I nodded.

"It's like . . . you're suddenly a part of everything around you. Something greater than yourself. Something beautiful."

I nodded again, still cradling the leather jacket to my chest.

Kellen squeezed my arm. "Don't worry. We'll get you there."

I stretched out on the couch with Rafe's jacket clutched tightly to my front, with the sleeve pressed against my nose.

What does it feel like to channel?

Rafe had tried to answer that question for me once too. But he hadn't used the same words that Kellen had.

Actually, he hadn't used words at all.

We pushed the motorcycle out of the shed as quietly as possible, toward the cornfield behind Rafe's house. His dad was home, but judging by the new bottles that had accumulated in the sink that afternoon, he was in no shape to interfere.

Rafe swung his leg over the seat. I went to jump up behind him but he shook his head.

"No, in front of me," he said.

I hesitated. That would mean sitting on what looked like the gas tank, and the handlebars looked too wide to hold on to comfortably. I would rather have just held on to him.

"Trust me," he said, and placed a gentle kiss on my bottom lip.

Thus reassured, I climbed up in front of him. I felt mildly encouraged that once he scooted up close to me and grabbed the handlebars, I was completely encircled by his arms. I was sure of him. What I wasn't sure about was the hodgepodge of motorcycle parts I was currently perched on. The engine under Rafe's seat was orange and had a faded "350" on it. The part under my butt was blue. And the headlight between my knees looked too rusty to even function.

Rafe aimed the bike for one of the lanes between the rows of corn and started the engine.

I don't know what startled me more, the worryingly loud, throaty roar beneath us or the way we jerked forward. But before I could react, we were racing between two walls of corn and the wind was slapping me in the face.

I could hear Rafe shouting in my ear.

"Feel that?"

"Feel what?" I yelled back. I wasn't sure he could hear me.

It was all I could do to hold on, one hand on the handlebars, one reaching down to clutch his knee.

It took three lengths of the field—two stops, two sharp turns, and two abrupt re-starts—for me to relax enough, to trust Rafe's driving enough, to realize that the wind was not, in fact, trying to keep me down.

It was trying to raise me up.

I sat up straighter.

"Feel it now?" Rafe yelled.

I had been gripping both the bike and Rafe like my life depended on it. Now I let go. Moving slowly, to test my balance, I sat up even straighter and brought my legs up and under me, until I was balancing on my knees on top of the gas tank, just behind the headlight. Then, very tentatively, I raised my arms into the air.

I closed my eyes.

And I felt it.

"It" was an assortment of things. The engine of the motorcycle, pushing me forward. The warm embrace of the wind, pulling me up and blowing back my long hair. Rafe's arms, still in a circle around me. Even the cornstalks on either side of us, stretched out for an acre in each direction. They had an energy too. And trumping everything else, there was the moon. I couldn't see it, because my eyes were closed, but I felt like if I reached up just a tiny bit more, I'd be able to touch it . . .

I felt the bike slow and skid to a halt. We had come to the end of the row.

I lowered my arms and twisted around to face Rafe. I couldn't imagine the expression on my face, but whatever it was, it made Rafe smile in a way I had never seen before.

"That," he said, "is what it feels like to channel."

I was saved from having to say anything by a gruff, angry voice coming from the direction of Rafe's house.

"RAFE!"

Rafe grabbed me by the shoulders and tossed me off the bike.

"RAFE! I warned you about that bike!"

The voice was closer now. So much for Rafe's dad being dead to the world.

Rafe grabbed my hand and pulled me out of the cornfield, toward the trees, leaving the motorcycle behind.

We ran until we could no longer hear his dad behind us. We must have passed the outer boundary of the Haven, but there was no formal border, no markings to tell us when it happened. The trees did not change much, except that they grew thicker the farther away from Rafe's house we got.

After a while, we burst into a clearing. Rafe stopped, dropped my hand, and leaned forward, resting his forearms on his knees to catch his breath. I did the same, and listened hard for anyone coming up behind us.

Nothing. The night had gone silent.

"I'm going to catch it tomorrow," Rafe said. Still breathing hard, he took off his jacket and laid it on the ground behind us.

"Don't go home," I suggested.

"I have to," he said, a glint of humor in his eyes as he sat down. "It's home."

I sat down beside him on the jacket.

"I'm sorry," I told him. "I didn't mean to get you in trouble—"

He stopped me, putting one finger to my lips.

"My idea. My fault. It was worth it to see you smile like that."

"Is that really what it's like?" I asked.

"Not always," he admitted. "Sometimes. On a good day."

"I hate being a Void," I said, making a face.

Rafe caught my chin, making me look at him.

"I don't hate anything about you."

He kissed me. We were both still breathing hard from all the running, so it was almost a relief when he moved from my lips down my jawline and then down farther to the sensitive skin on my neck. After that, everything got a little fragmented and fuzzy.

There were so many things vying for my attention all at once: Rafe's lips, the softness of his leather jacket on my (eventually) bare back, the feel of his hands on me, the sound of us breathing not quite in unison but together, the sight of the half-full moon above, keeping guard over us. All the practical thoughts, all of the impractical ones, and the blazingly romantic look that was in his eyes whenever they met mine.

But the main thing I was feeling was the sense that I was in the right place. For the first time in my life, I truly felt as if the

Goddess—Laverna, if you like, or whatever guise you prefer to think of her in—was smiling down on me.

I had never wholly participated in any ritual I had ever attended—I had always felt like an outsider, always had to hide behind an act. But not this time. Now, then, I could give myself up completely, lose myself, and not worry I would be found out. Because here there was only Rafe and the smiling Goddess above me. Both of them knew what I was.

And both of them loved me for it.

CHAPTER FIFTEEN

I woke up blurry-eyed, stuck somewhere between trying to forget the cornfield and wanting to pore hungrily over every little detail, just to torture myself.

I rehid Rafe's jacket underneath Laverna's altar, even though I didn't have a lot of faith it would be safe there. The thought put me in no mood to find a perky, curly-headed little person lurking just outside the apartment door.

"Hi, Macie! Wanna play?" Aimee asked, bouncing on her tiptoes.

I shook my head. I wasn't sure what I had done to gain her approval, but ever since that day by the creek, she had been popping up everywhere I went. Like a cute stalker.

My little shadow.

"Sorry, kid," I said. "I have things to do. Does your dad know where you are? Or Talya?"

Grinning wickedly, she shook her head side to side.

"I ditched them," she announced proudly. "I got away. Like a spy!"

Like a thief, the thought came to me, along with an uncomfortable twinge. I wasn't looking for a protégé. I couldn't afford a little tagalong, so I gave her the sternest look I could muster.

"Go find Talya," I commanded her. "She's probably worried about you."

She stuck her tongue out at me and took off running.

I shook my head.

Kellen was leaning against the Depot door, waiting for me. There was a cardboard box at his feet and a half-eaten breakfast sandwich in his hand. It was a croissant, egg, and cheese thing, wrapped in biodegradable waxy paper that had the Crescent Roll logo on it.

The mouthwatering smell launched a new attack on my already traumatized senses. I had eaten a handful of raw carrot noodles for breakfast that morning, which I had had to scrape clean of my homemade sauce in order to avoid another overdose of raw garlic. My stomach had not been willing to accept that as a proper meal and was now strongly encouraging me to rip the sandwich out of Kellen's hand. I came very close to doing just that, especially when he held it out for me to take.

"Bite?" he offered.

With a supreme act of will, I shook my head and reached

into my pocket for the Depot key. I was not my mother. At least one of us needed to keep up appearances.

"Oh, that's right," Kellen said. "You don't eat this kind of stuff."

I nodded at the box.

"What's that?" I asked.

"Just some stuff I thought might be useful."

Curious, I knelt to take a peek inside. There were a couple of sage smudge sticks, a small container marked "Saltwater," an obsidian arrowhead, a large gray stone, a smaller stone with a hole through its middle, a horseshoe, and a bag of beans.

I picked up the beans and looked questioningly at Kellen.

He shoved the last of the sandwich in his mouth and chewed carefully before answering.

"Supposedly if you spill something, like beans or coins, ghosts have to stop and count each one."

I pointed at the Depot door.

"Do you really think *that thing* is going to stop and count beans?" I asked.

Kellen shrugged. "I don't know. It's worth a try. Why? What's your idea?"

Instead of answering, I stood up and busied myself with the stubborn door. I had shoved the key in the lock and taken a deep breath, preparing to throw my weight against it, when I was distracted by voices on the other side of the square.

Kellen and I both turned around.

Mayor Bainbridge was coming out of Good Karma Coffee. She stopped and held the door open for six or seven people in dark suits who emerged behind her.

My gut twitched. I couldn't recognize everybody in Witchtown by sight yet, but my instinct was telling me that these people *did not belong here.*

"Who are they?" Kellen asked. And I could tell by the caution in his voice that he was thinking the same thing.

"Those must be the investors," I surmised, recalling what the mayor had told my mother in our living room.

"Oh, right," Kellen said, and the worry drained out of his voice. "The expansion."

Well, at least I knew something that Kellen didn't.

I squinted over at the suited figures. Witchtown's last hope. I wondered if the mayor had given them the fake books yet, or if my mother had been too busy fooling around with Percy to forge them.

I opened my mouth to say more about the suits, but suddenly there was a buzzing noise in my ear. I let go of the doorknob, swatted at the sound, and slapped something. It felt like a bug, but it hit the ground with way too solid a *thwack* to be a mere fly.

"Ew!" I cried, revolted. I covered my head in case there were more of them.

"What?" Kellen asked, startled, and I pointed down at my feet.

The bug was brown, with a cylinder-shaped body, about

the length of my palm. It had long, folded-in legs, two anten-nae, and transparent wings. I had wounded it, and the wings were making a disturbing scratching sound as they twitched in vain, trying to get it back up into the air.

I shuddered.

"Is that a grasshopper?" Kellen asked.

"Aren't grasshoppers green?"

"I don't—ugh, look out!"

We both ducked as two more insects dive-bombed our heads. They made a screechy humming sound, like someone playing loud notes on a severely out-of-tune guitar.

The bugs flew away, but the sound did not disappear with them. If anything, it got louder.

I straightened up. The sound was all around us. No, that wasn't exactly right. It was *above* us.

Hesitantly, I raised my eyes to the sky. There was a dark cloud hovering over the ritual area. A cloud full of flapping wings and darting, solid little bodies.

"Not grasshoppers," I said ominously. "Locusts."

Kellen knelt to pick up his box, without taking his eyes off the swarm.

"Let's get—"

Before he could say the rest, the cloud broke apart and suddenly there were locusts everywhere. Across the square, I saw the mayor and her investors duck, and all around me I heard screams as people ran for cover.

Kellen dove for the Depot door, but I grabbed his arm and

pulled him away. We couldn't escape into there—not when there was an angry poltergeist in residence who could probably do more damage to us than the locusts. I pulled Kellen toward Tenjin's Tomes next door instead.

We ran inside and it took both of us together to slam the door shut again against the cloud of insects that tried to follow us in. At least two dozen winged bodies smacked into the door behind us, then fell motionless to the pavement.

Kellen reached out and gently brushed two locusts off my shoulders. I shuddered in disgust and ran my hands frantically over my hair, down my arms, over the folds of my sweatshirt, and through my hair again to make sure I had no more on me.

"What on *earth?*" the shop owner exclaimed, her long blue cape swirling as she came out of a back room. I hadn't met her before, but now hardly seemed like the time for introductions. She joined us behind the glass door so we could all stare out into the square together.

The swarm was now obscuring the sun. It was hard to see anything besides the occasional shimmer of wings. Individually, the bugs were moving very fast. But as a group, they were moving in a slow, counterclockwise circle. They seemed to be centered on the square, which struck me as odd. Why should a giant cloud of biblical insects be attracted to the ritual area of a town full of witches?

"Look!" I said suddenly, pointing to the altar.

One of the dark-suited investors was standing there, seemingly unconcerned with the locusts that were swarming all around him. He raised one arm above his head, almost casually. When he opened his mouth, I blanched, imagining bugs flying into it.

He said only one word. Had I been outside, I'm sure I would have heard it, because whatever it was, it shook the entire square with its intensity. It sent a tremor through the bug cloud and for a second that felt like it lasted several minutes, the locusts all froze, motionless in midair.

Then they all fell to the ground, carpeting the square in small brown bodies.

Now that there was light again, I could see the man more clearly. He was middle-aged, probably fortyish. Tall, with a trim black beard. He was looking down at all the dead bugs, his face twisted in disgust.

The mayor and the other investors ran up to him. I couldn't hear him speak, but his lips seemed to be saying *I'm fine, I'm fine.* He raised both hands, assuring everyone that they could back off. I froze.

There was a sliver of silver on the second finger of his right hand.

My eyes moved quickly over the other suits; there was a silver ring on the right hand of everyone who surrounded the mayor.

A wave of fear washed over me, and I grabbed Kellen's arm to steady myself.

The mayor's investors were Naturals.

———

"Stop panicking," my mother snapped.

I had run back to the apartment, wincing at the crunch of freshly dead locusts under my feet. I don't even remember what I said to Kellen. But, sadly, I think he was probably starting to get used to me running out on him.

"Why shouldn't I panic?" I shouted at her. "They're *Naturals!*"

"Shhh!" She put a finger to her lips and motioned to her closed bedroom door. Only then did I register that her hair was disheveled and that she was wearing only a hastily thrown-on robe.

I stared at the bedroom door, then back at my mother, who was sitting at the kitchen table.

"*Percy?*" I whisper-squeaked.

My mother rolled her eyes.

"Grow up, Macie. Yes, Percy is here. We're adults. We know what we're doing."

"He's married! To the *mayor.*"

"Weren't you going on about something?" my mother inquired, feigning boredom. She leaned over, poured herself a glass of wine, and sipped it, watching me carefully over the rim.

I pinched the bridge of my nose. I only had the space to deal with one disaster at a time. I had to put the mayor's husband out of my mind for now.

"The Naturals," I reminded her. "They change our game."

"How?"

"Well, for one thing, they're going to figure out what I am!"

"We don't know that," my mother whispered calmly, but the gulp of wine she took betrayed her true anxiety level. "The moonstones have always worked before—"

"We've never tested them on a Natural," I reminded her.

"*I'm* a Natural," she growled at me. "I created them. We have no reason to think they won't work as they have always worked and kept both Naturals and Learneds from sensing the Void in you."

I pinched my nose harder, trying not to groan. She hadn't seen the man in the square. She hadn't felt his eyes. Sure, my mother was a Natural. But he was something more. I had felt it. He had looked right through me.

My mother took another enormous gulp of wine and closed her eyes. When she opened them again, her usual calm had taken over.

"They are only here for the day," she informed me. "To take a tour and pick up the books I forged. Brooke doesn't think they'll be back until they decide to invest. That's *if* they decide. They have a week or so to accept the offer Brooke made them."

She had known they were here. She had known, and she hadn't warned me.

And here she was, casually talking about Brooke. While her husband was right in the next room. Probably naked.

Shuddering, I grabbed the bottle of wine and poured myself a glass. My mother did not object.

"What about the rest?" I asked. "Like the memory spell? We don't know that that will work on Naturals either."

"We don't know that it won't."

"Are you willing to take that chance?" I asked, taking a deep sip of my wine. It made my empty stomach curl up on itself uncomfortably, but I ignored the feeling and took a second, bigger sip. "How's the vault coming?"

"Poorly. How's the shop?"

"Still standing," I muttered. Which was more than the last tenant had managed, but not good enough. Not for our purposes.

My mother put down her glass.

"You were the one who wanted to stay here," she reminded me. "You made the decision, Macie. Don't tell me you're second-guessing yourself already."

I bit my lip. She was right. It *had* been my decision.

"If we leave now," she added, "we leave with nothing. I don't like the idea of running in fear from a pack of Naturals, but I don't relish the idea of them catching us any more than you do. Let's just keep the con going for another week—until Solstice—and then we'll see what our options are, okay?"

I stalled, taking another sip of my wine. Just two days ago, I had been so sure I was done. But now . . .

This was my chance to leave. To pull the plug. It was the perfect excuse.

But I couldn't bring myself to do it. I had no idea why, but I couldn't make myself say the words.

"Okay . . ." I said tentatively. "We'll stay."

My mother got up from the table and turned back toward the bedroom.

"I'll make sure Percy didn't hear anything."

"How are you going to do that?" I asked, out of sheer morbid curiosity.

She faced me and grinned wickedly.

"Never hurts to get a little practice with that memory spell. He's such a willing subject. Darkness and clouds, darling. Darkness and clouds."

Then she practically skipped into the bedroom.

I considered throwing up. The idea of her using poor Percy as her plaything, both mentally and otherwise, made my heart ache and my stomach turn, respectively. But I couldn't let myself succumb to the mood of either body part. Instead, I gulped down the rest of the wine in my glass and bolted out of the apartment.

I saw no sign of the mayor and her entourage of Naturals as I walked, but I kept my head down just in case. I needed to see a friendly face.

The Crescent Roll was jam-packed. The chalkboard on

the wall proclaimed that it was "Only 7 Days Until Solstice!" and reminded patrons to "Preorder Your Honey Cakes and Litha Loaves Today!"

I spotted Gayle behind the counter, and even though there was a sea of people between us, I waved my arm excitedly at her. She waved back.

"Hello, Macie! Make any progress with your ghost?"

My heart sank at her words, but I tried not to show it.

"Some!" I lied, and tried not to grimace as her face broke into a broad smile.

"I knew you could do it!" she said, handing a box of pastries to the woman at the front of the line. "I'd love to visit, but I'm a little busy at the moment. What about tomorrow evening? I think I could slip away then."

"Great!" I said, calculating the probability that I would find a way to deal with the poltergeist by then. In order to avoid having to admit to Gayle that I was woefully out of my depth, I would have to think of something brilliant between now and then.

It felt strangely good to have a goal.

I left the shop quickly, my blood pumping at the thought of a challenge.

CHAPTER SIXTEEN

Someone had done a good job of cleaning up the locusts; I only had to kick one or two carcasses out of my way as I headed to the Depot that evening.

An odd feeling of calm had come over me, a sensation I hadn't felt since the Haven before Rafe's. I recognized it immediately for what it was: focus. The thing that I had been grasping for in the bathroom that first morning in Witchtown. I wasn't sure what had brought it on. But whatever it was, I thanked it. For the first time in a long while, I was seeing things clearly.

I didn't know what I thought I had been doing these past couple of days. Magic lessons? Funerals? This town was doing its best to suck me in, to make me forget what I was really doing here. But I wasn't going to let it.

This was strictly business. And I couldn't afford to waste any more time getting down to it. Not now that there were Naturals in play. They had all left town that afternoon, with the books my mother had forged. They wouldn't be back until after Solstice, at which point I had to have something to show for myself or my mother was going to pull the plug on this whole con.

Which was why I called for reinforcements.

Talya and Kellen arrived at the Depot at precisely the same time, although they came from opposite directions.

Getting my unruly poltergeist to fall into line was number one on my list of priorities. But I also had a number two priority that was long overdue. And thanks to my newfound clarity, I saw an opportunity to take care of both of them in one shot.

"Talya," Kellen said, acknowledging her with a slight nod as he tucked his box of supplies more securely beneath his arm.

"Kellen," Talya said in return, blinking at him from behind a thick layer of black eyeliner. She had a duffel bag with her; she had come prepared too.

I let us all inside. Bradley was nowhere to be seen, but the destruction caused by our last encounter was more than obvious. Boxes of merchandise were strewn everywhere, several shelves had been knocked over, and oddly, a door I hadn't noticed before in the very back of the shop had been ripped off its hinges.

Talya noticed the door as well.

"What's back there?"

"I don't know," I answered, walking over to investigate. Talya and Kellen followed.

Passing through the doorway, we climbed a steep flight of

wooden stairs, which led to a small living area directly over the store. There was a kitchenette with the basics: a refrigerator, a sink, and a one-burner stove. Next to the kitchenette was a dumpy old couch and a large wood-frame bed without a mattress. There was even a very small bathroom.

"Did you know this was up here?" Kellen asked me.

An odd idea came into my head: *This is mine. I could live here.*

I shook it off.

"No," I answered. "I had no clue."

"This is perfect," Talya said, and she set down her bag and sank to her knees beside it. She pulled out an armload of white candles, a tape measure, a piece of chalk, a sprig of fennel, and a large silver bell.

"What's all that?" Kellen asked, looking it over with interest.

"Everything you need for a ghost trap," Talya said, as though it was glaringly obvious.

"You've done this before," I observed. She hadn't mentioned it earlier when I had asked her to come by.

"Yes," she said. "Once. My mom — she's a realtor — was trying to sell this one house, but the ghost inside wouldn't let anybody in. So I trapped him and asked him what was wrong. It turned out he just didn't like the yellow daisies my mom had planted out front. So we replaced them with pansies and the ghost went away. My mom sold the house the next day."

"Well, that's one more ghost than I've ever banished,"

Kellen said, setting his box down out of the way and walking back to sit beside Talya. "Tell us what you need us to do."

Talya stiffened at his nearness and scooted a couple of inches away. Kellen looked surprised. Maybe a little offended.

But I knew it was nothing about Kellen in particular that bothered her. Talya just didn't like people close to her.

She looked up at me briefly, and I flinched.

Did she know what I was doing?

I couldn't tell. She looked away too quickly.

"You said his name is Bradley, right?" she asked. When I nodded, she continued. "That'll make things easier. And it would also be good to have some bait. Was there something in particular that made him come out before?"

I thought for a second, then ran downstairs to get one of the mislabeled bags of dried basil. It was only a hunch, but that's what Kellen and I had been discussing right before the poltergeist had materialized the last time.

When I got back upstairs, Kellen was holding the tape measure and Talya was using the chalk to draw two nine-foot-wide circles on the parquet floor. Once the candles were arranged around the edges of the two circles, Talya lit them with a wave of her hand. She herded Kellen and me into one circle and threw the bag of basil into the center of the other. Holding the fennel, she walked clockwise around both circles, chanting softly to herself. I couldn't understand everything she said, but I was pretty sure the Goddess she called upon to guide the ritual was named Shechinah.

Talya didn't seem to expect either Kellen or me to participate, which was a relief. I held my moonstone necklace with one hand and tried not to let my nerves show. Kellen watched everything Talya did with silent curiosity.

Once both circles were cast, Talya joined us in the center of ours, picked up the bell, and cleared her throat.

"We summon you, Bradley," she called out. "Come in peace, or not at all."

She rang the bell three times.

We all stared at the other circle, which was empty except for the bag of basil.

Nothing happened. Not even Bradley's telltale cold wind.

"We summon you, Bradley." Talya tried again, louder this time. "Come in peace, or not at all!"

Three more rings of the bell. Still nothing.

Kellen shrugged.

"Maybe he doesn't want to come."

"Maybe he doesn't want to come *in peace*," Talya said, and raised a questioning eyebrow in my direction.

I gestured to the empty circle.

"Are you sure that'll hold?" I asked her.

"It should . . ."

"Okay then," I nodded.

"Wait a sec —" Kellen started, but Talya cut him off.

"We summon you, Bradley," she said again. *"Come."*

This time, on the third peal of the bell, Bradley materialized inside the circle. He was huddled in his coat and when he looked over at us, his model-sharp features looked pissed off.

"What the *hell?*" he demanded.

Then he looked down and saw the bag of basil. He picked it up with a snarl and threw himself in our direction.

All three of us jumped, but Bradley was thrown back the instant he hit the edge of his circle. He landed hard, back in the center, right on the seat of his designer jeans.

I crept as close to the edge of our circle as I dared.

"I just want to talk," I said.

Ignoring me, he picked himself up with a grunt and tried to fly off in the opposite direction, only to hit the same barrier on the other side. He flew around like that for a while, like a fly trapped in a jar, swearing his head off and causing the temperature in the room to drop to near-Arctic levels.

I hugged my arms to my chest and raised my voice.

"I want to talk about Stan!"

He paused. His back was to me, but he turned slowly with boneless grace until he was looking right at me. The red around his oversize pupils pulsed with not-quite-restrained rage.

"So talk," he said, and I was surprised to hear that he was using his conversational tone, not his dangerously creepy whisper.

I took a breath.

"You said this was Stan's place," I said carefully, watching his eyes. "Is he here too?"

"No, it's just me," said the poltergeist, and flashed me a smoldering grin that reminded me of fire.

I decided to get right to the point.

"The people in town think you don't want the shop to have a new owner," I said. "But I don't think that's true."

Bradley raised one immaculately groomed eyebrow, but said nothing.

"I think," I pressed on, crossing my fingers in hopes that my hunch was correct, "that you just don't want the shop to have the *wrong* owner."

I gestured to the bag of basil in his hand.

"The last one planned to cheat his customers," I said. "What was wrong with the one before that?"

Bradley's eyes flickered down to the basil. He didn't answer right away, and my heart started to pound as I tried to plan an escape route. Just in case Talya's circle wasn't enough. Just in case his fire wasn't contained by the circle at all . . .

"The second one was a horrible person. And an idiot," he mumbled finally. "She would have run this place into the ground."

I relaxed slightly, mentally high-fiving myself. I *knew* there was a reason he had stared at me for so long, rather than just incinerating me on the spot. He had been sizing me up. And apparently, he hadn't liked what he saw. I was going to have to try to change his mind about me.

But before I could try, Kellen opened his mouth.

"You didn't think the previous owners were good

enough, so you *killed* them?" he demanded, from over my left shoulder.

The poltergeist looked in his direction. Before I could lose his attention entirely, I broke in, "What about me? You tried to kill me too. Why don't you think *I'm* good enough?"

His eyes snapped back to me.

"You're a kid," he scoffed.

"So? I'm not an idiot," I told him, then I pointed to the basil again. "And I would never sell crap like that. I'm not looking to cheat anybody."

To my shock, I realized that was true.

"Give me a shot," I challenged him. "Let me open the place, get it running. If you don't like the way I do business, you can ask me to leave. And I'll go. But no more fire."

Bradley crossed his arms and rocked back on his heels— odd, considering that he was floating above the floor. He did not respond.

"And no more breaking things, or flying around scaring customers," I added, recalling his stunt with Autumn and Royce. "An out-of-control poltergeist is not good for business."

The ghostly eyes narrowed.

"You can't make me leave."

I paused, wondering once again what had happened to cause the first Depot fire. I was becoming morbidly curious about it, but I didn't dare ask him about it now. Not when I was finally starting to make progress. He had totally lost it the last time I brought the subject up. But why would Bradley *want* to stay in the place where he had died?

Filing that question away for later, I squared my shoulders and said, "I never told you to leave. You can stay, if it means that much to you."

I heard Kellen draw in a surprised breath, just as Talya grabbed my hand. But I ignored him and shook her off.

"You can stay," I repeated. "But you have to behave. *No more fire.*"

As Bradley pondered my offer, I thought about what I was getting into. I had no illusions about what would happen to me if I got on Bradley's bad side. He was the type who would get what he wanted or burn the world down in a rage-filled snit if he didn't. Without feeling guilty about a thing.

Luckily, I was quite well versed in dealing with that personality type.

"What's your name?" Bradley asked me.

I looked sideways at Talya, thinking about Gayle's thing about names and power. Talya shrugged.

"Macie," I told him. "My name is Macie."

"Okay, *Macie,*" Bradley said, drawing out the pronunciation of my name as though he enjoyed playing with it. "I agree to your terms. But only because I find you . . . interesting."

He flashed me that seeing-right-through-to-your-bones stare again, and I had a sudden flash of panic. Could ghosts sense Voids?

"Macie—" Kellen started to say something, but I stopped him with an upraised hand.

"Deal," I said to the poltergeist. "Um, I guess we can't shake hands, huh?"

"Guess not," he said, gesturing to the trap all around him. "But you could let me out."

I turned to Talya.

"Let him out," I said. When she raised her eyebrows at me, I added, "Please."

Talya said a few words and walked around both circles counterclockwise to open them. The moment she was finished, the poltergeist started to become more transparent.

"I'll be seeing you," he said to me, ignoring Talya and Kellen completely.

And then he vanished, with one last wisp of cold wind.

I turned triumphantly to Talya.

"That was amazing!" I exclaimed. "How did you—"

But Talya was not looking at me. Her wide-eyed, glassy stare was fixed on Kellen. Through him, actually. Beyond him.

"What is it?" I asked, unable to keep the eagerness out of my voice. *"What do you see?"*

Talya didn't answer right away.

Kellen looked back and forth between us, his eyes wide with confusion. I wondered if he knew about Talya's strange affliction. He seemed to have a way of knowing things, even things that people preferred to keep private. But judging by his expression, he had no idea what was going on.

"What do you see?" I asked her again.

When Talya did speak, it was to Kellen, not me.

"Your mother," she began, then clamped a hand over her mouth.

Kellen's eyes widened, and I saw his chest rise and fall as he drew in a deep breath.

"Say it," he said.

It was obvious that she wanted to. Needed to, maybe. Her face was pinched from the pain of keeping her mouth shut.

She removed her hand.

"Your mother," she repeated. Then she paused for a moment and closed her eyes. Like she was seeing it all unfold behind her eyelids. "She killed herself. And you think it's your fault."

What?

"I *know* it's my fault," Kellen corrected her. "Go on."

"There was a pond," Talya said. "Water lilies. Moss. You found her there. You tried to pull her body out of the water, but you couldn't."

"I was eight," Kellen said. "I was small for my age."

No, no. This was not what I had meant her to see at all . . .

What would Kellen have looked like at eight? Big blue eyes, scruffy brown hair. An angelic little boy. I was stricken by the image.

I could see shades of that boy now, in the seventeen-year-old who stood next to me. Gone was the cocky, swaggering do-gooder whom I had marked early on as a fraud. The pain in his eyes was real, just like at the funeral. But this was fresh. It could have happened yesterday.

What have I done?

"Why did she do it?" I couldn't help but ask.

He looked over at me.

"Remember I told you that I'd seen a Void, that I knew what they were like? I was talking about my mother. She burned herself out. She was never the same after that. She just couldn't live with it."

"Why was that your fault?" I asked.

Kellen didn't answer. He looked at Talya, daring her with his eyes to say it.

But Talya looked away and settled herself back onto the floor. If she had seen the rest of Kellen's mother's story, she wasn't telling. I knew better than to ask.

Kellen leaned against the empty bookshelf at his back.

"So now you know. My deep dark secret. Everyone has one, right?"

My mind was reeling. Had I been reading him wrong this entire time? I had known that his Golden Boy act was just that, an act, from the moment I met him. But I had assumed he was using the act to cover up something nefarious, something deceitful.

Like me.

Guilt gnawed at my insides like acid. Was I really so far gone? Had I prayed to Laverna one too many times, so that now she threw a veil over my thoughts as well as my misdeeds?

"Anyway." Kellen interrupted my self-pummeling with an attempt at a light tone. "Wow, Talya. That's some gift you have there."

"I'd hardly call it that," Talya said. "A curse, more like. I'm sorry. I can't help what I see. And ritual work makes it impossible for me to control what I say."

Kellen glanced at me then.

He knows. He's never going to forgive me. He probably shouldn't.

He looked back over at Talya.

"No worries," he said, and smiled. At least, it was a half smile.

"It's late," Talya pointed out.

When we got back downstairs, Kellen headed straight for the door. He opened it, said goodbye to Talya, then addressed me in a voice that contained no hint of his usual playful tone.

"Second lesson. Tomorrow. Early. The Tor."

"Okay."

He left without looking at me.

Talya slung her duffel bag onto her shoulder.

"Thank—" I started.

"Did you get what you needed?" she hissed. "From him?"

"I—"

"Because the next time you're going to use me like that, I'd appreciate a little heads-up."

"I—"

"You could have asked, you know. I would have said yes."

"I—"

I cut myself off that time. I had no idea what to say.

"'Night, Macie," she said icily, and slammed the door shut behind her.

CHAPTER SEVENTEEN

I didn't dream of Rafe that night, but that was probably because I didn't sleep.

I lay there for a long time, in the dark, waiting for exhaustion to overtake me. But it never did. Finally I gave up, got up, and pulled out *The Art of Raw Vegan Cooking.*

I busied myself making a Lavender Cheez Cake. The result looked surprisingly edible, even though the recipe had called for ground-up cashews instead of cream cheese. Maybe I'd give it to Gayle. The only friend who wasn't currently mad at me.

When the "cake" was done and setting in the fridge, I ground up a few sprigs of rosemary and steeped them into a tea. Then I sat, sipping and fidgeting, until the sun came up and it was time to head to the Tor.

I felt pretty lightheaded as I started walking. Probably because of all the tea. And the two sides of my brain that had been quietly warring all night continued their sparring, although I could have sworn that both of them were trying to cover yawns.

They're marks, nothing more. Talya, Kellen, Gayle—all of them. They're a means to an end. You'll be leaving them behind soon anyway.

No. It's different since Rafe. You know that.

The Tor was a modest mountain. More of a large hill, really, just north of downtown and west of the forest where Kellen had tried to kiss me. There was a winding path up the south side to the summit, which boasted a three-story stone bell tower and vast views in every direction.

Kellen was already there. He was sitting on the grass at the base of the tower, arms draped over his drawn-up knees, facing east. The sun was hitting him pretty much full in the face, but he didn't seem to mind. He did not turn around as I approached.

I stopped a few paces behind him, nervous about what to expect. Kellen had not yelled at me the way Talya had, but he hadn't been able to look me in the eye either. Maybe he was just waiting to chew me out in private. I deserved it, but that didn't make me any more eager for the experience.

I looked warily at the back of his head. I had misjudged him, that was clear. But by how much?

"What do you know about ley lines?" he asked suddenly, still not turning around. How long had he known I was there?

"Ley lines?" I repeated. His voice had sounded normal,

very Kellen-like, not angry at all. That gave me the courage to go over, drop down, and kneel beside him on the grass. "Not much."

"Do you know what they are?" he persisted, still looking out to the east.

I followed his gaze. The day was clear and we could see for miles, to the arc of the wall that surrounded Witchtown and far beyond.

"Ley lines are invisible lines of power that crisscross the earth," I answered. "People like to build things in places where the lines meet. Like, important spiritual places, monuments—"

"And towns," Kellen interrupted. "Three ley lines converge right under this hill. That's why Reginald Harris chose to build Witchtown here. It's a very powerful place, spiritually speaking."

"Oh," I said.

He gestured to the tower behind us.

"Harris designed the tower, too. The bells are bewitched to ring of their own accord, if Witchtown is ever in danger."

"Oh," I said again. But privately, I was pretty sure that couldn't be true.

After all, they hadn't started ringing when I got to town.

Kellen turned his head and looked at me out of the corner of his eye. "I thought that since you have such trouble channeling power to yourself, I'd bring you to the power and see what happened. Lie down with me."

"What?" I asked, skeptically.

Kellen straightened out his legs and lay on his back, resting his head on the grass.

"Lie down," he repeated. "Flat on the ground. See if you feel anything."

Trying not to think about bugs, I lay down and copied his pose, so that we were about an arm's length apart on the hillside. I could have reached out and touched his left hand if I had wanted to. Part of me *did* want to, just to make him talk to me about something other than ley lines. But I settled my hand firmly on the grass beside my hip instead.

"Close your eyes," he said, which I was already doing because the sun was shining almost directly into them. "Feel anything?"

"No," I said honestly, squirming to get my shoulder blades into a more comfortable spot. "What am I supposed to feel?"

"Just wait," Kellen said. "Give it time. Be still."

I did as he said and stopped moving, trying to ignore a rock that was digging into my back. This whole exercise was pointless, but it hardly seemed like the time to complain. So I gritted my teeth and tried to enjoy the feeling of the sun on my face.

I'm not sure how long we lay there, side by side, before Kellen spoke again.

"Last night—" he began, then paused, and I held my

breath, ready to defend myself. But all he said was, "The poltergeist. I thought we were there to banish him. But you let him stay. You were . . . kind to him."

"That surprises you?" I asked. *Why, because I wasn't kind to you?*

"I'm not sure he deserves it," Kellen went on. "The things he's done—"

"Everyone deserves a second chance," I said. Then, thinking about it, I added, "Okay, maybe in his case it's more like his third or fourth chance. But still. People can change."

"You think so?"

"I hope so," I muttered.

Kellen said nothing to that, and we lay in silence again for so long that I started drifting off. It's hard to fight sleep when your eyes are already closed. I'm pretty sure I dozed. And I didn't wake up until I heard Kellen's voice again, closer this time.

"You knew Talya was going to see something about me, didn't you?"

I opened my eyes. Kellen had rolled over onto his side and was looking at me.

I rolled over too so I was facing him. There was no need for me to respond. He already knew the answer.

"Why did you do it?" he asked.

The hurt that had been so evident in him at the Depot, the hurt that had eaten away at me while I tossed and turned and "baked" last night, was mostly gone now. He sounded more curious than anything else.

"Because I wanted to find out more about you," I answered truthfully.

"You could have asked me," he pointed out.

I looked away. Talya had said something similar. The truth was, the thought of asking either of them anything straight out had never occurred to me. I wasn't used to people giving me what I wanted.

I was used to taking it.

"I'm sorry," I told him. "I had no idea. You can hate me if you want to. I'll understand."

"I don't hate you," he said slowly. "But maybe now you understand better why I think, why I *know,* you're not a Void."

I gritted my teeth again. It was wrong to be mad at him right now. Not when he had every reason in the world to be mad at *me.* But I couldn't help it.

I sat up.

"Why are you so obsessed with proving that I'm not a Void? Why do you keep insisting that I am something more than I am?"

"Why do you keep insisting that you're something less?"

He sat up as well, and he was very close. As close as he had been that night on the log. My nose was filled with the scent of juniper, and I had to stop myself from closing my eyes to breathe it in even deeper. I held his gaze, trying to give him my best steely-eyed glare.

"You don't even know me. Why do you think you know so much about me?"

"Because I *see* you, Macie O'Sullivan." He reached out a hand to cup my cheek. I was too lost between anger and guilt to do anything but freeze. "And I don't think you see yourself at all. I know you don't see what you really are."

"Which is *what*, exactly?" Still unable to move, I dared him with my eyes.

He brought his other hand up to my face. His eyes were suddenly very soft in the bright sunlight.

"Beautiful," he said simply. "Strong. A little bit too secretive, maybe. Way more suspicious than is healthy. But definitely the least empty person I've ever met."

He kissed me, and his lips were surprisingly tentative, given his usual cockiness. But they were sincere, and as he pulled me into him, I felt myself letting go, letting my guard down. Forgetting my anger at him. Forgetting most of all that I was supposed to be here for one reason and one reason only, and that reason did not include forming yet another hopeless attachment.

Yet for all that, I was kissing him back. My lips parted against his and I felt my arms slip around his waist. For one moment, a blissful, heady moment, I believed the things he said about me. I *was* more than an empty, soulless vessel who would never be part of something bigger than herself. I was not a monster who used her friends and exposed their darkest secrets on a whim.

But then I saw a flash of Rafe, on his knees, clutching at his throat. His dark eyes were vacant. Scared but vacant. Frantically searching mine but finding nothing.

And then, suddenly, the eyes faded to a light blue. They became Kellen's eyes, and the face around them became Kellen's face. The empty, frightened look was even scarier on Kellen.

"No," I moaned into his mouth.

I pushed him away.

I *was* empty. I *was* soulless.

"I can't," I gasped, and I vaguely recalled having said the same thing to him on initiation night. "I can't—I can't do this again!"

"Do what?" he exclaimed, breathless and confused. The faintest bit of hurt crossed his face and I ached with it.

"I can't," was all I could say. I lowered my head, tears clouding my eyes.

"It's that guy, isn't it? The one from before."

I hung my head, not contradicting him, even though it wasn't Rafe. Not really. Not in the same way it had been the first time. Shaken loose, my tears fell onto the ground between us. Like rain. Like the rain that had come down that night. So hard, so unrelenting . . .

I felt a hand lift my chin, and Kellen was staring down at me. Hurt. A little bit angry. Frustrated in the extreme.

"It's more than that. What aren't you telling me?"

"I can't—"

"Yes, you can. I'm not Talya. I can't read people. So I'm asking you, the way you should have asked me. Tell me, please. Who are you, Macie?"

Who are you? echoed Rafe's voice inside my head.

It had been raining all day, but it started coming down hard after sunset. Buckets. Sheets of water. I was thoroughly soaked after running the short distance between my house and Rafe's.

"Rafe!"

I threw myself through his front door, which was blessedly unlocked. He was in his room, fiddling with some engine part. He dropped it and caught me as I skidded into the room and came to a squeaky, dripping halt in front of him.

"Macie! What's wrong? What happened?"

"She's doing it!" I babbled. "She's doing it now! We have to go!"

"Shhh!" He put a finger to his lips and let go of me with one hand so he could close his bedroom door. "What's happening? Go where?"

I looked frantically around the room, and my eyes fell on the cluttered desk.

Keys.

I grabbed them and shoved them into his hand.

"We have to go. How much gas is in the bike?"

"Whoa, whoa." He took the keys and took one of my hands

in both of his, as though he could will his calmness into me. "Slow down. Tell me what happened."

"Do you trust me?" I asked.

He looked startled. And I don't think it was the question as much as it was the panic in my voice.

"Of course I trust you," he said, his tone starting to match mine in urgency.

"Then please, you have to do what I tell you. We have to get on your bike and leave. Right now. This second."

He stared down at me. Trying to read me, to gauge my seriousness. To figure out what I didn't have time to say.

"Okay," he said hastily. He kissed me quickly. Not the romantic kind of kiss, but the kind you do for reassurance. "Let's go."

He grabbed his leather jacket from the back of a chair and tossed it to me. "There's enough gas to get us out of the Haven at least."

"Thank you," I murmured. It was only partially to him, but he grabbed my hand and kissed my knuckles in answer before he let go to open the door to his room.

A blaze of lightning framed him in the doorway. It blinded me but I kept moving anyway. I was startled when I walked right into him, slamming my nose between his shoulder blades.

"Ow!" I blinked back tears and cradled my aching nose in one hand, shoving him in the small of his back with the other. "Rafe, go!"

He didn't budge; it was like trying to push a concrete wall.

"Rafe?" I ventured, squeezing myself between him and the door. He was dead-eyed and staring straight ahead . . .

My mother was standing in the hallway, directly in front of him. Had she followed me here? I wondered how long she had been standing there.

"I warned you," she said darkly.

"Please—"

"It's done, Macie. We have to go."

"No!"

I could already feel her pull on me. Part of me wanted to follow her out into the rain, into the car and away from here. Part of me was already miles away.

But then I looked at Rafe. He seemed bewildered. Now he was looking in my direction, but his usually sharp eyes were staring through me, squinting, as though he was trying to make me come into focus.

"Who are you?" he asked.

No.

I didn't know why I was surprised. This was what she did. What we did. We took what we wanted and then erased ourselves.

"I warned you," my mother said again, in a voice so carefree and light that it made me want to rip her throat out. "You know the rules. 'Don't get attached.' I thought you were old enough to know better."

"It's not like that," I informed her coldly. "I love him. And he loves me."

She laughed and motioned to Rafe, who immediately slumped against the door frame and slid down until he was sitting on the floor, still staring at me without really seeing anything.

"Loves you? He doesn't even know you. Did you tell him why you were here? Does he know we just took everything this town has?"

Her words were damning. True, and damning. But I would not let the truth derail me. I would tell him the truth, eventually. I had promised. He would forgive me; I knew that he would. It was something I couldn't possibly expect my mother to understand.

"I did you a favor, Macie," she continued. "Now he'll never know. We must go now."

She breezed down the hallway, so sure I would follow her that she didn't even glance over her shoulder to see if I was there. I lost her in the dark until she opened the front door. Then I could see her silhouette in the porch light.

I summoned every bit of strength I possibly could and threw it all into one word:

"No."

She froze. I'm not sure she'd ever heard that word from me before.

I stood between her and Rafe, feeling suddenly vulnerable. All I had to face her with was a determined glare. There was no way that was going to be enough.

She walked briskly back down the hallway, toward me. Her calm demeanor fell away more and more with every step, and there was real fury in her eyes by the time she stopped in front of me.

"I am not going to jail because you let some farm hand get into your pants and you think that's love. Stop wasting time and get in the car."

"No," I said again. My voice was shaking with emotion, but I forced the words out clearly so she would have no choice but to hear me. "I'm done with you. Done! Just fix him and we'll never tell a soul. You'll never have to see us again. Just—"

The slap came before I even saw her raise a hand. It spun me halfway around, shocking me more than it hurt.

"Ungrateful little slut," she hissed, as I rubbed my stinging cheek. "You think you're old enough to play games with me? With me? You have no idea what I'm capable of."

She looked pointedly over my shoulder at Rafe. He was still sitting on the ground, watching us but too confused to see much. He certainly hadn't seen her hit me. I could only imagine what a clearheaded Rafe would have done about that.

His eyes flickered up to mine. And for a second, I thought I saw the fog fade. There was a glimmer, a split second when I could have sworn that he knew me.

"Rafe?" I ventured.

But then his eyes widened and his hands went to his throat. He gasped for breath but found nothing.

I looked at my mother in horror.

"What are you doing?"

"Whatever it takes to get you in that car," she replied. The breeziness was back. She smiled as she looked back and forth between me and Rafe. "I'll release him then, and not a second before."

"No!" I felt a tightness in my chest. As though I was the one who couldn't breathe and not Rafe. This could not be happening.

But then Rafe started to make choking sounds, and I knew it was real.

"Stop this!" I begged her. "Please!"

Rafe fell forward onto his hands and knees. His choking grew louder and more desperate, and the fist inside my chest squeezed harder.

"You're killing him!"

"What do I care? Leave with me and he lives. But he won't remember you. Stay, and he dies. But you'll be the last thing he sees. Either choice has its poetry, you've got to admit," she quipped.

She meant it. She would really let him die.

Even knowing my mother as well as I did, the realization appalled me. But there it was, spelled out plainly in her eyes. She would kill to squash my disobedience. Without a thought. Without breaking a sweat.

My rebellion, such as it was, died right then and there.

Rafe fell back onto his heels and I sank down in front of him. He held me at bay with one hand and continued to claw at his throat with the other. There was no recognition in his eyes now. Just panic. And a plea that I could somehow make it stop.

"I'm sorry." I dodged his hand and got in close, caressing his cheek. I looked straight into his eyes, trying to get past the fog and into the place where my mother's spell couldn't touch.

"I'm sorry," I said again.

His face was turning gray. I pressed my lips to his, then used his shoulders to pull myself up. I turned and threw myself down the hallway, running for the car.

I got in and slammed the passenger door shut as hard as I could. So she would hear. I pressed my face against the window, and I saw Rafe collapse face-down on the floor.

Because she had released him? Or because he had passed out? Or worse . . .

My mother strode out of the house then, blocking my view. She didn't look at me as she rounded the front of the car and let herself into the driver's side.

I kept my face against the window. The engine roared to life and my mother brought her foot down on the gas, slamming me back in my seat as she sped us away from the small gray house.

But not before I saw Rafe turn onto his side.

Alive. He was alive.

Five days later, we arrived at Witchtown.

Kellen sat quietly in front of me, listening as I recounted the gist of what had happened that night. It was the only answer I had to his question.

"Say something," I pleaded, when I had finished and he had been quiet for too long.

"What did she do to him?" Kellen asked. "What was the spell? The first one."

"She made him forget. But she didn't just do it to him. She cast it over the whole Haven. So they would forget we were ever there."

He blanched, incredulous.

"She can make a *whole Haven* forget just like that?"

"She's very powerful."

"So an entire town has a giant blank spot in their memories, covering the whole time you were there?"

"No, it doesn't make people forget entire periods of time. Just us." I paused, trying to figure out how to explain it. I wasn't exactly sure how it worked; we always left immediately after she cast the spell. "She makes us into ghosts. They remember everything that happened, but they don't remember us."

"Everything that happened . . ."

"They remember being robbed," I said quietly. "They just don't remember who did it."

"So you're thieves."

"Yes," I said to my feet.

"That's what you do? You go from town to town robbing people, then bewitching them to forget?"

"Yes."

"All your life you've done this?" he persisted.

"Yes."

"So everyone you've ever met . . . they've all forgotten you?"

"Yes, everyone," I said slowly.

"But it never really mattered to you," he said, watching me carefully. "Not until *him*."

"Until Rafe. No, it didn't."

"Did he know?" Kellen asked. "Did he know you were there to steal from him?"

"No," I said quietly. "He knew I was a Void. But you're the first person I've ever told about . . . the rest."

"Then he didn't know you. Not really."

"Maybe not," I said. The idea was sobering, and not one I wanted to dwell on.

"The jacket I bought you the other day. That was his, wasn't it?"

"Yes," I admitted. And for some reason, I felt more ashamed about that than I did about being a thief.

Kellen's expression hardened.

"No wonder you get along with that ghost so well," he muttered. Then he stood up and looked down at me with a look of total disgust. "So I'm the first one to know you're a thief? Then I'm the first one to really know you, Macie O'Sullivan. And you know what? I don't think I like you very much."

He turned on his heel and walked off, then disappeared around the side of the bell tower without looking back.

I stayed where I was. Suddenly, the sunlight on my face felt accusatory instead of soothing.

Well, you didn't want it to happen again, a voice in my head sneered. *Now it won't. You scared him off before it could get serious. Mission accomplished.*

Then why did I feel like the ground had just fallen out from under me?

CHAPTER EIGHTEEN

I stayed up on the Tor until it was so late in the afternoon that the sun started to disappear behind the west side of the bell tower. Kellen did not return. By the time I walked down the hill and back downtown, the sun had set almost completely.

I headed back home. As soon as I got to the square I got that nagging feeling.

The feeling that someone was following me.

I stopped dead in front of the Gaia Grill and closed my eyes. I was *so* not in the mood for this.

"Aimee!" I snapped.

She slunk around the side of the building. There was a guilty smile on her face, which I might have found endearing if I hadn't been so on edge.

"Quit following me," I snarled at her. "Why can't you bother somebody else?"

Her face fell. And she disappeared back around the side of the restaurant.

I bit the inside of my lip. That had been uncalled for. But I just couldn't deal with my little shadow right now.

It's better for her if she stays away from me, I consoled myself as I continued walking.

I was hoping to have the apartment to myself. But when I let myself in, I found my mother. And Percy. They were sitting at the kitchen table, leaning close to each other and laughing about something. They were both holding forks.

Sitting on the table in front of them, right next to a bottle of wine, was the lavender cake that I had made the night before. Half of it had been eaten.

The sight of the cake made something inside me snap. I narrowed my eyes at Percy.

"Get. Out," I said, and I barely recognized the voice that was coming from within me. It sounded dangerous. Like it belonged to someone who was capable of causing pain.

Percy dropped his fork and scrambled to his feet. He looked like he was about to bolt out the door until my mother reached up and grabbed his arm.

"Wait for me in my room, Percy. I need a quick word with Macie."

Percy retreated into her bedroom, as ordered, and my mother turned her attention back to me. I remained standing, keeping the table between us.

"That cake was not yours," I growled at her. "*I* made it. For a friend."

"Friend?" my mother said carefully. "Since when do you have friends, Macie?"

"Since now."

She licked her fork clean, seemingly unconcerned with my tone. She was not as easy to frighten as Percy.

"I would have thought you learned your lesson last time. With that boy. That's what happens when you get attached. You get hurt."

"You should talk," I said, with a pointed glance toward her bedroom.

"That's different. I know how to keep my emotions out of it. You don't. It's something you need to work on."

"He can *hear* you, you know," I pointed out. "It's not like these walls are soundproof."

My mother threw a carefree hand into the air.

"I'll alter his memory later."

She stood up, silently declaring our talk over, and headed for the kitchen door, carrying the empty wine bottle with her.

Nothing ever mattered for her. Because all she had to do was wave her hand and she could undo it.

But could she really? Would the pain that Percy must have felt at her callous words ever really go away, just because he might consciously forget them? Is Rafe walking around somewhere heartbroken, empty, and unable to figure out why?

I moved around the table and blocked her path.

"Why did you sell my jacket?"

She raised an eyebrow.

"*Your* jacket?"

"Rafe's jacket," I corrected myself. "Why did you sell it?"

At the mention of his name, my mother's expression shifted from carefully constructed boredom to rage. Just like that. Like I had flipped an invisible switch.

"Why? You know why!" she thundered. "It was a weakness, Macie. I did you a favor."

"I don't see it that way."

"Well, that's why you have me. To teach you how to see things properly."

She sidestepped me and continued toward the kitchen door. As she did, she gave my shoulder a painful squeeze. Her warning was clear: *Drop this now.*

I chose to ignore it.

"I'm done," I told her, without turning around. "I'm finished with all of this."

I heard the wine bottle hit the bottom of the recycle bin, then silence.

I turned around. Her back was to me.

"We've always talked about how we'll settle down one day," I said. "Wasn't that always the plan? Why can't we do it here?"

"Here?" she asked, still not turning around.

"Why not?" I asked, and I felt my pulse start to race as

I thought about all the possibilities this plan presented. "We have a business here. We have people here who we . . ." I trailed off. How to put this in terms she would understand? "People who we spend time with," I finished.

I took a few steps toward her and put a hand on her arm.

"This could be our place. Our ending."

She threw my hand off.

"No."

That was it. No debate, no discussion. Just *no*.

"Why?" I asked as she skirted past me into the living room. "We'll never find a better place than this. Why can't we—"

I stopped. The answer had hit me like a ton of bricks.

"You don't want to find a better place," I said quietly. "You don't care if we get a big score from Witchtown. That's why you were so willing to let me take the lead on the con. You don't want it to work. Because if it did, we'd have to settle down somewhere, like you promised. And you don't want that. Do you?"

She didn't answer, but she didn't have to. I could see in her eyes that I had hit a nerve.

"You *like* the moving around," I said, and I couldn't believe I was seeing that for the first time. All these years—she had been enjoying herself. While I had just been waiting for it to be over. "You like how we've been living all these years."

"What's wrong with the way we've been living, Macie?"

"*Everything.* Everything is wrong with it—"

She waved me off.

"Fine. You got me. You're right. The idea of settling down, being stuck in one spot—forever. It doesn't appeal to me. I wouldn't want it. And even if I did, it would never be here. Witchtown?" she wrinkled her nose. "I don't like it here."

"Well I *do*."

"*Do* you?" came a condescending, slurred voice.

It wasn't my mother; Percy had reappeared. His baggy sweater vest hung crookedly on his bony shoulders, and he seemed to have lost a shoe. I hadn't realized he was drunk before, but it was more than obvious now. He was holding on to the door frame for support and staring at me in a rather confused way. When he pointed at me, his finger shook.

"First thing you need to learn about this town, Missy. It's not all it's cracked up to be."

"Thank you, Percy." My mother smiled, as though he had just put the perfect cap on her argument.

"It was a stupid idea," Percy muttered, stumbling into the room and lurching to the table, where he fell into the chair he had vacated a few minutes earlier. He picked up his fork and started jabbing aimlessly at the cake. "Witchtopia my ass. It'd be worth more if we burned it to the ground."

I rolled my eyes at Percy's drunken rant, but my mother crossed back to the table and sat in the chair next to him.

"What do you mean by that, Percy dear?" she asked him sweetly, prying the fork from his shaky fingers and feeding him the minuscule amount that was still stuck on the prongs.

Percy swallowed and smiled idiotically at her.

"Insurance. Reginald Harris was in insurance, remember? This place is insured up to high hell. Especially for fires. Harris was always so paranoid about that."

He burped, and looked vaguely startled at the noise.

My mother loaded up the fork with another bite of cake.

"You mean, if there were to be an accident, damage of some kind, the insurance companies would have to pay?"

"Brooke would get a big fat check," Percy blurted, eating off the fork my mother held up for him. "It would solve all her problems, I keep telling her. But she won't do it. Stupid woman. Never listens to me . . ."

"Thank you, Percy."

He smiled, and then put his head down on the table.

My mother gave me a meaningful look, and I felt my insides tighten into knots.

"No," I said, before she could say anything. *"No."*

"It's perfect," my mother said, staring down at the table. I could practically see the thoughts racing around inside her head. "An accident would scare off the investors. As long as it's big enough. We'd have to make sure the fire was big enough."

"No," I said again.

"Then we'd just have to wait for the insurance money to go into the town account. Once it's there we grab it and go. Easy. Hardly any work at all."

"We're not doing this," I said. "Listen to yourself. You're talking about *burning down the town.*"

"So?"

"*So?*" I repeated in disbelief. "That's crazy. People would get hurt. Maybe die. We don't do that!"

"For this much money, Macie, we have to be willing to take a few risks."

"Not with people's lives!" I exclaimed.

My mother stared at me, and I could sense the switch flipping again—to a setting I knew all too well. She stood up and came around the table until she loomed over me, and I felt myself shrinking. Her face was thunderous. She glared at me, beautiful and terrible. When she spoke, her voice was scarcely audible, and yet it was the only thing in the world I could hear.

"You will do this, Macie. You will do exactly what I say."

"I won't," I said, but I was shaking so badly my teeth were chattering.

My mother smirked at me.

"Do you really think you have a choice? Remember what happened the last time you tried to defy me."

I blinked away an image of Rafe, on his knees.

"You've got nothing to hold over me this time," I told her. "Not if you're going to burn down the town anyway."

"Oh, but I do, Macie," she said, and then she pointed, right to my moonstone. "So you like this town? You think they like you? I wonder what would happen if they knew there was a Void in their midst."

I swallowed. *She wouldn't.*

My mother put her hands on my shoulders. I wanted to shrink from her touch, but I couldn't move.

"It's a simple choice," she said, her voice switching back to its usual calm. "You can shut your mouth, get with the program, and help me, so we can both walk away with a lot of money. Or, you can defy me. But let me be very clear what will happen to you then, Macie."

She put a finger under my chin, making extra sure that I was looking her right in the eye.

"I swear—with Laverna as my witness, I swear—that if you get in my way this time, I will set you adrift. I will leave you here, in the ruins of the town you love, and everyone will be able to see you for exactly what you are. We'll just see how long it takes them to send you packing. Right after they brand that pretty little cheek of yours."

She slapped me, lightly, on my left cheek. Then she reached down and tugged on the chain of the moonstone.

"This necklace is the only thing preventing them from seeing the truth. I gave it to you, and I can take it away. Just think about that."

She let go of me and stepped aside so suddenly that I fell forward. Then she walked into her bedroom, alone, leaving Percy snoring into his folded arms and me gasping for breath, clutching the side of the table.

I could not stay in this apartment for another second.

I reeled toward the front door. I was so numb it took me

three tries to turn the knob. Once I got it open I ran until I was in the center of the town square. I leaned heavily against the altar, and slumped as I felt cool air fill my lungs.

When I had gotten my breath, I let go of the altar and stood back to find the Witchtown motto staring me in the face:

To grow in knowledge
To live in harmony
To harm none

The motto had annoyed me on the night of my initiation. It still kind of did. It was hopelessly idealistic. An aspiration, a dream. But it was also more than that. I'm not sure when I first started seeing it that way. I'm not sure it mattered. It was as clear to me now as the words carved into the marble.

Witchtown *was* a dream. An impossible, hopelessly optimistic dream.

A dream that needed to be protected.

CHAPTER NINETEEN

I couldn't go home. So I headed for the Depot, the only place in Witchtown that would have me.

For now, I thought, as I trudged toward it. *Once the mayor and everybody else finds out you're a Void, there will be no place left for you in this world.*

I fought back the images from my old nightmares; the brand coming toward me, the sound of my screaming as the hot metal touched my cheek, the smell of burnt skin . . .

I shook my head. Really, that was the best scenario I could hope for, now that Kellen knew everything. The absence of police cars in the square right now made me think he hadn't told anybody yet. But that didn't mean he wouldn't.

I had been a Void forever, but I don't think I had ever felt truly powerless until that moment.

"Hello, dear."

I jumped. Gayle was standing at the door of the Depot.

I had totally forgotten I was supposed to meet her tonight.

She looked different outside the bakery. No aprons or flour smears or hairnets. Her muscular arms were hidden beneath a loose, flowing tunic top and her gray-white hair was free of its tight bun, flowing in loose waves to her shoulders. Her smile was the same, though. Even in the dim light coming from the street lamp, I could still make out her grandmotherly, all-knowing smile.

But once she got a good look at my face, her face fell into a concerned frown.

"Dark thoughts this evening?"

"You could say that." I dug the key out of my pocket and let us both inside.

She walked in without hesitation and headed straight for the light switch. "Well, let's see what we can do about that," she said, as she flipped on the lights. "Any sign of Bradley?"

Gayle's eyes swept the ceiling, searching for the poltergeist. We both waited expectantly, but the surly ghost did not materialize.

"Did you know him when he was alive?" I asked.

"A bit," Gayle said vaguely, turning around to take in the entire room. "So this is your place! How exciting!"

I cringed at the mess of boxes, packing materials, and scattered merchandise all over the floor. I hadn't gotten around to cleaning up.

"I'm still getting things organized," I said lamely, and then I remembered my manners. "Um, can I get you some water? There's a sink upstairs . . ."

I trailed off, remembering the half-eaten cake back at the apartment.

Gayle sat down on one of the stools in front of the burnt counter and patted the empty one next to her.

"I don't need anything. But I think you might. What can I help you with, Macie?"

I sat down heavily on the offered stool. Gayle's kindness made me want to cry. I didn't deserve it. I couldn't even begin to think of how to explain to her what was wrong. At this point, it would probably have been easier to tell her what was *right*.

Which was pretty much nothing.

When I didn't respond, she scooted her stool directly in front of mine and looked me right in the face. She didn't say anything, just stared at me intently, leaving no part of my face unexamined. I could imagine feeling very uncomfortable with anyone else doing that, but not Gayle. Her no-nonsense expression was so sincere, I found it impossible to do anything but sit there and let her scrutinize my too-big nose, my freckles, and my jagged haircut.

It was when she got to my haircut that her expression brightened.

"Well, let's start with the obvious. How about I even that out for you?"

My hands flew self-consciously to my shorn locks. So one side *was* longer than the other. I *knew* it.

"You do hair?" I asked.

"I cut Maire's all the time," she said, standing up, and then she searched behind the counter until she came up with a pair of scissors. "These will do."

Gayle motioned with her fingers for me to turn around on my stool. While I did, she fished a large piece of tissue paper out of a nearby box of candles and draped it around my shoulders, like a smock. She combed my hair briefly with her fingers, and then I started to hear the brisk *snip snip* of the scissors.

"I'm curious what you did to pacify Bradley," she said conversationally.

"I made a deal with him."

"Really?" Gayle sounded surprised. "If you don't mind my asking, how did you manage to talk to him? I haven't been able to get a word in edgewise since he died. Not since he went all whispery and firey."

"Talya trapped him," I answered.

"Really?" Gayle said again. "Talya, the girl who works in the Archives?"

"Yeah. She and Kellen have been helping me out with the Depot."

"Well, I approve of your choice of friends," she said, and I could feel her pull slightly on two strands of hair on the opposite sides of my head, checking for evenness. The *snip snipping* resumed. "Talya I don't know well yet, but she seems to have a nice way about her. And I've been Kellen's mentor ever since he got to Witchtown. A very impressive young witch, that one."

"Yes," I said noncommittally. I didn't feel like dwelling on the fact that probably neither Talya nor Kellen was speaking to me at the moment. So instead, I asked her the question I had been dying to ask Bradley at our last encounter: "Do you know how the first Depot fire started? The one where Bradley and Stan died?"

I looked cautiously around the Depot, trying not to move my head too much and mess up my haircut. It felt wrong to talk about someone who could very well be listening, even if I wasn't getting that telltale prickly sensation.

"I don't know," Gayle answered. "I suppose you could always ask Bradley, but . . ."

"But what?"

Gayle hesitated: the *snip snip* of the scissors stopped.

"It's not always wise to ask people about their past," she said. "Especially in Witchtown. We're all misfits here. Refugees from the real world. I mean, we live behind *walls* for pity's sake!"

She came around to the left side of my stool.

"Whatever we did before, wherever we came from, we're here now," she said, and out of the corner of my eye I could see her frowning at the left side of my head as she raised the scissors to trim a little bit more. "We all have our secrets and our oddities and our embarrassing stories. Witchtown lets you embrace them, to let them all hang out. It's a gift this place gives you."

She paused. The sound of the scissors stopped. She walked in front of my stool and looked me right in the eye again.

"This town is very special to me, Macie. I would never let anybody hurt it."

My breath caught in my throat; I did not blink.

"Neither would I," I told her, meaning every word.

"Good."

Gayle made one last snip, then stepped back to admire her work.

"*There.* If only we had a mirror."

"I trust you," I said, running my fingers through my newly evened-out locks. They felt slightly shorter than they had been, but also less choppy.

Gail set the scissors on the counter and turned to face me, a serious expression on her face.

"Whatever it is that's troubling you, Macie — you don't have to tell me. But I think you ought to tell Kellen and Talya. That's my advice. And the giving of good advice has always been my greatest talent, aside from baking."

"Everybody listens to you?" I asked, believing it.

"Mostly. I'm still working on Brooke . . ."

"What do you tell her?"

"Mostly that she needs to learn how to delegate. She's been politely ignoring me for years, but I'll get through eventually. I always do."

I nodded, and stared down at my feet. Suddenly, all I could see was Kellen's face after I had spat out the whole story of Rafe, and of why my mother and I were really here.

I don't think I like you very much.

"Talk to them," Gayle said again, drawing my attention off the floor. "Your friends will see you through this. Whatever *this* is."

I looked at her. I was tempted, despite her warning, to ask what *she* was doing in Witchtown. She didn't seem like a misfit to me; what was she running from in the real world?

But before I could think of a way to ask her that, Bradley materialized behind her. He had the scissors Gayle had just used, and a wicked gleam in his eye. For a split second, I thought he was going to stab her, and I practically fell off my stool.

But then he winked at me. And he reached for a chunk of the baker's shoulder-length curls.

I opened my mouth to warn her, but before I could, Gayle rolled her eyes.

"Bradley!" she snapped, not even bothering to turn around. "Don't even think about it!"

To my surprise, Bradley immediately dropped the scissors and backed up.

"Yes ma'am," he mumbled, and slinked back into the shadows, like a puppy caught chewing on something he wasn't supposed to.

Apparently even Bradley was smart enough to listen to Gayle.

My first order of business the next morning was to invite Talya over. To my immense relief, she came.

It was much easier to tell her everything than it had been to tell Kellen. I don't know if that was because it's easier to break the rules the second time you do it, or because her dark eyes were a lot less judgey and a lot less distracting—than Kellen's.

Or, it could have been that she already knew.

She let me cough it all up, let me spill my guts all over the Depot floor. And when I was done, she smiled and leaned back casually against the counter. We were sitting on the stools that Gayle and I had sat on the night before.

"I saw you at the mayor's office that night, remember?" she said, with a slight smile. "I suspected you might be a thief then, and I got confirmation when I read your mom at Odin's Tavern after the funeral. I didn't see anything in her head about the burning-down-the-town—"

"She hadn't thought of it yet," I cut in.

"—but I figured you must have some plan in mind for Witchtown, otherwise you wouldn't be here. Thanks for finally telling me, though."

"Why *did* you cover for me?" I asked. "When the mayor asked who had been prowling around her office. I've been dying to know."

Talya shrugged. "You covered for *me,* that day in the square. I had a feeling about you. Like, maybe we could be friends. You kept my secret. Plus," she said as she wrinkled her nose, "I never liked Lois. She was the main one who spread the rumor about me being a Void."

I nodded, enjoying the feeling of getting several of the outstanding questions in my head answered at the same time.

"You have no idea what it's like, Macie," Talya continued, "seeing people the way that I do. So you're a thief? That's not the worst thing I've seen, not by a long shot. Everyone has secrets. You should see the things most people are hiding . . ."

Her face plummeted into a frown. And suddenly, I had to hand it to Talya. I wouldn't have blamed her at all if her unwelcome gift had turned her into a dark, warped soul. She might be odd, maybe even a little dark at times, but she was definitely not warped.

"I wasn't sure you'd come today," I said. "After what I did—"

"I almost didn't," she admitted.

"I'm sorry for using you," I said, then paused, trying to find the right words. "I've never . . . I'm not used to having friends."

Talya smiled.

"Neither am I."

"I'm trying to get better at it," I told her, then sat up straighter. "At everything, really. I may be a thief, but I am *not* an arsonist. I don't want to hurt people."

Talya nodded. "No, I didn't think that you did."

"I want to stop my mother. I need your help."

"Okay," Talya said. "What should we—"

The door to the Depot swung open and Kellen walked in.

I swallowed, my mouth suddenly very dry.

Talya looked back and forth between us.

"Does he know?" she asked. Quietly, but not so quietly that Kellen couldn't hear.

"Yes," I said.

"Good." Talya sat back on her stool and folded her arms. "Because I think we're going to need him if we're going to figure out how to stop your mother from burning down the entire town."

Kellen's eyebrows shot up, and I cringed. I guess he didn't know *everything*.

Kellen was quiet for a moment. He looked at the boxes on the floor around us, and settled himself down on one after poking it to make sure it was solid.

"I'm in," he said, still not looking at me.

"Good," Talya said briskly. "Let's figure out a plan."

"Well, obviously we could go to the mayor. Or the police," Talya said for the second or third time, after we had been kicking ideas around for half an hour without agreeing on anything. "But if we're going to save the town without implicating Macie, I think we're going to have to stop Aubra ourselves."

"Okay," Kellen said, sounding unconvinced. "How do you suggest we go about stopping a Natural?"

"The same way the Inquisitors did," Talya replied, remarkably cheerfully considering the subject matter.

"You mean angelica," I filled in.

"Exactly."

"Wait a sec," Kellen interjected. "I thought angelica was banned? Only law enforcement can get it."

"That's true," Talya agreed. "Unless you find it growing wild. Which Macie did."

"Here?" he asked, amazed. "In Witchtown?"

"By the river," I told him. "That day we figured out there was rowan in the water."

Kellen let out a low whistle.

"What will it do to her?" he asked. "I'm not an herbalist, so I only know the basics."

I looked over at Talya. I didn't know much more than the basics either, but I had a feeling she did.

"Based on what I've read, it varies," she said. "Depends on the strength of the witch and the potency of the herb. I still haven't seen the angelica you found, but since it's summer, it's probably pretty immature. Potency might be an issue. But at the very least, it should prevent her from using magic against us. Even in its weakest form, it takes away a Natural's most important advantage."

"And what about its strongest form?" I asked.

She sucked in a breath.

"It kills. But only in large amounts, which we don't have, and only when it's at peak maturity, which ours isn't. I can almost totally guarantee that we won't kill her."

"*Almost* totally?" Kellen echoed worriedly.

"Well, nothing in life is certain," Talya reminded him,

and then she slid off her stool. "I need to see what we're working with before I speculate any further."

I started to get up as well, but she stopped me with a hand on my arm.

"I think I can find it, based on what you told me. You stay here. And *talk*." She cocked her head over at Kellen.

She left before I could argue with her, and when the door of the Depot closed behind her, the silence that was left behind was painful.

I looked down at my feet. Gayle had said that Kellen and Talya would see me through this. But the truth was, she had no idea what *this* was. That was the entire problem with taking her word for it.

"Macie?"

"Yeah?"

I looked over at him. He looked tired, like he hadn't slept well the night before. I wondered if that meant he was regretting what he had said to me. Or maybe he was regretting not having said even more.

He drew in a breath, and I got the strangest feeling that he was about to tell me something. Something important. My ears perked, and a shadow of my old doubts about him peeked over my shoulder.

But he only said, "What are we going to do, once we have your mom under the influence of the angelica?"

I let out a slow breath, and my misgivings about him fell away.

"I don't know. Let's just see if it works, okay? Then we'll figure it out."

Because honestly, and with all due respect to Talya, the thought of a simple, innocent-looking plant taking down Aubra O'Sullivan made me want to laugh.

I was going to have to see it to believe it.

Even after Talya returned, angelica in hand, and we hammered out a plan, I was still having a hard time summoning up much confidence. Which turned out to be kind of a good thing, because it's hard to be nervous about something when you're ninety-nine percent sure it isn't going to work. That was the only way I was able to sit across a table from Kellen and sip my water in relative calm at Odin's Tavern for the hour and a half it took for Aubra to walk in.

I drank water. Kellen worked his way through three pints of Odin's ginger ale, explaining that he was the only one in town who actually liked it.

When my mother finally breezed in, arm in arm with Percy, the first stab of true apprehension hit me.

I had never had the guts to face her with anything other than attitude, and I was pretty sure she was immune to that. Part of me was desperately curious, in a wide-eyed-child kind of way, to find out what it would feel like to hit her with something substantial.

Something like the herb that Talya was, at this moment, hiding under the bar.

My mother noticed me right away, but gave me only the barest of glances before taking a seat beside Percy at the bar. I squirmed and turned all of my concentration to looking like I wasn't about to fall off my chair with anticipation.

Kellen must have been thinking the same thing, because he leaned forward suddenly and took my hand, which was resting on top of the table.

"Talk to me," he said. "We can't just sit here silently; it looks weird."

"What should we talk about?" I asked. Over his shoulder, I had a perfect view of the bar. Odin was nowhere to be seen. Talya had talked him into letting her work a daytime shift, and she was putting napkins down in front of my mother and Percy.

Kellen squeezed my hand.

"Why didn't you tell me?" he asked. His tone was more inquisitive than demanding.

"What do you mean?" I squeaked, even though I was pretty sure that my mother was too far away to hear anything other than the rise and fall of our voices. "I told you everything!"

"Not everything, no. You didn't mention that you were working *against* your mother now. From everything you told me . . . you know, last night, after we . . . I assumed you were onboard with whatever her plans were for Witchtown."

"Surprise," I said, watching his eyes.

He looked down at the table, at our hands, and shifted his fingers so that they were between mine.

"I've never had so much difficulty figuring a person out," he said. "Just when I think I'm getting close, something happens that makes me doubt everything."

I blinked. I could have said the same thing about him. At least, I would have said that before I found out about his mom.

"Do you think you could ever let somebody know you for real?" he asked.

"I don't know," I said truthfully. Rafe had known me. Not totally, not everything, but enough. He hadn't wanted to know the rest. Hadn't needed to. But Kellen did. What did that mean?

"I wonder if that's why I like you so much," he said, mostly to himself.

"I thought you didn't," I said.

"I lied. I thought that was obvious. I *do* like you, Macie. More than I probably should."

"I like you too," I said, stretching out my fingers between his. "I don't . . . I don't want you to forget about me."

"I won't," he promised, his blue eyes catching mine across the table.

Over Kellen's shoulder, I saw my mother throw her head back and down the last of whatever had been in her glass.

I stiffened, waiting.

Kellen felt it through our intertwined hands. He didn't

look over his shoulder, just watched my face carefully. He would be able to tell by my reaction what was going on.

My mother put the empty glass down on the bar, in front of Talya. Then she turned slightly on her stool and regarded the chandelier that hung down from the center beam on the tavern ceiling. It was a tangled web of interconnected metal candleholders, but only about half of the candles were lit.

"A bit dim in here, don't you think?" I heard her say.

She pointed, and the unlit candles burst into flame, instantly brightening the entire room.

Then she winked at me and turned back to Percy.

Talya picked up the discarded glass and shook her head slightly at me.

I let out the breath I had been holding.

The angelica hadn't worked.

"Did you give her enough?" Kellen asked, as we walked back to the Depot.

"I gave her a lot," Talya said. "I put twice as much into her second drink. Nothing."

"Maybe it's too immature?" I suggested.

"Maybe," Talya said, sounding unconvinced.

"It's too bad we don't know any other Naturals to try it on," Kellen said.

I blinked as I caught sight of a small, curly head peeking out from the side of the Depot.

"Aimee?" I called.

The curls disappeared, and I heard the sound of running feet.

"She's a bit scared of you right now," Talya informed me. "She said you yelled at her the other day."

"She's been following me around like a shadow," I said, with more than a twinge of guilt. "I might have lost my temper. I'd like to apologize, if she'll let me."

"She'll come around," Talya assured me as we arrived at the door of the Depot. "And as for the angelica, I think we should try again."

Reaching into her bag, she pulled out a fistful of angelica blossoms. She extracted a few stems and held them out to me.

"Try grinding these up and putting them in her tea or coffee. Whatever she drinks in the morning. Maybe it'll have more of an impact when she has an empty stomach."

I shrugged, and reached out my hand to take the flowers.

"I guess there's no harm in —"

The moment my fingers closed around the angelica, my eyes rolled up and the sidewalk tilted strangely upward to hit the side of my face with a loud *smack*.

Then there was just darkness.

CHAPTER TWENTY

*T*en thousand eight hundred and sixty-two."

"What?" I asked.

"Dollars. I checked with the bank today. And I need ten thousand eight hundred and sixty-two dollars to pay off my father's mortgage."

"Oh, is that all?" I teased.

"And ninety-seven cents."

I was ready to tease him again, but his eyes were suddenly very serious, so I shut my mouth.

"That's maybe six months of work," he said. "Then I'm free. We're free."

"Free?" I tried out the word.

Rafe took my hand and held it between us on the pillow.

"I can leave my dad then. And you can leave your mom."

"I can't. She protects me—"

"I can protect you."

"Not the way she can."

That silenced him for a moment.

"Then we'll go where it doesn't matter that you're a Void. We don't have to live in a Haven, you know."

"We don't?"

"It's not only witches who need furniture. I could get an apprenticeship. On the outside. With the regular people."

I frowned. I had no memory of living outside of a Haven. I hadn't, not since Seattle. What would it be like to go from a world full of witches to one with no witches at all? I could probably do it. I could go without the community, the rituals, the weirdness. But could Rafe?

"You'd do that?" I asked. "For me?"

"Yes, I would. For you, I would."

I laid my head on top of our hands and closed my eyes.

"And what would I do?" I asked dreamily. "Outside of a Haven?"

"Anything you wanted."

I woke up to an unfamiliar smell assailing my nose.

I was stretched out on the dumpy couch in the apartment above the Depot. The smell was coming from the kitchenette. I couldn't quite place what it was, but it was making my mouth water.

"Kellen, she's awake."

Talya, who had been perched on the arm of the couch at my curled-up feet, jumped down, walked to the other end of the couch, and knelt in front of me. Her large eyes, un-eyelinered today, looked concerned, and also faintly purple around the edges of the corneas. She must have been wearing colored contacts.

"Almost done," Kellen called from the kitchenette. He opened the small oven and used mitts to extract the source of the smell: a huge, gooey, piping hot piece of pizza.

I had to look away before I started to openly drool. I turned back to Talya.

"How long was I out?"

"About half an hour," she said. "But you were breathing and everything, so we figured you'd wake up eventually."

Bradley swooped down from the ceiling. I flinched, bracing myself, but all he did was hover just above Talya's head.

"Checking up on me?" I asked him. Then, because his eyes looked marginally less scary than usual, I added, "Don't tell me you were worried."

"Hmmphmm," was his noncommittal reply as he slowly faded from view.

"Order up," Kellen announced, and Talya moved aside so he could approach and wave the pizza under my nose.

I tried to breathe through my mouth. My stomach woke up anyway and demanded that I inhale the pizza or else. I could already taste the cheese, feel the grease running over my tongue, imagine the crustiness of the bread on the outside and the fluffiness on the inside . . .

If I didn't stop this soon, I was going to pass out again.

"I can't eat that."

Kellen crouched down, still holding the pizza plate right in front of my face.

"Is that you talking or your mom?"

I glowered at him. My stomach glowered at me.

"Do you really object to pizza?" he persisted. "Or are you still just following your mom's orders?"

I blinked. He was right, damn him, and not just about the food.

I took a deep, deliberate breath through my nose.

No, I most definitely did not object to pizza. Quite the opposite.

"Give me that."

Kellen brightened and put the plate into my hands.

"Fresh from Gayle's bakery," he informed me. "She calls it Pentagram Pizza: it's the best pizza in town."

"Also the only pizza in town," Talya added, settling herself on the arm of the couch again. "Kellen thinks that if you hadn't been doing the raw vegan thing, you wouldn't have reacted so strongly to the angelica."

I closed my lips around my first bite of the pizza and had to stifle a groan. It was still a little too hot to eat comfortably, but I didn't care. It was even better than what I had been imagining. Why, oh why, had I ever voluntarily given up cheese?

A few bites later, I emerged from my revelry to find Talya and Kellen both staring at me. The combination of their serious expressions and the unaccustomed heaviness of the processed food made my stomach lurch, when I had expected it to be rejoicing.

I swallowed hastily.

"Why did the angelica affect me at all?" I asked, voicing the question we all had to be thinking.

Kellen and Talya exchanged a look.

"We have a theory about that, too," Talya said, a bit uneasily. "Tell her, Kellen."

Kellen ran a hand through his hair.

"Well, for one thing, you're immune to rowan."

"You know why that is," I countered, stuffing another bite into my mouth. Suddenly, I felt the need to argue. To prevent him from spelling out their theory.

"I know why *you* think it is," he corrected me. "I have always disagreed. Especially now."

"I used to think you were a Void too," Talya said, jumping in. "When I couldn't read you, I assumed that's what it meant. But I've done some research since—"

"You thought I was a Void and you didn't say anything?" I snapped, angrily.

"You thought the same thing about me at first," she said calmly, not rising to the bait. "I didn't have to read you to figure that out. You never said anything either."

"Yeah, but you *researched* it," I said. It was the only thing I could think of to accuse her with. It was lame, but it was all I had.

She took a deep breath. Determined, I think, not to let my attitude bother her.

"The Archives house Reginald Harris's personal library," she said, crossing her legs and flashing me a temporarily violet-eyed glare. "Why else do you think I took that boring job? I wanted to find out about myself. About other people like me. I thought I couldn't read you because you were a Void. But I think I was wrong about that. I don't think it's Voids who are immune to my readings; it's Naturals."

"But you read my mom," I blurted.

"Yes," Talya said pointedly. "I did."

I bit my lip.

"Look at the facts, Macie," Kellen said, in his teacher voice. "You're immune to rowan. So you're not a Learned. And the angelica knocked you out cold, but it *didn't* affect your mother."

I bit my lip even harder. Why was I forcing them to lay it all out for me? I wasn't an idiot. But regardless of all the facts, and the theories, I needed more. I couldn't alter a lifetime's worth of thinking on so little.

"Tell her the other thing," Kellen suggested. He was still crouched in front of me, kind of protectively, but also like he was blocking me from getting off the couch and running out the door. I felt trapped. I reached down to find solace in more pizza, only to find that the plate in my lap was empty.

Kellen stood up, took the empty plate, and walked it back

to the kitchen. Talya eased down from the arm of the couch until she was sitting right next to me, effectively trapping me again.

"I saw something else when I read your mom," she confessed. "I told you that I saw everything about the stealing, the vault, the other towns, all of that. But I didn't tell you the rest because it didn't make sense to me. Not until now."

She trailed off. Her face was suddenly stiff. I could almost hear her teeth grinding together.

She hates this, I realized. *She hates telling people what she sees about them.*

I reached over and took her hand. Her fingernails were covered in badly chipped black polish, and she was wearing so many rings that when I squeezed her fingers together, they sort of clanked. Her violet eyes reminded me of the flowers on an anise plant, which was interesting because she smelled a little bit like black licorice. I had never noticed that before.

"I only saw a glimpse of it," she said. "The vision came right at the end, before I started getting dizzy. But I saw two things very clearly. One was Pendle Bishop. The other thing was *this.*"

She pointed to my moonstone, and my hands rose up protectively, covering it from view.

"What is that?" she asked. Rather casually, as though she was changing the subject. Even though I knew she wasn't.

"It keeps people from sensing that I'm a Void," I said, the words sounding a bit hollow.

Talya shook her head.

"I don't think that's what it does," she said gently. "I think that's what your mother *told* you it does."

Still gripping the stone, I thought back to our second day at Witchtown, when I had seen Pendle Bishop for the first time. She had looked at my moonstone. The old Natural, who could barely see, who could barely focus her old, clouded eyes. She had definitely noticed my moonstone.

"Well," I swallowed. "I don't know what it means. It's not like we can ask Pendle Bishop to fill in the blanks for us."

Kellen returned from the kitchenette.

"Maybe not," he said. "But we can do the next best thing."

The grass outside of Pendle Bishop's house looked like it had grown more than should have been possible in the days since I had last walked by. It was as though it knew that no one was going to bother to cut it now, so it might as well just go nuts.

"I don't have a clue what we're looking for," I admitted, as the three of us walked up to the old Victorian. "Do we even know if her stuff is still inside?"

"The mayor told me she's keeping everything the way it is until Pendle's sister can come and look through it all," Kellen said, leading us around the back. "She lives up in the Northeast, somewhere. The mayor has been trying to get ahold of her."

I stepped up to examine the lock on the back door.

"This is a very basic single deadbolt lock," I said to Kellen and Talya, feeling a touch of excitement. Finally, a way to put my ill-gotten skills to good use! "No sweat. It'll take me five, maybe ten minutes to pick once I get my — what?"

They were both staring at me. Kellen was holding up a key.

"I used to water her indoor plants, too," he explained, sliding the key into the door. "She'd forget, and they would start to smell."

"Oh." I couldn't think of anything else to say.

Inside, the house was fairly neat. Neater than I had expected. I had pictured a slightly crazy scene, full of empty cat food cans and stacks of old newspapers. But the kitchen was clean, and filled with the scent of a large basil plant near the window, which was just starting to wilt. The living room was dark but clutter free except for a pile of large-print books and a pair of very thick glasses on the coffee table. There wasn't a cat in sight.

Talya went over to examine the books.

"Looks like the old broad had a thing for bodice rippers," she said, causing Kellen to look vaguely scandalized.

"We need to find personal stuff," I said, looking reluctantly at a door I was pretty sure led to a bedroom. It seemed wrong to pry into the old woman's things.

Talya walked purposefully into the bedroom. I followed, still feeling uneasy, especially when we were confronted with the intimacy of an unmade bed and a threadbare bathrobe that had been laid across the comforter. As though Pendle Bishop could return at any moment and find us there.

I shivered and tried to concentrate.

There was a desk in the corner covered by more books, all with covers depicting bare-chested men and windswept women. There was also a small calendar, a lot of loose papers, and a lap desk with a half-finished letter on old-fashioned stationery.

Before I could stop myself, I reached for the letter.

Pendle Bishop's handwriting had been shaky. I could picture her sitting at her desk, wearing her thick glasses and laboring intensely over her words. The first page began: *Dear Trudy.*

"Is her sister named Trudy?" I asked Kellen, who was hovering in the bedroom doorway, looking at least twice as uncomfortable as I felt.

He shrugged, and I went back to the letter.

I flipped through the pages, stopping cold when I got to the last one. The nearer to the end of the letter, the shakier the handwriting got. But it was still legible:

I never would have done it. Not if I had known what she was going to use it for. But she was so insistent, and I needed the money so badly, I didn't ask the questions I should have. Had I known it was for a child . . . a Natural child.

She would have been too young to know what she was. Or what it would do to her. Does she suspect, I wonder, where her mother's strength comes from? I cannot bring myself to even talk to her. But I must, Trudy, I know I must. I must make this right . . .

At the bottom of the page, there was a sketch. It was even shakier than the handwriting, but there was enough detail that there was no mistaking what it was.

My moonstone.

I ran right out the front door and sank to my knees in the too-tall grass.

The chain around my neck was just long enough so that I could see the moonstone when I looked down. I held the stone up in my hand and stared at it. It was something that had always brought me comfort before.

But now, the milky blue and white stone stared back up at me like an evil eye. I dropped it hastily.

"Macie?"

It was Kellen's voice. I didn't look up, but I saw his gray tennis shoes and Talya's black, high-heeled boots come up on either side of me.

"Is it true?" I asked. I wasn't asking anyone in particular.

"If your mom were really a Natural, the angelica would

have worked on her. And I wouldn't have been able to read her," Talya said matter-of-factly.

"I never questioned her," I muttered, blinking at the pointy toes on Talya's boots. "All these years. She told me I was a Void and *she* was a Natural. And I believed her. Just like that."

I looked up at Kellen.

"*You* knew I wasn't a Void. And you'd only just met me. Why didn't I know?"

I looked back down at the moonstone, and suddenly I couldn't bear the thought of wearing it for another second.

I reached behind my neck and fumbled for the clasp. But before I could undo it, I felt two pairs of hands on top of mine, stopping me.

"Macie, wait," Talya said. "Let's think about this."

"No!" I shouted, shaking off the hands and jumping to my feet. "You don't understand! I found that angelica *days* ago. And I never thought of using it against her. Not even for a second. Until you brought it up. This thing"—I glared down at the moonstone—"it clouds my brain. It keeps me from thinking straight!"

I reached for the clasp again, and this time it was only Kellen who stopped me.

"You're probably right," he said, gently pulling my fingers away from the clasp. "When Pendle Bishop put a spell on it, to allow your mother to pass off your power as her own, she probably added an element of concealment to it. Something to make you trust your mother, so you wouldn't suspect. But if you take it off—"

"I'll be able to think clearly," I finished for him. "And I'll have my power back."

"I doubt it's that simple," he said, sounding apologetic. Still holding both of my hands, he looked over at Talya for help.

"You must have taken it off before, right?" Talya asked. "To go swimming? To shower?"

"Yes," I admitted.

"And does anything ever change?" she persisted.

"No," I said, looking at the ground.

"Your mother wears one too," Kellen said, and it sounded like he was thinking out loud. "I'll bet you *both* have to take them off, plus who knows what else you have to do to break a spell that old? How long have you worn that thing?"

I thought back. I had been five years old when we entered our first Haven, and I remembered wearing the necklace then. But not before then. I hadn't had the necklace in Seattle.

"Eleven years," I muttered. "Give or take."

I shuddered, and blanched when I felt the metal chain shift around my neck with the movement.

"She can probably tell when you take it off," Talya added. "If she suspects that you figured it out—"

"She'll alter my memory," I finished for her. "I'll forget all about this."

"Exactly," Kellen said, sounding sorry. "You have to keep playing along. Just for a little while longer. Until we figure out how to stop her."

"When will that be?" I asked pleadingly. Every minute of wearing the necklace now felt like a minute too long.

"Soon," Kellen assured me.

Talya rolled her eyes. "I wish I had your confidence. Last time I checked, we were out of ideas."

"On the contrary," Kellen said, "I think things are looking up."

Talya and I shot him simultaneous *you're crazy* looks, but he just smiled.

"We've got a Natural on our side now, don't we?"

He watched me carefully as I considered this. Finally, I nodded slowly.

"I guess we do," I said.

A Natural who doesn't even have the power she was born with.

I had never heard of anything so pathetic in my entire life.

When I returned to the Depot, without Talya and Kellen, I found a glum-faced Percy waiting for me at the door.

He was holding an enormous Solstice wreath decorated with yellow and red flowers.

I groaned under my breath. I was still reeling from the events at Pendle's house. That, plus the pizza I had eaten earlier (which had hit my enthusiastic but unprepared-for-processed-food stomach like a brick), was not exactly putting me in the mood to deal with Percy. I needed to lie down.

I nodded to the wreath.

"You shouldn't have," I told him.

"I didn't," he assured me, without smiling. "This is Brooke's thing. Mind if I put it up now?"

"You want to put *that thing* on *my shop?*"

"It's for the Solstice celebration," he explained. "Every building in the inner circle has to have one."

He turned and pointed. Over half of the shops facing the square were already adorned with identical wreaths. They matched the yellow and red streamers that had replaced the black banners on the streetlights.

I looked dubiously at the ugly thing in Percy's hands. It was so loud and the flowers on it were so obviously fake that it seemed like a weird thing for the mayor of the greenest city in the world to insist we all decorate with.

But, as the newest business owner in town, I wasn't about to make a fuss.

"Sure, Percy. What do I need to do?"

"Nothing. I can hang it up for you," he said. "I just need to get up on your roof."

"Sure," I said again, unlocking the door and holding it open for him. "Um, Percy? Is everything okay? You seem kind of . . ."

"I'm fine," he said, flashing me a very forced smile and nearly knocking me over as he hauled the wreath inside.

I shut the door behind us with a sigh.

Whatever my mother had done to upset him, I hoped she would make it right soon. Or at least erase it from his memory. Sad Percy was sort of infectiously morose.

And I already had enough to worry about.

CHAPTER TWENTY-ONE

*D*espite Kellen's assurances that we would come up with a way to stop Aubra "soon," and despite the fact that Talya had been doing so much research in the Archives that she was all but sleeping there, three days went by without any of us coming up with anything useful at all.

I had been spending a lot of time in the Archives myself. After I cleaned up Bradley's mess at the Depot, I found that I had nothing to do except shut myself up in the dingy room with Talya and help.

So it actually felt good to come out into the fresh air on the afternoon before Solstice. Kellen and I had both signed up to help decorate for tomorrow's celebration. Talya remained behind, saying she'd rather die than spend the day getting ordered around by Autumn.

As it happened, it was the mayor, not Autumn, who was directing the setup for the ritual. Kellen and I joined the rest of the volunteers in a clump around the altar, as Brooke and Teresa (the mayor's new assistant) sorted through papers and assigned everyone a job.

I heard a familiar, affected laugh and followed the sound across the square. My mother was in fine form this evening. She was wearing a short dress that made her legs go on for days, very high heels, and an intentionally wild and curly hairstyle. She was clutching a masculine arm and tossing her head back to laugh. Her moonstone necklace was prominently displayed amid a ridiculous amount of cleavage.

I drew in a disapproving breath. Half the town was here. The mayor herself was within spitting distance. What was my mother thinking?

But when the crowd shifted, I saw that the arm she was clutching was not Percy's. It belonged to someone taller, with a familiar shade of brown hair that curled slightly over the top of his collar.

Kellen's dad.

My stomach dropped to somewhere around my knees. And before I could get it together enough to somehow head him off, Kellen followed my line of sight.

"Well," he said dryly. "That's unfortunate."

"My thought exactly," I said. No wonder Percy had been in a bad mood.

"Quiet down, everyone!" the mayor commanded, her voice tinged with excitement as she stepped up to the altar.

"Thank you all for joining the preparation committee for our Solstice ritual! We have a lot to do and very little time to do it, so let's get organized . . ."

Teresa appeared at her side and started handing out sheets of paper.

I looked worriedly over at Kellen.

"Are you okay?" I whispered. I didn't know what to tell him. *Yes, my mother hooks up with inappropriate people all the time. But usually she does it monogamously?*

Kellen didn't look to be in the mood for jokes. Even true ones. His eyes were locked on his father, who had his arm wrapped around my mother's waist and was nuzzling her hair.

Teresa moved through the crowd handing out work assignments, and the mayor kept right on giving us the details of the ceremony.

"And the highlight, of course, will be the lighting of the bonfire by our very own Natural, Aubra O'Sullivan!"

There was a polite round of applause. My mother acknowledged the clapping with an embarrassed wave as she continued to cling to Kellen's dad.

Her eyes met mine. They were filled with an intensity that I recognized. I had seen it dozens of times before, in dozens of other towns. It was as if an invisible, silent alarm had gone off somewhere. It was time. All of a sudden I *knew* what she was going to do.

"The bonfire," I whispered to Kellen.

I looked over at the mountain of brush and logs that some

of the volunteers were piling in the eastern part of the square. Did Witchtown have insurance coverage for a Solstice bonfire gone out of control? I was sure they did. Reginald Harris would have seen to that.

And what would happen after the smoke cleared? The mayor might be able to convince the townspeople to hang on and wait for the insurance money so that they could rebuild. But the investors would be history. There would be no more money to maintain security on the wall. The town would be vulnerable, a sitting duck for anyone looking to take out their anger on those who were different from them.

The townspeople would turn to Aubra to protect them. And she would, dutifully, right up until the second the insurance money arrived. Then we would be history. After that, whatever was left of the town would crumble. Reginald Harris's dream of witches looking after their own would be reduced to a pile of rubble. And those who were here to witness its fall would never be able to recall exactly what had happened.

All of them—Kellen, Talya, Gayle, even little Aimee —would forget that they had ever known a girl named Macie O'Sullivan. *She* would make them forget.

I narrowed my eyes at my mother. Her gaze turned from cheerful to annoyed, and she dropped Kellen's dad's arm in order to make her way toward me.

"Incoming," I muttered to Kellen.

"Once you've gotten your assignment, please get to work!"

the mayor intoned, with mock sternness. "Have fun! And let's have a great Solstice, everyone!"

There was more applause, which ended quickly as people broke up to attend to their appointed tasks. My mother had reached us by then and stood so that she was blocking us from the rest of the people in the square.

I had to look up to meet her eyes; she was wearing the damn heels again.

"Angelica?" she asked, quietly, so that only Kellen and I could hear. She giggled mockingly. "Nice try. You didn't think something so trivial was really going to get in my way, did you?"

"It was worth a shot," I said, trying not to flinch as she glared at me. "What are you *doing,* anyway?" I demanded, gesturing toward Kellen's dad. "What happened to trying to open the vault?"

"I warned you about what would happen if you interfered," she reminded me, ignoring my question. "You really think you can hack it on your own?"

"I'm not afraid to try," I told her, struggling to keep a lid on my temper.

I felt Kellen take my hand and squeeze it. I could practically hear him imploring me to keep my mouth shut. I took a deep breath and tried to calm down. As much as I wanted to rip off the moonstone and scream right up into her face, as loud as I possibly could, that *I knew,* I couldn't do it. Not without risking everything.

Because Talya was still buried in the Archives, looking for

a way to break the spell. And until she found something, we were all at my mother's mercy.

My mother mistook my momentary silence for uncertainty. And she moved in for the kill.

"You know," she said, reaching out a hand to touch the side of my face. "If it wasn't for the fact that I gave birth to you, I would never believe you were my daughter. You don't have any sense at all. You haven't even figured out the truth about your boyfriend, have you?"

"What?" I asked, wary of this unexpected line of attack.

She turned taunting eyes onto Kellen.

"Ask him who his father is."

I looked at Kellen. His hand was still in mine. He was glaring a warning at my mother, who was smiling sweetly back at him.

I rolled my eyes.

"I've *met* his father," I informed my mother. "I know him. And you made it pretty clear tonight that you know him even better. What of it?"

But Aubra wasn't looking at me; she was still smiling at Kellen, as though this conversation were entirely between the two of them.

"Your uncle has such interesting pillow talk, Kellen. Not that he remembers telling me anything, of course."

"Uncle?" I repeated, sucking in a deep breath. "Kellen, what is she talking about?"

"Tell her," my mother commanded him, her fake smile

fading. "Tell her who you are and why you're here. Tell her who your *real* father is."

I looked over at Kellen and waited for him to contradict her, to tell her she was mistaken.

But he didn't. His expression was impossible to read: the only other time I had seen his face this devoid of humor was when he had told me about his mother.

If any of that was even true.

He turned to me.

"I'm not going to lie to you, Macie," he said.

He was still holding my hand; I ripped it away from him.

"Who is your father?" I asked. My voice sounded toneless, dead.

With the barest of glares over at my mother, Kellen squared his shoulders and stood up tall. There was not even a hint of an apology on his face or in his voice when he turned to me and said, "My father is the minister who leads the group camped outside of the wall. I moved here two years ago, with my uncle, so we could tell him what was going on in Witchtown. I am the spy."

I turned away. I didn't really have a destination in mind, just anywhere but here. My thoughts were churning and I was never going to be able to make sense of things with both of them just staring at me like that.

It was hours until the official Solstice Eve celebration was supposed to start. But a four-piece string band had already set up on the outskirts of the square. Talya's uncle Odin was front and center, plucking a huge cello and singing. Royce was right beside him, on guitar. And even though everyone was supposed to be setting up, the dancing had already started. I skirted around the makeshift dance floor, intending to give the music a wide berth.

Just behind the band I caught sight of Percy, sitting glumly in the shadows. He was holding a bottle of something and staring, slightly cross-eyed, at the ground.

I turned away, unable to deal with yet more evidence of my mother's wake of destruction. But before I could take another step, I felt a tug on my wrist. I was pulled into strong arms and hauled onto the dance floor.

Kellen.

"Just listen," he said quickly, holding me trapped in dance position. One arm was wrapped like an iron band around my waist, the other was holding my arm out to the side, my hand in his. He wasn't hurting me, but his grip made it clear that I had little hope of escaping him. Not without making a scene.

"I'll scream," I threatened.

"If you tell them what you know," he said quietly, cocking his head at the whirling couples all around us, "I'll tell them what *I* know. And who do you think they'll believe? You or me?"

He had me there. No one in Witchtown would believe their charming Kellen was a secret Zealot spy. He wasn't the kind of person it was easy to believe bad things about. Just look how long it had taken me to find out the truth about him. Even Gayle loved him.

"I'm not trying to scare you," he said, pulling me closer and talking directly into my ear. "I just want to explain myself."

"Fine," I said through gritted teeth, trying to ignore the familiar scent of juniper and how warm I felt in his arms. "Go ahead and explain. But I won't believe any of it. You *lied* to me."

He laughed at that, a laugh that was full of genuine amusement. He seemed to have recovered, somewhat, from my mother's assault.

"*You've* been lying to *me* since the day we met!" he pointed out. "You're only mad at me now because you found out I'm better at it than you are."

"You are *not* better at it."

"Yes, I am," he said, saying it as though it was an obvious fact. And I was bothered, to the point of fury, by the truth of it. He had really had me going. Luring me in with his ridiculous Prince Charming–Eagle Scout routine. Making me feel *guilty* for suspecting him. Playing me. The entire time, playing me. He was a Laverna-blessed God of Liars, complete with an irresistible grin and nice arms.

And yet, part of me was glad that the dancing was giving me an excuse to be close to him.

Get a grip, Macie.

I wasn't sure if that was my mother's voice in my head or my own, but either way it seemed like good advice. Until he pulled me even closer, so that I was pressed up against him in a way that made it impossible to think clearly.

"Actually, I only lied to you once," he said in my ear. "When I told you I didn't like you. But you knew that wasn't true. And as for the rest of it, I didn't lie, exactly. I just didn't tell you all of it."

"What about the bullshit story about your mom?" I demanded.

I felt him wince, and I immediately regretted my words.

"That was true," he said. He was still talking into my ear, so I couldn't see his face. But I could imagine his expression, the sad, lost one I had seen after Talya's ritual. In spite of everything, it tugged at my heart. "I found her dead and I ran away. I was only eight, so I didn't get far. My uncle took me in. I've lived with him on and off over the years, whenever it became impossible for me to be under the same roof as my father."

"Why didn't Talya see that?"

"I don't know," he said thoughtfully. "Maybe she doesn't see every secret at once. Or maybe she only sees your biggest ones?"

Or maybe she saw and didn't tell me.

That was something to think about later.

I thought back to the night when the Zealots had invaded Witchtown, to the priest on the roof who had been reading the Bible. Kellen's father—how could that possibly be Kellen's father?

"You said what happened with your mother was your fault," I reminded Kellen. "How did she burn herself out?"

He drew a deep breath.

"My mother was a Natural. But she never told my father. She knew he wouldn't—couldn't—understand. She taught me, starting when I was very young. It was our secret."

He paused. I could feel his breath on my cheek. Warm, just like that time in the woods when he had tried to kiss me. And the time on top of the Tor, when he had actually kissed me. I tensed, steeling myself not to believe him.

He lied to you. He's a liar.

But had he? Was he? He said he hadn't lied. And so far, he hadn't contradicted himself.

I couldn't blame him for keeping secrets. Not without being incredibly hypocritical.

"I wasn't supposed to do magic by myself," Kellen continued, his voice even softer than before. "But one day, my father caught me practicing in my room. He must have always suspected what was going on, because he knew what I was doing immediately. Later I heard them fighting, heard him say he was leaving her and taking me with him. So she Voided herself. On purpose. I don't know how she did it, exactly, but she must have reached for some power she knew she couldn't control. Because after that she was never the same. She was *gone*. Empty."

"And you think that's your fault?" I asked. My heart was breaking with the pain in his voice. In spite of the fact that he was basically holding me captive on the dance floor.

"I know it is," he muttered. "If it wasn't for me, she'd still be alive. How much clearer can it get?"

You were eight! I wanted to scream. *Even if you had gone to your father and told him everything—which you didn't—You. Were. Eight. You didn't know any better.*

But instead of saying that out loud, I blurted out another thought.

"If all that's true, then how can you spy for him? How can you be a witch and help him?"

"How can you ask me that?" he snapped. "You of all people? Do I really need to explain to you the twisted psychology of trying to prove yourself to a parent who's impossible to please?"

Damn him, he had me again. But I wasn't about to let it show.

"Is that what you're doing here? Spying to please Daddy?"

"Partly. It was an opportunity. To live in Witchtown, to be a part of the world my mother belonged to. What's wrong with that? And as long as I'm here, I can ensure that he and my uncle don't do any major damage."

"Oh, is *that* what you've been doing? Protecting us all?"

"*Yes.* And I've been doing a damn fine job of it. Better than you, anyway."

"Sabotaging the grapes? Poisoning the water with rowan? Calling up a locust swarm? You call that protecting people?"

"No, none of that was me. And it wasn't my uncle or my father either. The worst we've ever done is sneak my father and some of his cronies into town so they can interrupt rituals, like on the night of your initiation. All of those other things, they weren't us. And I will swear to that by any God or Goddess you want."

"Then who's doing all these things?" I asked.

"I don't know. *We* don't know. I'll swear to that, too."

I bit my lip and stared hard at his shoulder. The locusts, in particular, had seemed pretty biblical, pretty *Christian*, to me.

But I believed him. In spite of everything, I believed him.

He stopped dancing and pulled away a little bit. I looked up at him. I had no idea what to say, but I felt like one of us should say something. Instead, we just stared at each other. A long minute went by, until he finally released my right hand and reached up to touch my cheek. His left arm was still around my waist, keeping me close to him.

"This town is a haven for me too," he said quietly. "And you may like to pretend you're this unfeeling, hardened criminal, but no matter what you say, I know you feel the same. You don't want to let your mother burn it down, and neither do I. Can we at least agree on that? Enough to try and stop her?"

"You're a *Zealot*," I said accusingly. "How can I trust you?"

He scoffed. He was still touching my cheek.

"I'm not a Zealot, I'm a *Christian*. There's a difference. And I'm a witch, too. Call it whatever you want, Macie, it's just religion. They're all the same. That's one thing I learned from being in both worlds. Witchcraft, Christianity, they're all about believing in something greater than yourself. The rest is just details."

I rolled my eyes. This was so *not* the moment to discuss religious philosophy.

"It doesn't matter if I can trust you or not," I informed him. "Don't you get it? No matter what I do, she's always one step ahead of me. She always has been. She knows me better than I know myself. We're not going to be able to stop her!"

"Look, I get that you're mad. But for right now, this moment, we're on the same side. We can't just let her win. This isn't like all those other towns, Macie. Your eyes are open now. You can't pretend you don't know the things that you know."

I bit my lip and said nothing. His words made something click into place in my head even though he was wrong. People conveniently blinded themselves almost constantly. Like the mayor, ignoring Percy's obvious affair with my mother. Like Talya, willfully blinding herself to Royce's devotion to Autumn. And Bradley, who was clearly hiding from whatever had happened in the first Depot fire. It's easier that way. People pretend not to know inconvenient truths all the time.

I could do it too, if I wanted to. Only I wouldn't have to pretend.

She would believe me if I told her I wanted to forget.

I found my mother on the edge of the ritual area. She was standing there calmly, a smug expression on her face. As though she had been waiting for me.

"Well?" she said impatiently.

"You were right," I said quietly. "Things are different now. I've changed."

She drew in an annoyed breath.

"But I don't like it," I added, before she could say anything else. Looking down at my feet, I bit my lip and added, "I want things to be the way they were."

When I looked up at her again, she had crossed her arms and was waiting for me to continue. I took a deep breath.

"I've been thinking about this a lot. And I want you to erase him."

"Erase who?"

"Rafe," I said, and his name stuck somewhere in my throat. "I should've listened to you when we got here. I should have put him out of my head. I shouldn't have let myself be paralyzed by thoughts of someone who wasn't even thinking about me."

She said nothing, just continued to eye me as though she was trying to figure out the catch.

"Rafe was where it started," I went on. "Where I changed. I want you to take him out of my head. Every single, solitary memory of him. And then, everything will be like it was before. I know it will."

She still didn't say anything. So I went on.

"Then I'll help you. Whatever you want to do in Witchtown, I'll help you. But when we're done, I want you to take away my memories of that, too. All of it. Kellen, Talya,

Gayle, Aimee—all of them. All of Witchtown. Like none of it ever happened."

She drew in a breath, buying time to think my offer through. She narrowed her eyes and looked at me, as though she was trying to read my thoughts. I knew that she couldn't, but it still felt like someone was stirring the contents of my brain with a sharp stick.

Finally she said, "I'll need somewhere private for the ritual. Our apartment isn't big enough."

I let out a relieved sigh.

"We can use the Depot."

She shook her head immediately, shuddering a little. Before she could refuse out loud, I added hastily, "I took care of the poltergeist."

She looked doubtful.

"You did?"

"I did," I assured her. "Ask Gayle if you don't believe me."

She considered this.

"Well . . . all right, then. I have a few preparations to make. They shouldn't take long. I'll meet you at the Depot at six o'clock."

"Okay," I said, giving her a very small smile.

She turned to go, then turned back around suddenly. I stiffened, fearing the worst.

"Six o'clock," she repeated. "If you're not there, Macie, so help me—"

"I'll be there," I promised. "I swear I'll be there."

CHAPTER TWENTY-TWO

A couple of minutes after six o'clock, there was a knock on the door of the Depot.

"Macie?" my mother's voice called out.

"Come in!" I called.

She opened the door and popped her head inside.

"Why's it dark in there?" she asked apprehensively.

"I'm just coming down from upstairs," I assured her. "Come on in."

She took a few tentative steps inside, then stopped.

"What's going on?"

I shivered as the temperature in the room plummeted and an icy wind rushed past my head.

Bradley materialized just above my mother's head. She didn't appear to notice him. Not until he leaned down and spoke directly into her ear, using the same fierce whisper he had used on me the first time I had dared to enter Stan's place.

"Pleased to meet you, Ms. O'Sullivan."

My mother screamed; a shrill, ear-piercing scream that made me jump. All my life she had told me how terrified she was of ghosts, but I had never before seen her encounter one. And this was an Aubra I never could have imagined; she was pale, small, and shaky. And quite pathetic, what with all the shrieking.

She bolted for the door but Bradley blocked her. She spun around, searching for another exit, but Bradley was there too, hovering just above the floor with his arms crossed, shaking his head slightly at her antics.

"Macie!" my mother cried, finally seeming to remember I was there. "Help me! Please!"

"The light switch," I said from the corner, where I was safely out of the way. "The light will send it away. Hit the switch!"

I had left a candle burning beside the closest light switch. My mother spotted it and bolted straight for it, then pounced on it like her life depended on it.

Just as I hoped she would.

The second her fingers touched the switch, the circle of candles she had stumbled into lit up with a blaze of yellowy orange light. Beside me, Talya raised her hands and stepped forward to seal the circle.

I could barely hear the words, even though Talya was shouting them. I was too busy watching my mother's face. Her expression went from terrified to confused to livid in a matter of seconds.

By the time she realized what was happening, it was too late. Talya had completed the circle and my mother was trapped inside. We had encircled the space with rowan branches, just to be extra cautious. I had left one quarter of the circle open so that she could enter, but I closed it now by kicking the branches back into place.

"Thanks, Bradley," I said, giving the ghost an appreciative nod.

He nodded back, gravely, then floated up to the corner of the Depot and disappeared.

Below me, Kellen flipped on the lights for real and then leaned against the wall, arms folded over his chest.

Aubra glared at me from the center of the circle.

"I should have known you wouldn't give up so easily," she said ruefully.

"Darkness and clouds, Mother," I singsonged. "You have always underestimated me."

She ignored me and closed her eyes. I could tell by her breathing that she was trying to channel. But after a couple of seconds, her eyes flew open and she fell forward onto her knees, gasping for breath and grimacing in pain.

"Hello, Ms. O'Sullivan," Talya said formally, striding forward until she was standing a few feet in front of the circle she had used to ensnare my mother. "You seem to have stumbled into what is known as a Thief's Trap. One of Reginald Harris's favorite spells. The breathlessness you're experiencing, that squeezing sensation around your neck? You're feeling that because you're in possession of something that isn't yours. That's what is causing the trap to collapse in on you. All you have to do is give up what you have stolen, and the trap will set you free."

My mother shot Talya a haughty look and closed her eyes again.

"Attempting to channel will make it worse," Talya warned her, her voice chillingly calm. "Particularly trying to channel with stolen power."

My mother gasped again, louder than before, and brought her hands up to claw at her throat.

"Let. Me. Go," she wheezed.

Talya had explained the gist of the spell to me earlier, but only now did I see the true brilliance of it. This was probably the one spell where my mother's strength, stolen or not, couldn't help her. In fact, it was working against her.

Talya was kind of a genius.

My mother seemed to be thinking along the same lines. She glowered at the black-clad girl standing in front of her. Then she closed her eyes again, but this time I could tell that she was trying to force herself to relax. She took a very deliberate deep breath. She was trying to buy time.

I stepped forward.

"The trap is sprung, Mother. Only you can get yourself out of it."

She opened her eyes.

"How could you, Macie? I've protected you for years. It's been you and me. And this is how you repay me? By letting your friend hold me hostage?"

That made me pause for a beat. Doubt flooded in. I shook my head to clear it, but it was still there. The pull, the power she had over me. It was like she had me on a leash.

I looked down at the moonstone. Then quickly, before the pull could get any stronger, I undid the clasp and let the necklace fall to the floor.

It hit the polished cement just outside the boundary of the circle, out of my mother's reach. Her eyes widened as she watched it fall, and I waited until she looked back up at me before I answered her.

"I want what is mine."

She cleared her throat. The calm that she was always so good at summoning settled over her face, and she sat back on her heels.

"What makes you think that I have something that belongs to you?"

"I don't *think* that the power you've been wielding all these years is mine," I informed her, surprised at how strong my voice sounded. "I *know* it is. And I want it back."

My mother laughed. At least she tried to. The trap was holding her tightly enough that she made a little choking sound.

"*Yours?* You've never done anything to deserve it. Real

power, true power, comes only when you've earned it. And you haven't."

"You have?" I asked coldly.

"Absolutely."

When all I could do was stare at her incredulously, she went on.

"So you were born a Natural? Who do you think was responsible for that? *I* birthed you. And after your father left us, *I* raised you. I could have left you at the nearest Haven. You would have been just another Natural orphan. But I didn't. I kept you. I gave up everything for you. If that doesn't entitle me to the power you happened to be born with, I don't know what does."

Really? That was it? I was certain there had to be more to the story than my mother's ego and her entitlement.

Next to me, Talya scoffed. "Seriously?" she said. "You think you deserve some sort of reward for not abandoning your child?"

Her words had some bite to them. I knew that her parents had essentially done just that — dumped her off at Witchtown when they didn't like what she had turned out to be.

We're all misfits here. Refugees from the real world, Gayle had said.

My mother rubbed her throat with one hand, then raised her chin proudly into the air.

"I don't need to justify myself to either of you," she said haughtily. "I found a way to survive —"

"By stealing from me!" I interrupted her. "By lying to me! By making me think, *every single day of my life,* that I was some awful thing that had to be hidden!"

"It was necessary. You can't be trusted."

"What does *that* mean?"

Her eyes narrowed.

"Seattle."

I blinked. That day, that image, had always been cloudy inside my head. But not now. Now that I wasn't wearing the moonstone, I could see it clearly, in a way I had never seen it before. There was far less to the memory than I would have thought.

I had been standing in front of a window, shaking with rage. I had called up to the sky and the rain had come. Just like that. As easy as breathing. And my anger had vanished.

"I *did* make it rain that day," I muttered.

"You made it *flood* that day," my mother corrected me. "You were angry at me. You asked me about your father, I refused to talk about him, and you threatened me. You said that you would make it rain until I told you more about him. And you did. Our whole street was under water. There were hundreds of thousands of dollars' worth of damage; it was a miracle that no one was hurt.

"After that, I knew I had to do something. We couldn't live on the outside anymore, not with you out of control like that. People were asking too many questions. So I brought us to a Haven. I learned how to channel. And I met Pendle Bishop.

She made our necklaces and arranged for the . . . transfer, of your power to me. So that I could use it for both of us."

"Oh, I see," I said sarcastically. "It was a selfless move on your part. You did it for me. It was all for me."

"It was for *us*," she said evenly. "It has always been the two of us, Macie."

"Were you ever going to tell me?" I asked her. "Were you ever going to explain things?"

When she didn't answer, I inched up as close to the circle as I dared.

"Were you ever going to give it back?"

My mother raised her eyes to mine. I expected a lie. An elaborate, made-up story. But instead, she shocked me with what could only have been the truth.

"No."

I drew back from the circle.

"I don't know why I'm surprised," I muttered, half to myself. "You're a thief. I guess I just never thought you'd steal from *me*."

My mother said nothing.

"You've made me into a thief too," I went on. Not accusing her, not getting angry. I was past all that. "You made me think that the world was out to get me, that I had no choice but to steal what I needed." I shook my head. "It was never the world, Mother. It was you. *You* wronged me. Me and so many others. And you did it all using *my* power."

I winced. That was the hardest part to stomach. The

power that had altered all those memories, in town after town; the power that had nearly choked Rafe to death—it had all been mine. Stolen, misused. But mine.

"It's time for me to take it back, Mother."

She smiled. A weirdly out of place, strange smile.

"And how do you think you're going to do that?"

She casually undid the clasp of her necklace with one hand and laid the necklace on the floor in front of her.

"You think that's all it takes? All this time we've spent in Havens and still you've learned nothing about magic? These necklaces are the mere artifacts of a spell, worked over ten years ago by Pendle Bishop. Funny thing about people who do spells for money; they always make sure they're the only ones who can break them. And now she's dead. There's nothing your silly Thief's Trap can do about that."

"Did you kill Pendle Bishop?" I demanded. I had asked her that once before, but I had never been satisfied with her answer.

"What if I did?" my mother asked. Coolly, calmly. Like we weren't even talking about a person. "Whether by my hand or not, she's still dead."

"You're a monster," I said, staring hard at the floor. My moonstone lay there, just on the other side of the circle from my mother's. I was free of my chains. And yet . . . it made no difference.

I looked over at Talya.

"What do we do?"

She spread her hands, and I noticed they were shaking slightly. The effort of holding the spell for so long was taxing her. The trap had been the extent of our plan. And I wasn't sure how much longer she could go on.

My mother was watching Talya too, and the sight of my friend's struggle brought a smile to her lips. She settled back into the center of the circle and sat cross-legged, content to wait us out.

"It's a shame you can't ask Pendle for help," my mother mused. "But unfortunately, I think you'd find the conversation a bit one-sided."

"Maybe not," came a voice from the back of the Depot.

Kellen stepped forward from his place in the shadows. He was holding a small brown earthenware jar. It was caked in dirt, as if it had recently been buried.

My heart skipped a beat when I recognized what type of jar it was: an urn.

Kellen held it up so that my mother could see.

"Why don't we find out what Pendle Bishop has to say?" he asked. His face was grim, worryingly devoid of even a hint of his usual humor. He started to chant.

I exchanged a glance with Talya, who had begun to go a little bit white in the face. I couldn't understand most of Kellen's words—they sounded like they might be Latin. But I knew what he was going to do when he reached his hand into the jar and stepped up beside me, right to the boundary of the circle that held my mother captive.

"Pendle Bishop, return to us!"

He tossed a handful of Pendle Bishop's ashes into the circle at my mother's feet. A cloud of ash dust flew into my mother's face and I blanched. Beside me, I heard Talya make a gagging noise.

My mother looked disgusted as well. She covered her mouth and scrambled backwards, but the cloud followed her. Instead of dissipating, it rose up and started slowly taking on form until there was a specter of Pendle Bishop looming over my mother, complete with messy braids and multiple layers of threadbare clothing.

"Pendle—" my mother began, but the specter cut her off.

"Give it back to her," the old Natural growled.

My mother went to speak. I don't know if it was to argue or agree, but Pendle Bishop didn't wait to find out. She reached out, grasped my mother's jaw, and used her other hand to reach *inside my mother's mouth.*

My mother screamed as the specter drew something out of her. It was light, it was dark, and it appeared to be stuck. Pendle Bishop yanked hard, once, twice, a third time. My mother screamed even louder, especially when, with the last tug, it came free.

Pendle Bishop threw it behind her and it hit me in the center of the chest, knocking me backwards.

I hardly noticed when I fell to the ground. The jolt from hitting the floor was nothing compared to what was going on inside me. The thing that Pendle Bishop had thrown burrowed and expanded until it filled every square inch of me. I gasped, and for a moment I thought it might burst right out through my skin. But as it reached its limit, it stopped and receded, curling back into itself and waiting, like a coiled spring, somewhere just below my heart.

I sat forward, shaking.

"Are you okay?" Kellen reached down and hauled me to my feet. I reeled for a minute, but then found that my feet were quite solid beneath me. I let go of him.

Is this what it felt like to be whole?

"I think so," I said. "What *was* that?"

"Part reverse exorcism, part summoning spell, I think. I was pretty much making it up as I went along."

"Great," came Talya's voice from just beside us. "But do you know how to turn it off?"

She pointed toward the circle.

Pendle Bishop was still standing over my mother, glaring down at her with a fiery intensity that had my proud mother quivering at her feet.

"I should have seen you for what you were," the old Natural snarled. "I have to make it right. I *will* make it right."

Even as she said the words, she was fading. She was almost see-through when she threw her arms into the air and said a word I couldn't quite catch. The rowan branches all around her exploded in flames, just as she disappeared completely, leaving my mother trapped, alone, inside a circle of fire.

Talya gasped. My mother screamed, but the sound was

cut off as she started choking and coughing. I stared helplessly at the flames. I saw myself, when Bradley had tried to kill me. And I tried to remember what Kellen had told the kids about channeling wind to put out fires. Could I do that now?

I raised my hand, but whatever it was that had tucked itself inside of me remained stubbornly coiled up. Dormant. The wall was still there. Even without the moonstone, without my mother, the wall was *still there*. What did that mean?

My mother screamed again and I was about to start panicking when there was a sudden burst of compressed air. Kellen was no longer at my side. When he came back into view, he was holding the fire extinguisher, the white bow still stuck to its side. He sprayed it slowly back and forth until most of the fire had been smothered beneath a blanket of white foam.

"Well, what do you know?" he said. "It *did* come in handy."

My mother was coated with a layer of white as well. I kicked aside a bunch of smoldering rowan and stood over her.

Wall or no wall, I was no longer her pale, empty shadow. I would never be that again.

I was the strong one now.

"I want you to leave here," I told her gruffly. "And never come back. You say you don't want to settle down, don't want to be stuck in one place? Fine. Don't. You can have the whole world to wander in. But leave me Witchtown. This place is mine. I never want to see you here again."

I was expecting a scene. Yelling. Cursing. Threats.

But all she did was glare at me through lowered lashes, and give a barely perceptible nod.

I stepped back, giving her room. She rose to her feet, and I thought I saw a trace of the Aubra I knew in the way she set her chin and marched determinedly out of the door.

I followed her as far as the doorway. I couldn't help it. In spite of everything, it was surprisingly painful to watch her walk away. It *had* always been the two of us.

She stopped a few yards away and turned to look back at the Depot.

"I can see what this place means to you," she said. "I've always wanted you to have something like this."

I swallowed. I opened my mouth to tell her . . . I'm not sure what. Goodbye? Please stay? I forgive you? I hate you? I'm not sure what I wanted to say. But before I could say anything, her eyes narrowed.

"And now that you have it, I want you to watch it burn."

She closed her eyes and channeled. It wasn't much — not nearly what she could have done before. She was only a Learned now. She had no power of her own. But she was able to channel enough to send a spark up toward the Solstice wreath that Percy had hung on the front of the Depot.

As soon as the spark touched the garish, reddish yellow flowers, the wreath exploded.

CHAPTER TWENTY-THREE

*T*he blast from the explosion threw me back inside the Depot. From flat on my back, on top of a pile of ashy rowan, I could see that the entire front of the building was on fire and the flames were spreading fast.

Kellen threw the empty fire extinguisher aside and hauled me to my feet. I was still a little stunned, so I didn't understand why he suddenly shoved me toward the front door. The frame was on fire, and there was a curtain of flames between us and the outside.

I couldn't see my mother anymore, but I knew better than to expect her to have stuck around.

Finally, after all these years, you're willing to face the truth about her.

"Cover your head and run!" Kellen yelled, pointing at the door as he pulled a coughing Talya to her feet.

I shook my head to clear it and looked appraisingly at the flaming door. Kellen was right; it was the only way out. I steeled myself to run through the flames, but then there was a high-pitched scream from upstairs.

"Aimee!" Talya yelled, throwing Kellen off and running for the stairs.

My little shadow.

I felt Kellen at my heels as I raced after Talya. In my mind I was kicking myself. I had no idea how Aimee had gotten into the Depot, and all the way upstairs, without any of us noticing. But I should have known that my mother was never going to just slink away without a final parting blow. If Aimee was hurt, I would never be able to forgive myself.

She was already wrapped in Talya's arms when Kellen and I burst into the space on top of the shop. And even though she was coughing like crazy, she didn't seem hurt. I breathed a giant sigh of relief.

Then I remembered that we were still trapped inside a burning building.

"Help me get her downstairs!" Talya yelled, starting to cough as well.

We were all coughing now, and my eyes were watering so much it was hard to see. Holding a hand over my nose and mouth—for whatever good that would do—I peered down the stairs. All I could see were flames. The fire must have reached the roof, because debris was raining down on the shop floor.

Kellen was looking over my shoulder.

"If we run—" he started, but cut himself off as a

smoldering beam fell at the base of the stairs, sending a cloud of heat and smoke up at us.

We both jumped backwards, exchanging identical looks of panic. No way were we getting out through that inferno. And there was no exit to the outside from up here.

But we had more immediate problems. *Smoke rises.* Aimee and Talya were just a few feet away from me, but I could barely see them. And it was getting harder not to choke with every breath I took.

Don't panic, Macie, I scolded myself. *Whatever you do, don't panic.*

I looked frantically around the small living area.

"The bathroom!"

The closet-size bathroom was barely big enough to fit all of us. But the door had been shut, so it provided a blissfully smoke-free pocket of air. We piled inside and I climbed up on the toilet to open the postcard-size window near the ceiling. It was far too small for any of us — even Aimee — to fit through, but it let in a welcome trickle of fresh air.

"People would have seen that explosion, right?" I asked. I peered out the window and saw nothing but thatch. Dry, flammable, easily ignitable thatch. I climbed down from the toilet. "Someone will come and help us?"

Talya and Kellen looked at each other.

"Witchtown doesn't have a fire department," Talya said quietly.

I just stared at her.

A rhythmic *bong bong* sound started coming through the open window.

"What's that?" asked Aimee, from Talya's lap. They were sitting on the floor.

"It's the bells," Kellen answered, as he shoved paper towels into the crack beneath the door to keep the smoke out. "The bells on the Tor. They ring when the town is in danger."

Percy had hung the wreath on the front of the building. At the mayor's insistence, he had said. But it wasn't the mayor who had put that idea into his head. It had to have been my mother. How else would she have known that it would explode with just a spark?

And there was an identical wreath on every building in the square. If the fire spread . . .

I wondered briefly what the ring of fire around the town square would look like. If the fire got out of control enough for that to happen, nobody in this room would be alive to see it.

"Are we going to die?" Aimee asked, her eyes bright with tears.

"No," Talya assured her, not sounding sure at all as she pulled her cousin's curly head closer.

"No," Kellen echoed. "No, Aimee, we're not going to die. Macie is going to save us."

"Me?" I exclaimed, feeling a rising sense of terror at the thought that I was somehow responsible for getting us out of this. "What about you? You're *always* prepared for everything. You always have the exact thing everybody needs right when they need it. You must have brought *something* with you that can help us!"

"I did. I brought you."

He finished cramming the last of the towels under the door and turned to me. His expression was tense but controlled. "This fire is too big for any Learned to put out. We need a Natural."

I stared at him.

"I can't! I tried when Pendle Bishop set the circle on fire. I wanted to put it out but I couldn't! Nothing happened!"

Kellen said nothing in reply and for a second, I saw a trace of the same panic I was feeling cross his face.

But then it was gone, and he was holding both of my hands.

"You used your power before. In Seattle, remember? The rain?"

"The flood," I corrected him.

"It doesn't matter," Talya said impatiently, still holding Aimee close. "You tapped into your power then, and you can do it again. Think about that day. What did you do to make it rain?"

I thought hard. Aimee began to cry again. The sound tugged at my heart and I tried desperately to block it out. I closed my eyes. It was hard to remember. I had stood in front of the window. I had been so angry. I had felt it in every part of my body, just like earlier today, when the magic had filled me and I had been afraid I was about to burst. I did not feel that way now.

"I felt different then," I said.

"How?" Kellen asked. "What was different?"

He was being patient with me. The effort that it was taking for him to do so was plain on his face. But he was doing it. Even though we were probably all about to be burned alive. If I had been in his place, I would have grabbed me and shaken me until my brain scrambled. But that wasn't Kellen's style.

"What was different?" he pressed me again.

"I was angry."

"Angry at who?" he prompted, trying to encourage the memory.

"My mother," I recalled. "She wouldn't tell me about my father."

Never say that word to me, Macie, she had said. *You don't have a father. I never want to hear you say that word again.*

"You were emotional," Talya inferred, drawing me back into the here and now. Which, unfortunately, was becoming hotter and more smoke filled by the second, in spite of the towels under the door. "Okay, so emotion is the key to unlocking your power. That's common."

I coughed. My eyes were starting to water like crazy.

Aimee coughed too. We all shifted position so Talya could set her on top of the toilet and angle her face up toward the open window.

Kellen squeezed my hands.

"Let's talk this out," Kellen said, in the same, patient teacher voice as before. "You do realize that we're probably going to die here? Do you have any emotions about that?"

I could barely see him now, through all the smoke. Aimee started to whimper again, and another wave of panic shot through me.

This is it. This is how we're going to die.

"Macie! Work with me!" Kellen sputtered, as a hint of tension burst through his mask of calm.

"I'm trying!"

I closed my eyes. I tried reaching for the coiled spring, for the well of power that had returned to me. It was still there. I could see it in my mind's eye. I could feel it, in the same weird sort of way that you know your stomach is there even if you can't pinpoint how you know. But I could also feel the wall. The damned wall was keeping whatever power I had in solitary confinement.

Kellen squeezed my hands again and Talya left Aimee standing on the toilet to come stand beside us.

"Don't you see, Macie? It's your mother. She's still in your head," she said. "If she can't have your power for herself, she wants to make you fear it. She wants to make you so afraid that you won't even touch it. Don't let her do it. None of it was your fault."

"The flood—" I started.

"Was not your fault," Kellen said firmly. "You were young, untrained. And your father leaving wasn't your fault either. None of it was your fault—" he paused, and took a deep breath. "Any more than what happened to my mother was my fault."

"I thought you said that *was* your fault," I said.

"I lied," he said, and even with all of the smoke, I could see the ghost of a grin on his face. "What happened back then, whatever we did, that was then. It's what we do now that matters. Right now, Macie."

He grabbed me around the shoulders and pulled me into him. I could barely see and my head had grown foggy, but I could feel his arms around me, and Talya's too, even as I felt myself drifting away, leaving my body behind and floating up through the burning roof above our heads.

I could see the town, as if I was looking down on it from above. There was a crowd of people gathered in front of the Depot. I could see everyone. Gayle, her face tight with fear; Maire and Brooke, both industriously trying to get everybody organized; Autumn and Royce; even Odin was there. They were forming a hasty circle in front of the building. When they had all linked hands, they started chanting.

Chanting for rain. On the eve of Summer Solstice.

Witches are nothing if not optimists.

I felt a surge of love for them at that moment. For all of them. For the whole town. Every wacky square inch of it. My love moved me to tears.

"You can do it," Kellen's voice whispered in my ear. His voice sounded dizzy, as if he was about to pass out.

"I know you can do it, Macie," Talya added, sounding equally woozy.

My mother had never believed in me. But Kellen and Talya did. The town did. And maybe that was the difference. I had things and people to protect now.

My coil of power was still there, still untouchable behind its wall. And I thought of something that Kellen had said once, when he had been talking about my mother.

She's a Natural. Magic is like breathing to her.

I stopped trying to force down the wall. I thought about all the people below in the square. I thought of the town. This dream of a town. This silly, romantic, magic-infused vision of a town. I breathed.

And the wall shattered.

I felt the spring begin to uncoil, letting loose whatever it was that Pendle Bishop had thrown at me earlier. I let it out, pouring it all down into the square, into Maire, who stood at the very center of the circle, arms raised. As though she was waiting for me.

Her eyes flew open as the first thunderclap sounded.

Suddenly, I was back on the floor of the bathroom. Kellen's

forehead was pressed against mine and Talya's arm was slung around my waist.

There was a second thunderclap.

"Rain!" Aimee yelled, pointing out the tiny window and jumping up and down on the toilet. "Rain!"

I looked up. The smoke had begun to dissipate. Water was pouring through the window, spilling onto Aimee's shoes and down to the floor, where it pooled around my jeans.

Talya jumped up to hug Aimee. Kellen didn't move; he was staring down at me with an expression I had never seen before. It was the most beautiful combination of relief and triumph I could have imagined. It was even better than his most Kellen-like smile.

"I breathed," I gasped up at him, just before I collapsed into his arms.

CHAPTER TWENTY-FOUR

*T*wo days passed before the Depot was declared structurally sound enough for me to enter.

There was a giant hole in the front of the building, where the wreath had hung. A large part of the roof had been burned off, and most of the upstairs living area had been flooded by the sudden deluge of rain I had called up. The main room downstairs was dry but littered with charred debris. I busied myself there, hoping I could tidy up my thoughts as easily as I could sweep up the remnants of the fire and our ritual.

My mother had vanished during the fire. Her things were gone from the apartment. Except for her silver Natural ring, which I found sitting on the kitchen table.

I hadn't been able to bring myself to touch it. I wasn't sure if I was ever going to be the sort of Natural who wore the ring.

I had spent the last few nights at the apartment by myself. On the couch. I also wasn't sure if I was ever going to be able to go into that bedroom again. Not when I knew it would still smell like cinnamon, like her. Odin had mentioned something about my moving in with him, Talya, and Aimee. I thought maybe I should take him up on that. At least until the upstairs space in the Depot could be repaired. I made a mental note to bring the subject up with Talya when we met up for pizza later.

While I was sweeping up at the Depot, I found the remains of our necklaces. Thanks to the fire, they were now two twin puddles of silver, dotted with blue-gray shards of shattered moonstone. They were probably a permanent feature; I couldn't begin to think of how I would remove them from the concrete floor. Maybe I could pass them off as mosaics.

Maybe I would invest in a rug.

I had swept all of the rowan branches into a pile, and I was looking around for a garbage bag, when I found the box of herbs the previous tenant had left behind.

It was empty.

There was a garbage can beside it, filled to the brim with bags of the cheap basil that somebody — I still wasn't sure who — had tried to pass off as other herbs. The remaining herbs, the legitimate stuff that had merely been mislabeled, had all been carefully sorted and laid out in neat rows on the floor. Ready for proper labeling and display.

I knew for a fact that I had been the first person allowed back into the Depot after the fire. The first *living* person, that is.

"Thank you, Bradley," I said softly.

I found a garbage bag and was stuffing the last of the rowan into it when Kellen walked in.

"Where have you been?" I asked. I hadn't seen him since I had woken up with my head in his lap, after the townspeople had managed to clear enough of the debris off the Depot stairway to get us out. And then, I had only woken up for long enough to realize I was safe, and to see Royce helping Talya and Aimee out of the Depot, before I passed out again.

"I went to see my dad," he said matter-of-factly. "The rain washed most of the Zealot village away. The church is still there, but most of the congregation decided to call it quits and go protest somewhere else. My dad is leaving today. My uncle is going with him."

"And you?" I asked, not looking up from the rowan.

"I'm not sure," he started, and I had to remind myself to take a breath. "I bumped into Gayle and Maire on the way here. They said something about maybe taking me in."

I looked up at him, and he shrugged.

"It's been a long time since I've had a mom. Maybe it'll be nice to have two."

"But you're staying here?" I asked. I needed to hear him say the words.

"Yes," he said, and he smiled that irritatingly cocky grin of his. "I'm staying here. This is my home. It may not have started out that way, but . . ."

He spread his hands as if to say, *What are you going to do?*

"I understand the feeling," I said.

He raised an eyebrow.

"So you'll be staying here as well?"

I pulled a piece of paper out of my back pocket.

"The mayor said she's going to transfer the Depot lease to me. I'm headed over to see her after this. Since I'm a minor, I'll have to get a cosigner to make it legally binding. I was hoping one of your new moms could help me with that."

"But you're staying?" he pressed me.

Maybe he needed to hear the words too.

I grinned at him.

"Yes."

"Good," he said. His attention shifted to the floor and he pointed to the urn, which was sitting at the base of the counter, badly burned but intact. "After all, I did rob a perfectly respectable woman's grave for you."

I brushed the remains of the rowan off my hands and picked up the urn.

"That's right, you did. That wasn't very Christian of you."

Kellen slipped an arm around my waist and pulled me into him, urn and all. He leaned down to kiss me. Just before our lips met, he rolled his eyes.

"Religion," he scoffed. "Does it really matter what kind of label you put on it? They're all the same, you know."

I pressed my lips to his. I wasn't going to argue with him,

even though I knew in my heart of hearts that I would never believe that.

Not a witch like me.

"I found something."

Brooke pushed a small, rectangular piece of paper across her desk and into my outstretched hand.

"What is it?" I asked, without looking.

"An account, in your mother's name. She opened it at the Witchtown Bank just after you got here."

I looked down at the paper. It looked like a deposit slip. But it was the amount that caught my eye.

Twelve thousand dollars. All the money we had in the world. The sum total of our lives of thievery. We had never been very good about saving.

The mayor sat back in her chair.

"I wasn't sure what to do with it. I know you don't want to file a missing person report on her. I respect your wishes on that. Why involve the authorities when we don't have to? So I thought I'd transfer the money into a new account. One that's in your name."

I looked at Brooke strangely. I had just assumed my mother had taken the money with her when she left. I hadn't known about the account. Why was she telling me about it now?

When I just continued to stare at her, she tucked a

chunk of her acid blond hair behind her ear and cleared her throat.

"The investors have agreed to back Witchtown," she informed me, as though that fact was totally unrelated to what we had been discussing. "I'd hate for anything to derail our agreement at this stage."

I thought of the forged books that my mother had prepared; the ones Brooke had shown to the investors. And the vault, which she had never managed to open.

Twelve thousand dollars. The price of my silence?

I'd take it. But not for myself.

I took a deep breath.

"Eight hundred and fourteen dollars of that belongs to you," I informed Brooke, just a touch uneasily. "For . . . um, the beautification project."

The mayor gave me a look that was too tired to be accusatory. Percy's arrest had taken a lot out of her. As had his confession that all this time, he had been the one who had been sabotaging Witchtown. To say nothing of his very public affair with my mother. Percy was now sitting in the one lonely cell of the Witchtown Police Department.

"Well, I guess that means I need to hire Lois back," she mused.

"What about Teresa?" I asked.

"I think I'll keep her on as well," Brooke said, with a small sigh. "I'm learning to delegate."

I made a mental note to tell Gayle.

"And the rest of the money?" Brooke continued. "Should I transfer it to your account?"

"Actually," I said, "I'd like the rest in cash."

Later that day, I addressed an envelope to Rafael Diaz, Haven #NE86C, Nebraska.

I included no return address and no note. Just the cash. Ten thousand eight hundred and sixty-two dollars and ninety-seven cents. Plus a few caraway seeds to keep the mail carrier honest.

It was time for Rafe to have his freedom.

I had already found mine.

ACKNOWLEDGMENTS

Thanks to my wonderful husband, Mark, who has never wavered in his support from the second I said the fateful words "I think I want to be a writer . . ." And to our kids, Sophia and Alex, for inspiring me (slightly) more often than they drive me crazy.

To my super agent, Sarah LaPolla, for immediately getting this book, loving it almost as much as I do (which is a lot!), and working tirelessly to make it a reality. I am ever grateful to be your client.

To my fantastic editor, Christine Krones at Houghton Mifflin Harcourt Books for Young Readers, for acquiring the book and helping me to push it even further toward all it could be—and for introducing me to Bat for Lashes. Darkness and clouds forever!

To everyone at Houghton Mifflin Harcourt who worked so hard on this book: Ann Dye, Mary Magrisso, Ann-Marie Pucillo, Toni Rosenberg, Jim Secula, Sarah Sherman, Kelly Dubeau Smydra and Tara Sonin.

To Jennifer Thermes, the artist behind the beautiful map and the herb illustrations throughout the book.

To the wonderful KidLit community of Austin, Texas, most especially Cynthia Leitich Smith, Nikki Loftin, Mari Mancusi, P.J. Hoover, Jo Whittemore, and the fine ladies of the Lodge of Death.

This book required a lot of research, and I would like to thank the following people for each enriching the book in their own way:

Beth Ebbing Johnson at Sacred Moon Herbal for being so friendly and welcoming, for answering my stupid questions, and for keeping me supplied with every herb under the sun and moon.

Ginger Webb at the Sacred Journey School of Herbalism for her wonderful herb walks, which helped me to see the world through the eyes of an herbalist.

Sasha Buntman of Midnight Jewitch for answering all of my questions and supplying me with a fantastic must-read list that answered other questions I hadn't even thought of yet.

Dr. Rachel for taking the time to talk to me about her practices and beliefs (and for introducing me to the secret menu of super-caffeinated drinks at Jo's — I may never sleep again!)

Caitriona O'Ceallaigh for helping me brainstorm Gayle's bakery and for her wonderful website, Recipes for the Pagan Soul.

Lee Klancher for knowing exactly what kind of motorcycle Rafe would build (down to the very last detail!) and for helping me make the cornfield ride slightly more realistic (don't try this at home, kids!).

The folks at Llewellyn who put out the Sabbats Almanac every year; The writings of D.J. Conway, Laurie Cabot, Silver RavenWolf, and Scott Cunningham; David Hoffmann and Jamie Wood; and Jordan Yin.

My mother. For being nothing like Aubra. (See, Mom? I told you nobody would think this book was about you!)

And last but not least I'd like to thank YOU, wonderful reader. There are so many amazing books out there — I'm honored that you chose to spend some time with mine. I hope you enjoyed it!

Darkness and Clouds,
C.P.O.